The Hunters Rage

Book Two of Rage MC

Elizabeth N. Harris

ISBN: 9781675974223

This is a work of fiction. Names, characters, businesses, places, events, and incidents are either the product of the author's imagination or used in a fictitious manner. Any resemblance to actual persons, living or dead, or actual events is purely coincidental.

Elizabeth N Harris
The Hunters Rage.
Book Two of Rage MC.

Cover by JanFillem@janfillem, courtesy of Unsplash.com.

The Hunter's Rage

She was left for dead, discarded, her heart and soul shattered. Her body torn apart, and the man of her dreams turned into the man of her nightmares.

He was betrayed by the one woman he loved. His heart turned to stone, and he became a machine for the MC. Not even his brothers pierced his heart.

Then a can of worms is opened, a tattoo seen that can't be unseen, wounds open that never healed, and an MC bleeds again. History is about to be re-written, but it's not going to be pretty, it's not going to be nice, and it going to be bloody.

Books by Elizabeth N. Harris

Rage MC series.

Rage of the Phoenix.
The Hunters Rage.
The Rage of Reading.
The Crafting of Rage.
Rage's Terror.
The Protection of Rage.
Love's Rage.
The Hope of Rage.
First Rage.
The Innocence of Rage.

Love Beyond Death series.

Oakwood Manor.
Courtenay House.
Waverley Hall.
Corelle Abbey.

Hellfire MC Series.

Chapters.

Dedication.

To Michael, Jordie, Connor, Jack, and Alex.

Love you always, Mum x.

To Mr White, My old English Teacher at Mayesbrook Comprehensive School, Lower Site. I've no idea where you are now, but you're the first person who believed in me! I'm afraid, Sir, that the Attic's Secret is still a work in motion, even thirty-four years on! Maybe one day I'll publish it!

To my Taekoran, no more needs to be said.

Elizabethnharris.net
Elizabethnharris74@outlook.com
https://www.facebook.com/groups/483099482281750

This book was written, produced, and edited in England, the United Kingdom, where some spelling, grammar and word usage will vary from US English.

Author's Foreword.

During the writing of this book, I did research on the injuries a person can survive. I needed Artemis's injuries to be believable. While Artemis's injuries may seem extreme and unrealistic to survive, I was shocked to find out that they sadly weren't.

Men and women have survived worse injuries than Artemis. I cannot imagine how they coped and rebuilt a life, but they did. The urge to live was so strong they wouldn't give up.

To my own horror, I read some awful real-life stories and spoke to a few people. The people that survived worse injuries than Artemis, the people who survived nightmares. Those that picked themselves back up and fought to live, for those who still suffer PTSD, you have my utmost respect and will always be in my prayers.

Elizabeth.

A Quick Note!

After a couple of reviews and emails commenting on grammar and spelling errors, I thought I'd explain. My work is edited thoroughly, and some grammar and spelling will differ from US English. For example, color to colour or focusing instead of focussing. But I type as I imagine the characters to speak. I've been around several MC's and also know a good many bikers, and believe me, they don't watch their grammar! So you may find errors when one of the characters speaks; that's intentional! Even educated characters may drop their p's and q's from time to time, and we'll let them off because we love them so much!

Drake may use *don't* instead of *doesn't*; *it don't make* sense instead of *it doesn't make sense*. Or I *be* angry instead of *I am* angry! Or Phoe may say, *me and you* instead of the grammatically correct *you and I*. They also drop words, possibly one of my own personal pet peeves! *You won't do it* becomes *won't do it*, or *it ain't right* turns into *ain't right.* However, typos are not deliberate, and if you find any, I sincerely apologise!

I hope you enjoy the book because I write from the heart and genuinely love my Rage MC characters and the world I'm creating around them.

Prologue.

February 2004

I gazed out of the truck's window as it sped out of town. Thunder and Misty sat in the front, not speaking and not paying much attention to me. I wrapped my arms around my slight bump for solace. I desperately wanted to ask how Ace was, but I didn't know them well enough. Just enough that when Misty approached me in the bar and said Ace had been injured, I'd dropped everything and followed her.

Thunder had been waiting outside in a truck, and I'd clambered into it without a second thought. Thunder belonged to Rage MC. That's all I needed to know. Lost in thoughts, I patted my abdomen when I felt what I now realised was a kick. For the last five months, I'd sensed something off with my body and last week, I'd noticed I'd a potbelly.

Worried I might have something medically wrong, I'd visited the doctors that very morning. I'd let the doc run the tests he required. In sheer panic, I'd listened as the doctor told me, congrats, I'm pregnant. I lingered in complete denial, so he'd taken me to another room, where he'd performed a scan and established I was twenty-eight weeks pregnant.

How the hell had I ended up pregnant? The question kept running through my mind. I'd never been regular, and long breaks between periods weren't unknown to me, but we never had unprotected sex. I took the pill, so I should have been protected. It didn't matter now. At the clinic, I'd seen little arms waving around on the screen and fell into instant love.

Ace would be okay eventually, no doubt of that. His sixteen-year-old girlfriend becoming pregnant wasn't on his short-term plans. In fact, having fun and settling in an apartment with me were Ace's short-term plans. But Ace would support me, he loved me, and I knew deep inside me that Ace would be over the moon. Well, once the shock wore off, I thought ruefully.

When I'd stumbled bloody and battered onto Rage's forecourt five years earlier, Ace and Drake had been the ones who discovered me. Curled tight into a ball and scarcely conscious, I cringed away from the two of them. They'd taken me into the clubhouse, trying to reassure me. One woman,

Marsha, cleaned me up in a room and then delivered the blow to those outside that I'd been raped.

In my barely conscious state, I'd heard loud shouts and several thuds against the wall. Voices telling someone, 'brother, calm down,' filtered through the door. Huddled in a ball, afraid, I'd listened to another explosion of shouting and hot temper and then silence descended. The door opened, and a kindly looking older man entered.

Backing against the wall in sheer panic, I'd tried to escape. The man explained he was a doctor and had been called to help me. In terror, I'd refused to let him near me, and Marsha had to return. I was an eleven-year-old child who'd been raped and savagely beaten, so I trusted no one.

Marsha calmly walked up to me in her biker-chic clothing, perched on the bed, and gazed at me as I huddled in the corner. Slowly and tenderly, she'd started speaking and persuaded me to allow the doctor to examine me and conduct a rape kit. The doctor seemed compassionate and explained everything he needed to do before doing it.

Marsha asked who'd harmed me and, eyes wide, I told her nothing. Just kept silent and hoped to God, no one returned me to my stepfather. If I refused to talk, they couldn't send me back. It was childish reasoning, but it worked. The truth was, several hours ago, Mom had passed out in a drug haze, as usual. And my stepfather made the move he'd been planning for the last six months.

Sly touches between my legs and grasping my burgeoning breasts (I developed early to my embarrassment), he'd started making approaches. Tonight, with Mom passed out, he'd beaten me into a near stupor and then raped me several times. When he collapsed drunk, I fled.

Shocked, I ran to Mom, who roused herself enough to tell me I'd got what I'd been begging for. I ran away then. Terrified, I grabbed money from her purse, and I limped from the hovel I'd called home. I'd run aimlessly, with no destination in mind. For what felt like hours, I kept going before crumpling, bloody and miserable on the forecourt of Rage MC. Unaware I'd fallen on Rage.

The doctor gave me an injection and then left the room, and I overheard voices roaring. Someone kept yelling, 'who rapes a kid?' At the raised voices, I'd headed back into the corner, and Marsha had to cajole me out. Sweet Marsha rocked me in her arms until sleep claimed me. Several hours later, I woke up and looked into the eyes of the most magnificent boy ever.

Black hair fell in a sleek curtain to his shoulders, and glittering green eyes watched me. The tall, lean boy, aged fifteen or sixteen, kept an eye on me. His shoulders gave promise of a broadness yet to develop, and his legs were long and muscular already. The youth had a strong jaw, chiselled cheekbones, and resembled the movie star, Lou Diamond Phillips. I'd recently seen him in the film Young Guns and had been fascinated by the actor.

Those green eyes didn't leave my face as he strolled towards me in slow movements. He sat on the bed and held out a hand. I gazed at it, and with no expression, he leaned forward and picked up mine.

"I'm Ace. How do you feel, princess?"

"Hurt," I whispered hoarsely.

"Wanna talk?" I shook my head. Ace tilted his chin towards the door and nodded once. "The brothers won't let anybody hurt you. I can promise that."

With a vicious shake of my head, I refused to communicate, mesmerised by eyes that hadn't yet left mine. Ace's mouth puckered in what I believed was anger, and I flinched, pulling my hand back.

"What's your name?" Ace asked, switching tactics and retaking my hand.

"Kayleigh," I whispered back. Ace leant forward, and a ferocious expression crossed his face. This time I didn't recoil.

"No fucker will hurt you again, princess. No one, I'll kill 'em first," Ace muttered. I nodded, agreeing with this fierce Native American warrior. Who looked like at that moment, he'd kill anyone who crossed his path and said a nasty word to me.

"Come here." Ace held an arm out, and I slowly curled my battered body into his. I looked down, surprised, when something clunked against his stomach and saw my wrist in a bandage. I then understood what I hadn't yet taken into consideration.

My left foot was in a soft cast, ribs taped up and rubbing my head, and I felt stitches in my cheekbone. My right shoulder was sewn up, and pain laid heavy between my legs. The doctor must have returned and tended to me while I slumbered.

"Don't want to go back," I mumbled to Ace. "Adrian might kill me next time." Ace's arms tightened and then loosened.

"Kitten, you're Rage's now. Marsha won't force you to go anywhere you don't wish to." I nodded, thinking how nice to belong to something. "But you're going to have to help. Can't just keep you here without knowing who to fight. I won't let you go, princess, you're mine," Ace added. What an odd claim to make, I thought.

Deep breathing to stave off panic, I told Ace everything. How Mom married a man with an enormously fat beer belly. How I succeeded at school, although Mom and Adrian were generally drunk or in a drug-fueled haze. When Adrian began to touch me at age nine, and Mom called me a liar. I told Ace everything about those harrowing hours last night.

Ace listened and kept hold of me, keeping me safe, even though I knew I wasn't. Intelligent and way more thoughtful than most of my age, I understood that these people couldn't keep me safe. I realised that if I got sent back, Adrian would continue his abuse.

Ace lay down and tucked me into him. At first, I was stiff, and then I relaxed and fell to sleep. The next time I woke, I was alone and several minutes later tumbled back into a peaceful slumber. Somehow, I knew Ace wouldn't hurt me. Sleep was the healer I required and for once it was devoid of nightmares. The time I woke after that, I'd found myself tucked back in alongside a warm, hard body.

I knew without checking it was Ace. Evidently, Ace had appointed himself my protector by his actions. For a child who'd never had protection, Ace became my world. It was no surprise that I latched onto Ace with the pent-up love and need, a rejected, abused child, mustered.

That night began my life with Rage. They were an MC, I discovered several days later, which meant loud men and louder women. Marsha and another girl, Silvie, who was seventeen, looked after me, and brought food and clothing. Ace constantly hovered in my presence. I'd been there four days when Ace visited early one evening, informing me he was going out for a few hours. Ace promised to be back as soon as possible and left me with the women.

I'd nodded and dozed off, waiting for him to return. When Ace did, he climbed into bed and held me tight. Sleepily, I noticed that his knuckles were bruised and bloody but said nothing. I'd enough awareness of MC's not to comment.

The next day Marsha and Ace walked in and informed me that Mom had signed papers that had been drawn up to sign away custody. Marsha and her man Fish now had guardianship of me. Fish was sergeant at arms of the club, and I'd met him often. They offered me two options. One, I could live with them, and they'd take care of me, or I could stay at the clubhouse.

Fish, a tall, broadly built man with a bushy beard and shaggy hair, had been kind. He was quiet and never had much to say, but when Fish spoke, everybody listened. Fish was twenty-one, and Marsha the same age as him. He wore the biker uniform of faded blue jeans and a Harley tee. Modestly, Fish tamed his hair by wearing a bandana, and Marsha teased Fish loads about it. I'd never seen a couple more in love with each other than Fish and Marsha.

Ace stood silently as Marsha delivered my options, and I sought his opinion. He told me I could choose, and when I asked where he lived, I hated the answer. Ace lived a twenty-minute ride from Fish and Marsha. How could Ace protect me from so far away?

I elected to live at the club under Marsha's vigilant

eye. Ace spent most of his free time at the clubhouse. If Fish and Marsha left the clubhouse, Marsha got there every morning at seven a.m. and didn't leave until ten p.m. Marsha and Fish had no children, which even my child mind could sense bothered them. Being free of commitments, they often stayed at the clubhouse, as Fish always had stuff to do. I badly wanted them to have a baby because Marsha looked sad sometimes, and I hated that.

A few days later, I met Drake, a calm talking, husky-voiced brother who was Rage's Vice President. Drake was twenty-four, older than the others. It'd been Drake, I learned, who'd been shouting the night they found me.

Ace had been locked in a room that first night and not allowed out until he'd regained control of his temper. Marsha told me that both Ace and Drake had strong morals, and what happened and didn't happen to a child was part of that. Ace was working towards prospect, he informed me, which was a trainee biker brother in the making. In other words, Ace was moving towards being a badass. Personally, I thought he was already there, which made him chuckle.

Ace would apply to the club at sixteen. His father was an enforcer at the club called, non-imaginatively in my opinion, Apache. I wondered if Apache thought his name was racist, and Ace told me it wasn't. His father had picked his own name. Apache's father had ridden with Rage MC and perished in questionable circumstances. Apache and his son were Rage MC through and through.

The offer to stay at the MC surprised me because Bulldog, the President, was an absolute bastard. I feared Bulldog, he was dangerous, but even Bulldog had a line no one crossed, no one raped and beat a young child. So, Bulldog doing the one nice thing in his life, let me live at the clubhouse.

Life settled. Each day Fish arrived at seven a.m., if he wasn't already there. Fish made sure I'd eaten and then popped me on the back of his bike and took me to school. Marsha moved me to a local school in Rapid City, one only ten minutes away from the clubhouse. Fish gave me ten bucks for lunch and a wink and then picked me up at the end of each day.

I fast became a curiosity to my new classmates. I kept my head down and worked hard. The other kids had questions, which I avoided, and many of them stuck their nose up at a biker's kid being in the class. Fish and Marsha hadn't fooled around and had got me into one of the best schools in Rapid City. Fish picking me up stopped any bullying. Who'd want to mess with a mean-looking biker? If only they knew how soft-hearted Fish was!

After a few weeks, I came home from school one day and found Marsha and Silvie had decorated the dingy room I'd been sleeping in. The walls had been painted black and purple, which they'd discovered were my favourite colours. Marsha had bought a comfortable bed, a mattress and a wardrobe, and drawers for clothes. They'd managed to fit into my space a narrow table and chair with a laptop perched on top. A night lamp sat next to it, softly casting out light.

Marsha replaced the naked bulb in the room and hung a girlie beaded light. Voile swatches of cloth hung carelessly around my room, gathered up and looking elegant. A poster of the MC's patch was stuck to one wall and there was two canvas pictures of motorbikes, Harley Davidson's, I discovered later. The room was far more beautiful than anything I'd ever been given before, and I burst into tears at the kindness.

Life continued, and I was content, happy even, and I began to blossom under Fish and Marsha's care. I lived at the end of a hall away from the common room where the MC gathered. I stayed out of their way so I didn't irritate Bulldog and others I'd become distrustful of. Fish and Marsha, Apache, Drake, Ace and a couple of others became my circle of people. Slick (who was twenty when I'd been found) helped me study, and Gid helped with math as I hated math, and so did Slick.

Silvie and Marsha became the main staples of my life. The women regularly bought me things, hair stuff, knick-knacks, jewellery, and clothes. Half of the women at the club were honest, kind people, but there weren't many old ladies. Marsha was one of ten.

Other women who regularly dated one biker were called biker bunnies. Women who wanted a relationship but didn't have one.

The rest were bitches. SKANKS, yeah, I stated it in capitals because they were nasty. These women slept with any brother indiscriminately and without hesitation. They didn't think any male off-limits, even those who'd claimed an old lady.

This caused tension. Most of the brothers who'd claimed an old lady put them in their place. But a couple had roving eyes, Marsha had to put the skanks in their place, which led to catfights. But Silvie usually got me out of the way. The skanks hoped to score an old lady position, but realistically they were perceived as easy pussy.

I learnt the hierarchy of the club quickly and the rank of the old ladies. Bulldog didn't have an old lady. Bulldog screwed when he wanted and who he wanted. The President made it clear he wanted no ball and chain around his neck. Bulldog wasn't nice or attractive. Disdain within my circle grew for the brothers who cheated on old ladies.

Apache had no woman. Tragically, his old lady had died, and Apache had let nobody take her place. For Fish, there was Marsha and only Marsha. No one else existed. As far as Fish was concerned, no one came close to the goodness and beauty that Marsha portrayed. As we got older, Ace grew into the promise of his body. Women started noticing, but he never went there. Perversely, Ace's disdain made him even more interesting to the skanks.

Silvie confused me. She wasn't much older than me. She knew Marsha and Fish well, and Silvie happily waded into several catfights. A few of the brothers turned their wandering eye towards Silvie. But a word from Fish or Drake forced them to leave her alone. Silvie was a wonderful person, yet she came across as lost. I didn't understand why. Drake and Fish both took Silvie under their wing and made it clear they protected her.

Silvie loved taking me shopping and worked cleaning offices. Marsha told me that Silvie lived in a hostel and attended school during the day. She never appeared until after nine o'clock at night, until one night Drake dragged her into the clubhouse, furious. The old guy Silvie worked for had made advances on the stunning girl, and Drake had caught him.

After Drake taught him a lesson, he hired Silvie to work at the clubhouse and garage, cleaning for the MC where she'd be safe. Drake paid Silvie a damn sight better than the old man. And with Drake, Fish and, in the end, Apache and Slick monitoring her, she became much safer. I saw Marsha give her money sometimes, even though Silvie tried to give it back.

Drake got around a lot! He'd no interest in settling down with a woman. Drake was a horn dog to beat all horn dogs, Ace told me. Slick was a horndog too, and Gid. When I asked why Ace wasn't the same, I received a single word response, kitten!

Ace's answer at the time perplexed me, but I knew one thing, I was madly and completely in love with Ace. He was mine. Ace became my entire world, and every minute I'd free, I spent with him. When I got home from school and Ace was available, he was my companion. Ace often fell asleep with me, him on the top of my quilt and covered up in his own duvet.

I wasn't naïve. Far from it, I saw the looks Apache gave us, and I noticed the glances and whispered comments from Marsha and Fish. Fish would frown, look our way, and then something gentle lit in his eyes and he'd turn to Marsha and tell her to stop fretting.

I once heard Apache tell Slick that Ace had discovered his one and had to wait for me to grow up and become legal. I admit I was delighted thinking I was Ace's one. Ace proved that when one day, when at fourteen and walking home from school, four boys, who were older than me but who'd attended my school, cornered me. Fish had been unavailable, and the next thing I knew, I got yanked down an alley.

The boys called me a biker skank and tramp, becoming free with their hands. One held a hand over my mouth so I couldn't cry out. The next instant, they were pulled off me, and Ace beat the shit out of them. Strong arms folded around me, and I looked up to see Slick.

I screamed, frightened that Ace would get injured.

He did, after all, fight four assailants. Slick shook his head as Ace systematically took them apart. Finally, leaving them in a heap on the ground, Ace pulled me from Slick's arms and planted my ass on his bike and sped off. Ace rode to a hilltop, and we looked down across Rapid City.

Then in Ace's no messing tone, he told me explicitly what was what. I belonged to him. No one touched what was his, and at sixteen, I'd become his. Ace was waiting for me. No one could claim me apart from him. My eyes wide, I nodded and attempted to kiss him. Ace gently took me in his arms and explained that as much as I belonged to him, I was jailbait right now. We had to wait until I turned sixteen and legal. Ace planned to do right by me, as no one else ever bothered to put in the effort.

I bit my lip at that, and Ace groaned and ran his fingers gently down my face. He told me I was killing him, but he'd be patient. Ace was eighteen to my fourteen, and he'd waited three years, so he'd wait for two more. At that moment, I learned my life had beauty, and that was Ace and Rage MC. Despite the ugliness Bulldog brought to the club, Rage still had beauty.

Misty appeared a few weeks after that, a stunning but bitchy blond twenty-year-old who set her cap at having Ace. Ace told her several times in brusque terms to take her skanky, bitchy ass away from him, and so she tried targeting me. It happened once, and

Ace went batshit at her, making her back away. But Misty didn't cease trying to throw herself at Ace.

So that brought me to the present day. Two months shy of seventeen and pregnant. I'd been with Rage MC for nearly six years. I'd gone to the club that Rage owned, called Hells Rage, in partnership with another biker club they owned it with. For months, we'd been hearing that Drake's cousin Chance was struggling to take over Hellfire MC and get it clean. I'd heard rumours Drake was preparing the same moves with Rage, and my people supported him.

Drake made a real go of the club's legit businesses, a shop which sold tee's, riding gear and other biker accessories. Drake owned the rights to the bike design and repair garage, as his dad had owned the clubhouse land and left it to Drake. Drake established the garage despite Bulldog's objections. Drake also owned the shop called Rage MC Shop. Unoriginal!

Drake grinned and told Bulldog it was his land to build on, and Bulldog couldn't stop him. Snidely, he told Bulldog, if he didn't want part of the garage, that was fine by him. Yeah, as if Bulldog would refuse money! Next, there was the parts store, which, again, Drake forced to be legit. Bulldog seethed that Drake stood up to him. Whatever arguments Bulldog raised, Drake won.

Drake surrounded himself with select brothers, ones he'd recruited or trusted. Apache, Ace and Fish, obviously. The rest of Drake's circle included Slick,

Gunner, and Manny. Drake also brought Mac and Lex in. These brothers Ace trusted implicitly. Then there was Jacked, Gid, Texas and Axel. Drake was often heard saying the new brothers were the future of the club.

Axel was a founder of the club and called the first generation or first-gen, as Rage shortened it. Axel supported Drake and not Bulldog, a big booming man with nothing but kindness in his heart. I loved Axel to pieces.

Texas was second-gen, someone who'd been recruited by the founders. Axel and Texas were the two most respected brothers in the club. Jacked and Gid couldn't decide whose side they were on. They kept flipping from one to the other. But Bulldog had plenty on his side, Rage being that large.

By now, at twenty, Ace was a full brother, and he'd made my sixteenth birthday a beautiful thing to remember. Drake treated Ace as his second in command to Bulldog's fury. The writing was on the walls. Ace, Apache and Fish had a huge pull in the club, but I stayed out of it, as old ladies did. I bolstered my man and did what I had to, to provide him with what he needed.

After the disturbing doctors' consultation, I'd gone to the bar to wait. Ace was picking me up there as he'd a run to do. Sat at the bar, it stunned me; when Misty approached and informed me there'd been trouble, Ace had been knifed. I shot from my chair and followed her out without doubting for a minute my man needed me.

Suddenly, I looked up from my musings and saw we'd left Rapid City and were heading into the Black Hills National Forest. Confused, I leant forward and tapped Misty on the shoulder.

"Misty, what are we doing out here? Where's Ace?" Misty turned to me, and the look of sheer hate on her face took my breath away.

"Ace is precisely where he should be, at the clubhouse," Misty bitched. Something bad sliced through me, and my stomach clenched in dread.

"What's going on?" I asked. Thunder pulled up into a clearing and turned to me, and I visibly shuddered at the unholy light in his eyes. Thunder wasn't likeable, but I'd never believed he'd hurt me until now.

"Well, bitch, what's goin' on is, we gonna play some, ya know? Gonna get what's been comin' to ya." I pushed back against the seat as Thunder got out. Opening my door, he seized my hair and dragged me out. I knew what Thunder planned, and I fought, clawed, scratched, and punched.

Thunder punched me in the face twice, and I slumped to the ground and seconds later, he'd ripped my jeans off. To my horror, he forced himself on top and inside of me. I screamed and attacked his eyes. Thunder punched me again as Misty stood laughing while he raped me and came. Thunder rose to his feet and smirked at Misty.

"Bitch is a shit lay," he said, "time to get inventive."
I crawled away as best as I could when he grabbed
me and held me down as Misty spat on me. Then,
kneeling, she showed me a bat in her hands, and I
screamed as Misty smashed it against my knees. My
left knee shattered, and tears rolled down my face.

I started begging and pleading as Thunder raped
me again and then again. In between rapes, Misty
took her time smashing the bat into my arms and
hands, and then she aimed for my stomach. With the
limited strength I'd left, I twisted, and it slipped out I
was pregnant.

Quietly, I prayed for the torment to end and to be
left alone. Begged God and all the angels in the
heavens to save me, as sheer evil hurt me over and
over. I passed out several times, but it didn't end.
Thunder and Misty merely waited until I regained
consciousness. The torture lasted hours.

Misty stabbed a blade into my shoulder on top of
my old scar. Stabbing straight through a tattoo that
Drake had designed for me. With Thunder holding
me, she raped me with the bat. I couldn't take any
further suffering and allowed darkness to retake me.
When I came to, Misty raped me with the bat again,
and once again, I blacked out. A body can only take
so much pain. Thunder beat me wherever his fists
landed, and I was black and blue.

This was worse than what happened to me nearly

six years ago. This was carried out by Rage, my family. When I next came to, I found them standing over me. Thunder had a bottle in his hands, and the way he was eyeing me, I knew I didn't want to know.

"Ace will kill you," I muttered through split and swollen lips. Both laughed, and Thunder leant into my face.

"Who do you think gave the order?" Thunder spat at me.

"No! Never!"

"Ace is done darlin', he wants a real woman, not a child," Misty laughed in my face.

"Brother gave us you to play with and make sure you got taught a lesson. A lesson I'm happy to provide," Thunder grinned.

"Ace knows you're pregnant, and he don't want it. Ace don't want you, he wants it, and you gone." I died then, died inside. Thunder began rattling off MC brothers, who were likewise in on it. Not Fish, Apache or Drake, but Slick, Gid, Manny and several others. My body went limp as Thunder took the bottle and thrust it inside of me. I lay there, allowing pain to drift over me as Thunder broke the bottle inside and tore me up. I welcomed the pain as a distraction from my broken heart.

"Ain't fuckin' no blood," Thunder said to Misty and turned me over and raped me anally. And I'd thought the pain couldn't get much worse. After several more hours, they finished. I was beyond screaming then.

My body lay in the dirt, broken and bruised.

My bones had been shattered, my skin slashed, anally and vaginally I was destroyed, raped with the bat, bottle and Thunder's cock. I was destroyed emotionally and mentally. Cruelly betrayed by a man I thought loved me, betrayed by a family I thought was mine. All that was left was the life I carried whose heart beat with mine.

Misty leant over me and spat in my face. She took the knife she'd used to carve up my body and, in the final insult, sank it into my stomach and cut me open. Misty rummaged around as I screamed weakly, and she dragged out the love I'd carried in my stomach.

Misty lay it on top of me, and I heard a weak mew before silence. I was dead. I closed my eyes as Thunder aimed a final kick at me, and I allowed darkness to sweep over me, and I, Kayleigh Mitchell, died.

The cop threw up in the bushes, far away from the crime scene. His stomach empty, he ambled back to the bodies. He had seen nothing too horrific in his career, which had been over ten years, until this morning. The officer called in to confirm the body and called the coroner. The girl had been cut to shreds and beaten brutally. There were boot marks on her body, and her stomach ripped open, and her insides spilt.

Vehicles approached, and more cars pulled up. The girl's body had been found just over the border from South Dakota and in Wyoming. A few feet to the right, and she'd have been South Dakota's problem. She was now his issue until a detective got there. He eyed the bodies lying on the ground again and wondered what piece of shit would cut up a pregnant young girl.

The detective approached, and he gratefully handed over. The coroner arrived on the scene alongside forensics, and the detective watched as they started doing their jobs. As the coroner crouched, he shouted as the girl's hand twitched. Fuck! The detective raced towards them, shouting orders.

Chapter One.

September 2014

I swung my car around the corner, hitting a slight drift, and floored it. In front of me, the brown 1980 Buick skidded and then righted. I was on his ass, and the perp realised it. The dirty fucker was mine, and that's what mattered. One of the best bounty hunters in the business, I never lost a target. I was well known in many states and often called in to find a difficult mark.

I hated the fact that Marco Strummin had run to Rapid City because I'd history with that city and truly hated the place. But Marco Strummin, known paedophile to the police, had bolted and ran here, so I gave chase. There was a two hundred-thousand-dollar bounty on his head, and it was mine to claim. My throat clenched as Strummin spun out of control and crashed his car straight into the wall surrounding

Rage MC. Teeth gritted, I skidded to a halt and slammed out of my car, a black Ford SUV. I jogged toward Strummin, who'd got out of his vehicle and was stumbling away. I caught his shoulder, and the asshole spun around, throwing a punch at my face.

Yeah, I was small, dainty even, but all muscle. I worked out two hours each day and held a black belt in mixed martial arts and ju-jitsu. Add to that, I kick boxed five times a week and was trained to handle guns and knives. Strummin's weak assed punch was just that, weak. I blocked the punch and threw one of my own, catching him on the jaw and then grabbed his right wrist with minimal effort. Without a care, I snapped it backwards as it flew towards me with a knife in hand. I felt it break, and Strummin screamed.

I kicked him straight in his groin, and he hit the ground, wheezing. Inwardly, I smirked. A blow to the groin was the easiest way to take down a mark, and why waste energy? The knife fell from nerveless fingers, and Strummin collapsed into a curled ball, cradling his dick. Without hesitation, I drew my gun and aimed. He looked up at me, his face red, and he sucked in his cheeks.

"Fuckin' bitch," he wheezed. I cocked my head and kept my gun on him.

"On your stomach, hands behind your back," I ordered. Figures came out of the Rage clubhouse, and after a brief glance, I watched as Strummin followed my orders. I bent, putting a knee on his back, and clasped a cuff around his wrist. Strummin yelped as I snapped it around his broken wrist.

"What's goin' on?" a voice asked. My stomach tightened as Drake's smooth, rich tones swept over me. I kept my knee in Strummin's back and, out of frustration, rapped his head on the ground. If only the idiot hadn't run to Rapid City!

"Don't fucking move," I snarled. I rose to my feet and gazed at Drake. The man wore tight, faded jeans and a white tee with his cut over the top. President was sewn onto his cut high on his left-hand side. Drake hadn't changed. He was as gorgeous as ever. A few more lines around his eyes, a few strands of grey in his dark hair, a hard, muscled body that would make a male model jealous. Drake was still Drake. And Drake had won the battle to take over Rage MC.

"I'll ask again, woman, what the fuck is goin' on."

"Takedown, I'm a bounty hunter," I snapped back. Disgusted, I rifled through Strummin's pockets, and I found the keys, which for a strange reason, he'd taken from his car. Stupidity, running from a bounty hunter, and you stop to take the car keys? Yeah, that wasn't fishy. I moved towards Strummins's car, knowing he'd only have taken the keys to stop me from finding something. I opened the driver's door and heaved at the smell that came from inside the car. Rubbish was strewn everywhere, and it stank of sweat.

Not seeing anything, I opened the boot and felt my stomach clench again. Hidden under a dirty sheet was a wooden box, and after taking photos on my phone, I put on gloves and opened it.

"Motherfucker!" I swore out loud as I stared at the contents. The bastard had found three more victims, and there were dozens of photos of them. My stomach clenched, and I swallowed bile. Yeah, I'd seen and done a lot, but kids were off-limits. Sickened, I snapped more photos and carried them to my car.

"Witness statement?" Drake asked.

"What?" I said, walking away. I dragged Strummin to his feet and cursed again.

"Great, you pissed yourself, just wonderful," I growled. By now, other brothers had appeared, they stood around in a semi-circle, and my gaze drifted over them. With an effort, I controlled my features. Until that is, I spied that skank Misty standing in the crowd. I wasn't able to stop myself from sending her a glare of pure loathing and disgust. Misty stumbled backwards at what must have appeared, a murderous glare aimed at her.

"Saw what you found, you removin' it darlin', may be a problem. Can give a witness statement to RCPD."

"Whatever," I muttered as I dragged Strummin towards the back of my vehicle. I opened the tailgate and pulled a blanket around and laid it out. Disgusted, I shoved the dirty bastard hard, pushed him in, and slammed the tailgate shut.

I turned to get back in my car and saw Drake's gaze on my shoulder. His body had frozen, and he gazed into my face. Drake's eyes searched mine, and he looked confused, shocked and horrified. I'd no idea why, but my gut told me to get the hell out of there.

"Get out of my way," I growled, pushing Drake. I'd the advantage of surprise, and he stepped backwards. As I pushed past Drake, his body suddenly moved, and he caged me against my door with his arms. I stared up with a blank face.

"Kayleigh?" Drake muttered, disbelief in his voice. Curious eyes raked me, looking for something, anything that could link me to the name he'd just uttered. I frowned.

"Who?"

"Kayleigh," Drake muttered again. I saw pain cross his face, and Drake looked at my shoulder and raised a finger to touch it. I grabbed his finger and forced it away.

Drake's brow furrowed as his gaze raked me again. I knew what he saw, short-cropped curly red hair, green eyes, a heart-shaped pixie face, full lips and straight white teeth. I was slender and muscled, a tiny frame.

"It can't be. You don't look nothin' like her, but..." Drake's gaze dropped back to my shoulder, and I cursed. The tussle with Strummin had torn my tee, and my tattoo was showing.

"Name's Artemis, you've heard of me being who Rage MC is," I stated. Recognition crossed his face, I shoved at his chest, and he didn't move an inch. Bloody Drake. "If you don't mind, I wanna get that scum out of my car before he stinks it up." Drake gazed at me for a few more seconds before his eyes dropped back to my tattoo.

"He'll get to the PD alive?" Drake asked.

"Yeah."

"You sure about that?" And I knew Drake realised how I felt about Strummin.

"Yeah." Okay, I'd taken in dead marks sometimes, not entirely my fault. They shouldn't fight back.

"I'll trust you," Drake said, and I bit my tongue hard. Drake stepped back. Without another look at him, I climbed into my SUV and sped away.

A quick glance in my mirror told me Drake was standing in the road; his eyes narrowed at my vehicle. He was alert, and I saw Slick come to him, and then after a final gaze, Drake strode into Rage. Hatred and bile rose in my throat, and I swallowed it back. Drake had caught me unprepared. That wouldn't happen again because I'd my own reasons for hating Rage MC.

I passed Strummin off at RCPD and handed over photos, and filed the paperwork. The families of the boys he'd abused had clubbed together for a two hundred thousand reward. I called in to Buzz as I walked through the corridors of the PD. Buzz sent a well done over the phone and told me that another mark had been spotted locally to my position.

I sighed as I told Buzz to get me the details. A bounty hunters work was never done. Tired, I put my phone in my pocket and left the PD. As I rounded the corner to where my SUV was parked, I froze mid-step as I saw Drake leaning against it. Alert, Drake watched as I walked towards him and didn't make a move to get out of my way. I stopped a few feet from him.

"What now?" I asked, exasperated.

"Wanna know who you are," Drake replied.

"Told you, the name's Artemis."

"That ink on your shoulder, seen it a long time ago."

"Bully for you," I snapped back.

"A girl I once respected, admired and cared for a whole fuckin' lot, had that same ink on her shoulder."

"Good for her."

"That tat darlin' was one of a kind, wanna know how I know that? I designed that ink for Kayleigh Mitchell."

"Again, good for you both, but whoever you think I am, I'm not. My name's Artemis, and I'm a bounty hunter." Drake took two strides and got into my space.

"You're Kayleigh," Drake snarled at me. Pain lurked in his eyes as he ground out, "what happened to you?"

"Do I look like her?" Drake's brow furrowed.

"No," he admitted, and I shoved past him.

"Then leave me the fuck alone." Drake reached out to grab me, and my phone rang.

"Stace!" Buzz boomed down the phone loud enough for Drake to hear it. God bless Buzz.

"Got details?" I asked. Today was shaping up to be busy. Buzz rattled them off and then confirmed he'd send a text. I ended the call and stared at Drake, who was staring at me in sheer puzzlement.

"Stace?" he asked, confusion in his voice.

"Now you know something very few do, my given name. I'll thank you to keep it quiet." I opened the SUV door, climbed in and drove off, leaving Drake standing behind yet again.

It was midnight when I opened the door to the cheap motel I'd booked. Dead on my feet, I wanted to hit the sack and sleep. I'd been scheduled to make a call tonight, but it was far too late. I checked my phone and saw a new message. 'Love you,' I read and smiled. Yawning, I kicked off my boots, shoved my gun under the pillow and closed my eyes.

It felt like I'd hardly been asleep when my eyes snapped open, and I woke, alert with my gun in my hand, pointing at Drake. He sat in shadows but leaned forward as I snapped awake, his elbows on his knees and his chin propped on one fist.

"Death wish?"

"Now we gonna talk, woman, without you drivin' away," Drake said.

"For fuck's sake, you got an obsession with me?" I
snarled, keeping my gun on him. My other hand
groped for my phone and clasped it.

"Want to know what's goin' on. How you have that
ink and why you denyin' who you are," Drake
growled.

"You want to know about the tat?" I growled back.
"Check out a website called Tripp's Tattoos. You will
find several images of that tattoo on several people. I
saw it in Tripp's shop, liked it and had it done." I
spelt out Tripp to him. Drake grew silent as he did
what I told him, and his jaw clenched. The ink was
distinctive, a skull surrounded by roses with a flaming
sword through the top of the skull.

"Don't mean nothing," he said, "that's precisely as I
drew it." I rolled my eyes at him. Drake, always so
damn stubborn.

*"Hey, little princess, I got something for you,"
Drake said as he walked into Kayleigh's room.
Kayleigh looked up at him.*

*"What?" Kayleigh asked. Drake handed her a piece
of paper, and she stared at the image on it, confused.*

*"This, see that sword? That's you, in all your glory
and strength, burning bright to light the way for my
brother. The skull, that's those you've survived and
beaten, the roses, the beauty you bring to the MC,
little Kayleigh. In two weeks, you're sixteen; we'll get
it inked over this." Drake slowly and within her line*

of sight raised a hand and touched a scar on
Kayleigh's shoulder left by Adrian.

Drake shook the flash of memory away. He remembered designing and drawing that tattoo for the girl like yesterday. Kayleigh had been so excited at Drake's thoughtful gift. Drake always looked out for the women he valued. It was inbred in him.

"The only thing I've in common with this girl is a tattoo and her height. I did a bit of research. Kayleigh Mitchell was slender but curvy, with long blond straight hair and blue eyes. The girls face shape is different from mine. Kayleigh disappeared nearly twelve years ago, just after your faction went to war with Bulldog's faction. Most of you think she ran away," I snapped. Drake focused back on me.

"Yeah," Drake muttered, "Kaleigh running away broke my brother." My heart hardened, and hate swelled in my heart. Shame his brother broke, fucker should after what he was party to. Please note my sarcasm. Hate welled deep inside.

"Not my problem Michaelson, now get out of my room. You've five minutes before the police arrive." I turned my phone, and he saw my 911 to Buzz. Drake rose to his feet and looked at me.

"You're Kayleigh, and you're not, darlin'. I'll find out the fuckin' truth, so run as far as you want. I have your scent now," Drake muttered and left my room. I kicked the door shut behind him and watched as his bike rode away. Only then, I allowed myself to curse out loud. Still cursing, I picked my phone back up and dialled a number.

"I need help," I said when a voice answered.

Two weeks later, Drake strode into Rage's clubhouse and gazed around, taking in everything and then marched to the inner sanctum. His gaze dropped to Texas, the MC's secretary, who sat at the table. Texas was tapping his finger on a file in front of him. Texas's gaze rose towards Drake, and it was solemn.

"What you got, brother?" Drake asked, sitting in his chair. Texas had sent Drake an SOS ten minutes ago.

"This came today, unsigned and not addressed to a brother. Lex brought it to me. Isn't good." Texas looked pale under his tan. Drake lifted one eyebrow and then tapped for the file. On the cover of the file was a handwritten note.

'Now back off, we're even.' It was signed with a bow and arrow with an initial A curved around it, "Artemis," Drake muttered.

"Brother, before you open it, warning ya, brace," Texas warned. Drake shot Texas a glance, and Texas nodded. "Freakin' brace, brother."

Drake nodded an acknowledgement and opened a police file. The front page held details of a 911 call from a citizen who'd driven past a body in a clearing.

It detailed the date and time and names of responding officers and the investigating officers. The transcript of the conversation was disturbing. The citizen described a young girl, cut up and dead, laying in the dirt.

Drake turned the page and gagged in his mouth as he took in the naked body of a young girl he'd cared about. Kayleigh's beautiful, battered face stared up at him from another photo. Drake flicked through close-ups of the wounds and turned to the coroner's report.

Someone had beat Kayleigh to a pulp, multiple bones broken, sliced and stabbed with a knife a multitude of times and kicked and punched. She'd been raped numerous times. Broken glass and wood shards were discovered inside her vaginally and anally. Kayleigh had been tortured over several hours, the report stated, left for dead and gutted like a pig.

"Kayleigh was fuckin' pregnant," Drake whispered. The babe had been twenty-eight weeks. He turned a page and read a further report. As she'd been dumped in Wyoming, it made sense why their searches hadn't found her. Drake was sickened at the damage and hurt caused to the girl. It was a contrast to how he remembered Kayleigh, laughing and joking and teasing Ace.

Images flitted through his mind, imagining her pain and terror, and Drake closed his eyes for a few seconds. Kayleigh was owed by Rage. Drake continued to read on, details of injuries and summaries of the investigation, but without an I.D, it went nowhere. Just another Jane Doe. Furious, Drake slammed the file shut and dropped his head to his hands.

"Kayleigh was a casualty?" he asked Texas, bitterness in his voice. Texas shrugged, but Drake saw the man swallowing his own grief.

"Thought the girl ran. Kayleigh realised what was happening, thought she ran."

"Should have known," Drake muttered. "She'd never have left Ace of her own free will. He'd have been a father. Fuck shit, Ace should have been a father." Pain shot through Drake on what his brother was soon to find out. It didn't bear thinking about.

"Kayleigh was a kid in a situation that was fast deteriorating."

"Kayleigh was a fuckin' kid!" Drake roared and shoved at the table and rose to his feet, his chair flying backwards and tilting over. With a primal scream, Drake punched the wall hard, his knuckles splitting. Wounded, Drake paced the room, and Texas ordered Lex, who'd rushed in, to get Phoenix. Lex left the room at a run.

"Gonna need to lock down Ace," Texas told Drake. "You need to get a handle on this and lock it tight."

"Lock it down?" Drake roared. For nearly twelve years, he'd watched his brother suffer. Drake hit the wall again, punching through drywall. Furious, he kicked a chair that Texas ducked.

Drake needed to hurt someone right now. The urge to hurt someone so bad clenched his fists, and Texas watched him warily. If Drake flipped, more than Texas would be needed to lock him down. Drake swallowed as he thought of Ace, his brother.

Ace changed weeks after Kayleigh disappeared. He'd searched, dragging his close brothers into the search and then he *shut* down. There was nothing, no trace, no calls, simply nothing. The openness Ace once had, disappeared, and he became mean, cold and bitter. And Ace began fucking up those in Rage's way without hesitation or thought.

More than once, Drake thanked God Ace had been on his side. He feared no one but Ace made him pause. Ace took Bulldog out himself, a bullet to each knee and then carved the ink off the bastards back with a blunt knife. Sliced the man's throat with the same dull knife, and when Bulldog neared death, Ace put a bullet straight in the man's head. This was after Ace had played with Bulldog for over twenty-four hours. Ace was beyond salvation, and the only thing Ace had left was his brothers and club.

Ace never engaged with a woman again. He fucked when he needed to. Didn't care if the woman enjoyed herself. Once he'd done what he needed, Ace made them leave. No softness, no spark of humanity was left in Ace. The only crack in Ace's shield had been Phoe.

"Lock it tight, brother, 'cause tellin' you Ace

won't." Drake realised Texas was right. Ace would lose it, totally apeshit. He gazed at the older man, his brother who'd stayed by his side when Drake took the club. At the same time, Hellfire MC, his cousin's club, underwent a leadership change. Chance kicked ass the same way Drake did. Hellfire and Rage were clean. At the time, without Chance able to take his back, Drake had relied on Axel and Texas.

Texas was forty-nine. He'd started coming to the club when he was a kid. Texas watched Bulldog take over and drag the club into places some brothers didn't want to go. But they did, as they were Rage. When Drake was older and gained VP, objecting to how the club ran, Drake began a slow takeover.

Most of the younger members backed him quietly, and on the side, they worked hard at getting the legit side going and lucrative. When Drake shut the not so legit side, the women, the drugs, the gun-running, no one took a hit on their pocket. The legit businesses were lucrative, more than Drake had dreamed of.

Texas sat on the fence until Bulldog pulled a knife on Drake while Drake's back was turned. Then he waded in, and with Texas wading in, Drake won. Drake gave his brother the secretary job as thanks, and the man excelled. Texas was loyal to Rage first and then Drake.

"Get the brothers, Ace last," Drake ordered, and his gaze lifted as the door opened and Phoe strutted her ass in. His wife took one look at her man, walked over to him and wrapped around him. A slender hand touched Drake's face and pulled his head to her shoulder. Drake clutched Phoe tight to him and shoved his face into her neck.

"Baby," Phoe crooned. Drake rested his hand over her stomach. Phoe was three months pregnant and was starting to show.

"History raising its head, Phoe," Drake muttered.

"And Rage will get through it."

"This could tear the club apart, wife. Gonna be bad. Ace is going to need you." Phoe stiffened when he mentioned Ace's name. The one brother she was close to was Ace after the man had taken five bullets meant for her. Ace had bled for Drake's wife.

Ace handled her affection in his usual way, ignoring it. But sometimes, Drake saw Ace gaze at her with a soft look on his face that quickly was wiped. Drake was sure that Phoe had wriggled her way into some small part of Ace's heart.

The brothers began to enter, and Phoe gave him one of her sweet kisses. "I'll be waiting," Phoe whispered and strutted away. Her ass wriggling in a way that usually made his cock hard. Not today.

Ace looked up as a brother knocked on his door. "Meetin'," Slick shouted through it, and Ace pushed the woman in his bed away from him. He rose to his feet and dropped the used condom in the bin. Misty rolled over and showed her ass. Her eyes gazed at Ace's tight, fit body and she hid her drool. Ace was as sexy as he'd ever been and was in his prime now.

"Want me to wait?" Misty asked him silkily.

"Get out. Fucked you, now leave." Hurt flashed across her face, and Misty rose on her elbows.

"We going to keep doing this, baby?" Misty asked. Ace looked at her as he dragged his jeans on.

"Doin' what?"

"Dancing around, I'll be your old lady, you know that."

"Why you think I want you as an old lady?" Ace sneered.

"Over ten years, we've been doing this dance. I'm the one you continue to take to your bed." Ace snorted as Misty sounded so sure of herself. He sent her the most mocking lock in his arsenal, and the bitch blanched.

"The fuck you'll ever be on the back of my bike, I'll never take an old lady. I fucked you, now get out; you're just a hole I stick my cock in when I need to. Nothing else." Misty's face turned nasty, and she got up on her knees.

"Always goes back to Kayleigh. Stupid bitch ran away, and you're still moping after her," Misty snapped. Misty flinched as her words hit Ace, and his face turned deadly. She'd just made a huge mistake. Ace grabbed Misty's arm and slung her against the wall, crowding into her face.

"Yeah, always gonna be her, stupid bitch, you think you'd ever be a patch on her? That you'd ever walk in her shoes? Don't you get it? I do enough to get you wet so I can slide in and fuck you. Minutes later, it's over. That's it, never made love to you; I fuck you. Don't care that you don't get off; who cares if a whore gets off? That's all you are!" Ace hollered. Misty flinched under the harsh words. Eleven years, she'd been on and off in Ace's bed, and he was right. It never lasted past him shooting his load. But she kept coming back, hoping he'd see her as more. She'd screwed his brothers, hoping to provoke a jealous reaction and got nothing.

"Why her? Ace, get over her. What did she have that I don't?" Misty whined, laying herself bare. She'd always wanted Ace, but the Ace she got wasn't the version Misty wanted. Misty had sucked up his scraps for a decade, never had Ace ever looked at her the way he had that insipid bitch, Kayleigh. Why couldn't she be what Ace needed? That fucking Kayleigh Mitchell had been dead for years.

"My kitten never fucked every brother in this club for one. You think I want an old lady that every brother knows what her pussy looks like? My kitten was innocent and beautiful, something you and your skanky whore cunt will never be.

You've had more cock than fucking Casanova had pussy. You're a whore, understand? Just a whore that every brother fucks, you mean nothing to none of us 'cept when we need a fuck. You must piss cum," Ace sneered, dislike and hatred written over his face.

Misty's head dropped.

"I waited years for you, Ace, and for nothing? I hate you, I'm glad Kayleigh's..." she whispered, breaking off. Horror crossed her face, and Misty glanced at Ace. He'd missed her slip.

"Good, because you disgust me, that's why I screw you from the back. Don't need to view your bitch face, just need a hole to fuck. You stupid fuckin' bitch, I hate you. Loathe you. You're lower than shit. So easy, you're pathetic. All I gotta do is click my fingers, and along you come running. Droppin' ya panties as you do. Chance was right, you got a fuckin' bucket cunt, and I'm done. Need something tighter now," Ace sneered. Ace landed cruel blow after cruel blow.

Misty's face paled as Ace's hate-filled words stabbed into her and cut deep. Misty realised, there and then, Ace never belonged to her. Kayleigh still owned him. All her dreams went up in smoke, the dreams she'd nurtured for nearly twelve years. Her plan to get rid of Kayleigh had backfired, and Ace didn't give a shit about her.

"You'll come beggin', needin' me," Misty said to him in a last-ditch effort. Ace got in her face.

"Look around, I fuck you, and I don't give a shit if you get off on it. You're nothing, just a cunt I can fuck, plenty more in the sea. You think I treated Kayleigh like that? Oh no, my girl was sweet and wild, innocent and greedy. Took my time getting her ready for my cock.

Never stuck my cock in her and just screwed her for a few minutes. You think 'cause I fucked you a few times for ten years, you mean something? How stupid can one bitch be? Get out. Need to disinfect my dick." Ace laughed bitterly at Misty and shoved her roughly towards the door, and slammed it shut behind her, not caring she wasn't dressed. Misty screeched her displeasure and hammered on his door, and Ace continued dressing.

Drake looked up as Texas re-entered the room, Slick, Apache, Manny, Lex and Gid on his heels. Fish came in minutes later with Lowrider, Ezra, Gunner and Mac. Rock and Lex were last, followed by Ace and Jacked. The four prospects remained outside as this didn't concern them. Ace sat at Drake's right, and everyone else took their places.

"Got news today. News that ain't good," Drake began, "a few weeks ago, that bounty hunter struck a nerve in me. Somethin' familiar, and I checked her out." He looked to Ace. "Thought she was Kayleigh." The man's head jerked towards him and Ace's brow furrowed as he thought on the woman.

"Looked nothing like her," Ace said shortly.

"Yeah. 'Cept Artemis had the same ink as Kayleigh, the one I designed." Drake rubbed his chin. His hand tapped on the file, and Ace's eyes narrowed on it.

"Brother," Ace snapped out. Drake slid the file to him.

"Artemis sent this," he said slowly and allowed Ace to pick it up and braced.

Drake's body language gave off enough warning that everyone else braced with him. Ace flicked through the file, his face displaying nothing. He gazed at the photos for several long minutes and then closed the file and slid it back to Drake. Ace stared at Drake, and then his gaze flicked around the room, and ugly crossed his face.

"Fuck!" Ace roared and sprang to his feet. Drake was moving when Ace picked up the edge of the heavy table and launched it sideways, tipping it.

"Fuck!" Ace roared again, and Drake threw himself at Ace. The man struggled, punched and kicked out. Manny, who was closest, got his arms around Ace the same time Drake did, and Ace threw them off. Other brothers moved to contain the man, and still struggling and fighting, they managed to floor him and grab his arms and legs.

"Lock him down!" Drake roared as they carried the fighting, raging man out of the room. There were women in the rec room looking terrified. Phoenix, Drake noted, looked calm and collected. Misty stood near his wife, and his lip curled up. Misty was whiter than white. Skanky biker whore, he thought and then turned his attention back to his struggling brother. They got Ace down the hallway and threw him inside his room.

Fury erupted as Ace began to tear up the room.

Furniture smashed, and fists hit walls, and there was the sound of drywall being punched through. Drake and the others waited in the hallway for Ace to calm. They waited half an hour before the room grew silent.

"Get my woman," Drake ordered Mac and opened the door. The room was destroyed; nothing recognisable left. Ace sat in a corner, blood on his head and hands. His tee was ripped and hung in shreds on his body. Holes were punched in the drywall, furniture turned into firewood. The door opened, and Phoenix entered. Ace ignored her like he was ignoring Drake.

Phoe hustled across the room and sat next to him, and drew Ace into her warmth. Ace wrapped his arms around her and slid down the wall, landing his head in her lap. Phoe stroked his hair and murmured soothing words. Ace broke, the first time ever, Ace broke. Tears streamed down his face, and Ace cried quietly into her lap and arms.

"My beautiful girl, my angel," Ace rasped out through his tears. Drake remained with his back to the door, which held several holes. He guarded his wounded VP with all the loyalty the man had shown him. Ace calmed and lay there gazing at nothing.

"Brother," Drake muttered.

"All these years, I hated, loathed her, and she lay dead. Couldn't stop loving her even though I hated her." Phoe stiffened, not knowing what was going on, and her eyes shot to Drake's. He gave her a look which said later, Phoe's hands continued stroking Ace soothingly.

"Aware now," Drake replied to his brother.

"Eleven years, man, I hated her. Eleven years, my girl lay rottin' and unknown."

"We'll find out, call in markers, set that hunter on it. Artemis found this in two weeks. She'll find more." Ace raised his eyes to Drake, hatred blazing from them. Phoe's head snapped up at the mention of Artemis, and Drake realised his wife knew her. Artemis had been the one that Phoe hoped would help her on child rescues.

"Kayleigh would have gone nowhere with a stranger. You saw how she was with them. A brother had a hand in this," Ace hissed. Drake stiffened, his eyes narrowing as he followed the thought process Ace already had. Drake realised that Ace's anger hadn't just been because Kayleigh was dead. It was because a brother had betrayed him. Someone Ace shouldn't have to worry about.

"Fuck, shit," Drake muttered.

"Yeah, one of them out there knows somethin' and when I find out..." Drake slashed his hand, raising his eyes to Phoenix, who'd gone pale. Ace cut his words on seeing Phoe's face.

"She was pregnant. Kayleigh never told me. Why?" Ace cried the last word, feeling a world of pain.

"Don't know, Ace. We'll find out, find everythin' out, I swear on our cut I will," Drake replied. Ace rose to his feet and pulled Phoenix up to hers. Ace grabbed her tight in a hug and buried his face in her neck. Phoe's arms rose, and she held onto him. Ace let her go and walked away. Texas and Slick waited in the hallway.

"Had to lock down Fish and Apache," Slick said, and Drake gazed across the hallway. Where he now heard similar sounds coming from Fish's room.

"Get someone on him," Drake ordered Mac as his eyes followed Ace. Mac chased after his brother. Drake knew Mac would take that job himself. He wouldn't let anyone near Ace.

"Marsha's locked in your room, Silvie's with her. Marsha saw the photos. Fish didn't hold back," Slick continued. Drake nodded, and his eyes went to Phoenix. Drake threw his arm around her waist and dragged her back to the inner sanctum.

Lex and Manny had tidied it and righted the table and everything. Wearily, sitting his ass on the edge of the table, he drew his wife between his legs and held her tight. Drake began to talk, and she listened without judgement. Phoe held him close as his own pain drifted out of him at the image of a sixteen-year-old girl brutally taken from life.

I glared at my phone as, for the fifth time today, Drake's number flashed up. The damn man had been calling for five days now. He'd left multiple messages at the offices with Buzz, and despite being consistently ignored, the man remained determined. Determined to the point of getting Phoenix involved. I snapped open my phone and snarled, "what."

"Wanna hire you," Drake replied.

"I'm busy, and Rage can't afford me," I snapped back at him.

"Can afford you darlin', you owe us this."

"I owe you shit. You kept on about this, Kayleigh, now you know. I owe you shit," I repeated.

"Owe us to follow it to the end."

"How you figure that out?"

"You sent us the file, could've let sleepin' dogs lie. Opened a can of shit this club wasn't expectin'. So, you owe us to follow this to the end."

"Your thinking is fucked up, Drake. I don't owe you or your damned club anything. But one thing I'll tell you for free, start internally. From what I read of Kayleigh Mitchell, a brother's involved and maybe not just one. Find your own lapdog."

"Askin' ya nicely, woman," Drake snarled down the phone with a bite in his voice. I laughed at him and then cut the call and drove away. The following three calls were from Phoenix, and while I cared about that woman, I ignored her. My phone beeped with a message.

I pulled up outside another ratty cheap motel and listened. Phoenix was begging me to follow through on this, I was the best, and we both knew it. She said

Rage was in an uncontrolled, chaotic and downward spiral. Ace and Drake watched everyone, and my heart hardened against Ace. Phoe asked me to get involved until this was resolved and save her happiness.

Phoenix didn't need the stress. Three months pregnant, this shit couldn't be good for her. Angrily, sighing, I sent a text that I'd be in Rapid City within two days, and I threw the phone, cursing Phoenix to hell and back.

Chapter Two.

1st October 2014.

Shown to the small conference room at Phoenix's HQ, I stared out of the window, bracing myself. The file in front of me detailed Kayleigh Mitchell's death, and I was tapping my fingers absently. I'd prepared myself as best as I could to meet with Rage.

I wore black jeans cut low on my hips, a skin-tight Harley tee and a black leather jacket over the top. One of my specially designed chokers adjourned my throat, specialised boots on my feet, and my hair pulled back. Minimal makeup, I wasn't into being a dolly girl, instead, I was a walking arsenal. A Glock 42 strapped to one ankle and a hunting knife strapped to the other.

Strapped to my waist was a G20 Gen4 10mm auto, and my shoulder holster held the same. At the back of my waist was another hunting knife, and a third knife hung on the opposite shoulder. On my wrists were specially designed leather cuffs that allowed triangular blades to shoot up from the leather with one jerk of a cord. They allowed me to slash at someone's arms if they held me from the back.

My choker had hidden blades, too, built on the same design as the cuffs. The boots held hidden knives if my arms were incapacitated. Two of my rings held flip out sharp thin blades to gouge out eyes if needed to. Buzz had designed many of my accessories, and he was a total nutcase.

Between us, we made sure that I was covered no matter what. My belt buckle unhooked at a touch and held throwing stars. Hidden thin blades were in the elbows of my jacket. A walking arsenal, I was ready for anything, thanks to Buzz and his insane genius. Who didn't love Buzz's insane genius?

I looked up as Phoenix entered the room, followed by Drake and Rage MC. I studied the men in front of me, and they returned the favour. Apache looked older but no less handsome than when I'd last seen him. His eyes held such pain; it was tangible. Turning from him, I studied Fish and saw the same pain. Fish wasn't even trying to hide it.

Ezra looked tired, suspicious, and unapproachable, and Lowrider was just pissed. I allowed my stare to drift past them and spied Ace for the first time in many years. Time had seen Ace right. His hair remained just past his shoulders and was pulled back in a ponytail. Shoulders had broadened, and Ace was lean at the hips and waist, and his tee showed distinct muscle definition.

Ace topped six foot two and came across threatening. His whole aura was one of danger. Ace's eyes were dead when they looked at me; his mouth was bitter and drawn tight, and his face expressionless. I thought I'd prepared, I hadn't, Ace hit me straight in the gut, and my breath stuttered. Even like that, Ace remained the most fascinating man I'd ever seen.

Drake took my attention as he dragged a chair out and sat on it. Phoenix took one near me. One by one, the others sat, Ace at Drake's right hand and even without reading his cut, I realised he was Drakes VP.

"What precisely do you want?" I asked without preamble, tearing my attention from Ace and focussing on Drake.

"Want to know who and what was involved. Bitches have no place in a brother's business, but brothers don't whack a brother's old lady," Drake replied.

"Not the way Kayleigh Mitchell died," I said and tapped the file.

"Not in any way, a brother manages his old lady, not for us to interfere unless he's too weak. No one in Rage is weak."

"So what do you want? Spell it out, Drake?" I leaned forward. Drake needed to be very sure on this.

"Want you to investigate, and I'll need the names of my brothers who were involved. Want to know who else and then want you to walk. You don't need to be involved in the next stage." Phoe glanced at Drake but said nothing.

"And if there's more than one brother Drake?"

"What ya got?" Ace asked, leaning forward. Eyes snapped towards me with an alertness that hadn't been there when Rage entered.

"A sixteen-year-old girl was brutally…."

"No woman, you fuckin' know somethin'," Ace interrupted me. I ignored him and concentrated on Drake, and then glanced at each man sat at the table.

"And what if someone here is involved?" The room turned hostile as Ace sat forward, and Drake's body stiffened.

"Then Rage will deal," came the soft promise back. The softness didn't hide the lethal connotations in Drake's voice.

"May not have an MC left, Drake, by the time I've finished," I said, checking my nails as if I was completely uninterested.

"There'll be an MC left even if I stand with one brother and rebuild," Drake stated empathically.

"Are you sure you want to open this can of worms, Drake?" I held his eyes. Pain and betrayal flashed in them and then was gone.

"Yeah, babe," Drake gritted out.

"Last chance Drake, I start down this road, there's no coming back from this. I'll see it through to the bitter end. Do you honestly want to do this?"

"Yeah," he ground out.

"Even if it means there's only one brother left standing, and you re-start Rage MC."

"Dammit, woman, you want it in blood?" Drake bit out, frustration showing.

"You ain't ready for this," I whispered to him, sorrow in my eyes. Drake's eyes caught mine, and I felt his inner flinch. Drake was aware there was a more significant betrayal ahead. He wasn't ready.

"What the fuck do you have?" Ace cut in again, and I switched my eyes to his.

"Lots of shit. But I'll tell you this, Texas knows something."

"Bullshit!" Drake snapped. Disbelief rang in his voice. Ah shit Drake, if you don't believe Texas as a possibility, how would you manage the betrayals coming your way?

"Speak to Texas because he knows something. By the way," I said, rising to my feet. "Rage forgot to look at several someone's." Ezra leaned forward.

"We did?" Ezra asked, sounding confused.

"Yeah, not just brothers at the MC." I pushed away from the table. Pausing near the door, I looked back over my shoulder.

"This'll cost Rage in more than my fee's, and they're expensive enough. My frontman will be in touch for the first instalment today. Pay by eight tonight, or I walk, and you don't get me back at the table." I walked away and left Phoenix's offices. I hit the stairwell and began jogging down the stairs. As I reached the second set, footsteps echoed, and then I was pushed against a wall.

Instantly reacting, I pushed back, ducking low and drawing my knife, and I had it at Ace's throat before he could blink. His hands came up fast, and they shot up the middle of us and thrust sideways, knocking my arms outwards. Ace came at me fast but not fast enough. I bent low, rolled, and pulled my Glock from my ankle. Landing in a crouch, I looked up at Ace, the gun pointed at his head.

"Question is Ace," I sneered the last word, "is, are you quick enough to kick me away before I pull the trigger and empty the clip?" Ace took two steps back. Wise move, keeping my weapon aimed at him, I strapped my knife back in place.

"You sittin' on more than you're telling," Ace spat.

"Prove it."

"Only wanna know who, who do I kill for this? Weren't no outsider woman." I glared at him, and my lip curled in disgust.

"No, it weren't no outsider," I mocked him and backed away, keeping my gun aimed at him. Easily, I turned my back on Ace, showing I wasn't afraid and jogged down the remaining stairs.

I exited the building and kicked the door shut. My hands on my knees, I bent over and took a deep breath, my head dipped, and I breathed in deeply again. Straightening, I raised my eyes and saw Drake in front of me near his bike alone.

Drake's eyes narrowed. I tossed him a jaunty wave and climbed on the back of my Harley Lowrider, and kicked it into gear. With a throaty roar from the Lowrider, I sped out of the car park, Drake's gaze following me.

I went home. I needed to go home for a few days and remind myself why I was doing this. Soak up the precious life there, find my balance again, before Rage dragged me through shit that was years old. And still not settled. So I left.

Ace, Apache, Fish, Ezra, and Drake faced off against Texas. The man sat puzzled at the end of the table and scratched his beard. Texas ran one hand through his hair and shrugged.

"Ain't aware what I meant to know," Texas said finally.

"Think Texas, you saw somethin', heard somethin'. There's somethin' you forgot," Ace pushed.

"Lemme be, need time to think."

"Time to think is gone. If I find out you're hidin' shit from me…." Ace let the threat trail off. Texas looked up and narrowed his eyes. He rose to his feet and paced towards Ace. Ace refused to back away, and Texas got in his face.

"If you imagine, brother, I was involved in

Kayleigh's death, you better say so now. 'Because I be tellin' ya, I knew nothing and got no clue what I'm meant to. Who's to say the bitch isn't messin' with our heads," Texas clipped out. "Was me who cleaned up your mess with Bulldog and others. I'm aware of what we are."

"Artemis has been right so far, but the bitch knows more than she's letting on," Fish agreed.

"Don't think you're involved, brother. But believe you got somethin', that you ain't aware you know," Ace finally said. Texas gripped Ace's arm at his elbow and drew him close, face to face.

"Let me chew on it."

"What do you think Artemis meant by there's more than brothers at the MC?" Ezra asked, changing direction.

Apache stared out of the window at the rec room. It was a big space; it needed to be for the traffic that traipsed through it. Battered sofas and cushy chairs were dotted around, a pool table stood in one corner, and a bar lined the back wall. Either side of the bar were two doors that led to the brother's clubhouse rooms.

Drake followed his gaze, and cursed out loud, sat on her ass at the bar was Phoenix. Next to her was Marsha, and Phoe was holding her hand. Next to them was Silvie, dotted around the room, draping themselves over brothers were the skanks.

"The women," Drake muttered, "ain't just brothers

here. It's them too."

"Jesus, a woman's involved?" Ezra said disbelievingly.

"Need to start breakin' this down instead of reacting. Make a list of brothers and bitches who were too young, they're free of suspicion," Apache said.

"What about brothers who weren't Rage and joined later," Fish asked.

"Nah, they stay. They could have offed Kayleigh and then joined. A rite of passage. Anyone under the age of sixteen when Kayleigh was murdered can come off the list."

"Why sixteen?" Ezra asked.

"You see them pictures, brother? Weren't no boy child that carved Kayleigh like that. Was a man with a man's hate and anger. Anyone over sixteen could manifest that anger," Drake replied, chewing his lip as he looked out. Sixteen removed the prospects from consideration and ninety percent of the bitches but still left loads to go through.

"Make your lists," Ace replied. Drake rubbed his chin and stared at the miracle that was his wife. He'd a bad feeling about this. He left the room calling the meeting to an end and headed to his wife.

Texas sat in the inner sanctum for the third day running, wracking his brains, and he was tired. Artemis said he had something, but he didn't have a scooby doo what. Texas was at the point of getting Drake to call her when his eyes fell on the police file.

Every brother had seen it now.

Not the old ladies, although they'd been told most of it. Texas drew it to him and saw the pictures. He flipped back to the beginning and read through the reports, something finally tugged at his brain, and he went wired. Outside Drake saw Texas react and walked swiftly into the room.

"Texas?" he asked. Texas waved him to silence. His brow furrowed as he re-read the front page. Texas heard the door open and close again as he re-read the page several more times, the tugging got worse.

Leant back in his chair, Texas frowned; something bugged him, but what? His gaze fell on the date of the report. Texas shot to his feet, placing his hands on the table. He had the damn thread now.

"On the twenty-fifth of February, for the last eleven years, a package arrived. Addressed to the club, I opened it and found a second envelope, marked confidential and addressed to Misty. Twenty-fifth of February is when Kayleigh disappeared," Texas spoke slowly as he worked his thoughts out.

"Misty?" Manny asked, surprised.

"The first year, Misty took it and looked puzzled but not worried. Second-year it arrived, Misty snatched it from my hand and left at once. Bitch was pale and looked scared. Skank reacts the same every year since, it's the only day the bitch is here before the mail arrives. And the cunt makes sure she gets that fuckin' package before I do."

"We ride now!" Drake snapped at brothers behind him, and there was movement, and Texas sat back heavily. His eyes rose to meet Ace's, which contained barely leashed fury.

"Had somethin' and it didn't register, it wasn't important. Fuck, brother," Texas said heavily.

"You got there, Texas. Got there in the end." Ace clasped Texas's shoulder and gripped it tightly before letting go and leaving the sanctum. Ace headed out to his bike. February was months away, there was no package arriving soon.

Ace kicked the door in and stormed into Misty's house. It was a shithole; there was clothes, plates, and shit strewn everywhere. House stank of smoke and pot, and he wrinkled his nose before marching through the rooms. Misty was gone, her closets rifled through, and it looked as if Misty had left in a hurry.

"Misty's gone," Ace snarled. Drake nodded.

"Bitch got warned. We'll find her." Ace punched his fist through the bedroom door.

"Search it. I want those packages found," Drake ordered as he and Ace left the house.

Parked up the street, their eyes fell on a black Harley Lowrider with glistening chrome. A small figure sat on it clothed in jeans and a black tee, and a black leather jacket. A helmet sat in her lap, and they looked upon Artemis. They walked up to her as she started the bike. Artemis jammed on her helmet and lifted the visor.

"Texas figured it out?" she asked. For the first time, Ace realised her voice was soft and melodic, and he felt a tug on his cock. Angrily, Ace pushed his reaction to the back of his mind.

"Could have saved us time and trouble," Ace sniped.

"No fun in that, anyhow, you're here now. Make sure you check the floorboards," Artemis replied and revved the bike.

"You think this is a game?" Ace asked incredulously.

"Do I think torturing, raping, sodomising a teenage girl is a game? You're messed up in the head. How fucked in the head are you, to know you've dipped your cock for eleven years in the skank that fucked up your woman? Then again, maybe Misty acted on orders," Artemis asked, turning to Ace and watching his face. Her cheap shot hit home hard. Loudly, Artemis revved the bike harder and rode straight at them. They stepped back as her bike shot past them.

"That cunt has answers," Drake said. Ace nodded. His eyes followed the tiny figure on the huge bike until she disappeared. Drake turned to Ace, checking him out, and Ace tore open at what Artemis had said.

"Fuck!" Ace roared. He'd dipped his cock into the skank who'd played a part in his old lady's death. Fuck him and fuck Misty, ten freakin' years he'd screwed Misty sporadically. Ace bent over and threw up on the curb. Jesus Christ, he'd fucked the woman who killed his Kayleigh. He'd never get over the guilt. Drake placed a hand on his back as Ace heaved again.

I turned the corner, drove up a way, coasted several more corners, parked my Lowrider, and dropped my head. The look of ravaged pain that had crossed Ace's face when I got my shot in about Misty had torn through me. I hated Ace, truly hated him, but that pain had cut me too. It had come across genuine, something I needed to be mindful of; Ace was fake.

I turned the bike towards Hell's Rage. The bar should be open now. I needed to interview the waitresses that were on at the time Kayleigh disappeared. See what they remembered. Find out if they remembered Kayleigh leaving with Misty and Thunder. If they did then they might fuck with the flow of information I intended to control.

I walked in and saw Gunner and Mac behind the bar. A woman was with them doing inventory. My lip curled when Jacked walked out of a door and crossed his arms and looked at me. Jacked had become one of those Kayleigh had hated. I approached Gunner, who turned to look at me, his calm grey eyes closed and wary.

"What do you want?" Gunner asked in a low tone.

"Need to speak to Tati, April, Sue-Beth and Cliff, Donny. And James," I named the waitresses and barmen who'd worked that night.

"Tati and Donny don't work here anymore. April is in the back with Sue-Beth, and Cliff and James are on at five," Gunner replied. The clock showed I'd an hour to wait.

"I'll speak to the women." I moved to walk past him, and Gunner reached out and grabbed my arm.

"Don't like you, don't like what you're doing. Don't enjoy an outsider meddling in MC business."

"I just bet you don't, do you, Gunner? All those little secrets coming to light." Gunner's eyes flashed a warning. "Take your hand off me before I make you," I warned him. Gunner slowly released me, and I met the hostile gazes of Jacked and Mac. Unafraid, I met them stare for stare before they turned back to what they were doing. Mac stopped me at the door.

"I understand why Drake brought you in, but I don't like it but understand it. If a brother is involved, Ace will tear the club apart. None of them can be impartial, Fish, Apache, Slick, Ace, or Drake. None of them can see past those pictures. For eleven years, I watched Ace die until there was nothing left except Rage. I want him to have whatever peace you can find, but you won't rip the MC apart bitch, I won't let you do that."

"I'd be more worried about yourself, Mac," I replied and walked through the door.

After a fruitless half an hour with the waitresses, I got nothing. They didn't remember Kayleigh being there that night. Hell, they didn't even remember that night. Which meant the only information would be what I fed Rage. I hung around and spoke to the guys and got much the same info, except for James. He remembered Thunder and Misty entering the bar and Kayleigh leaving but couldn't recall them leaving together.

I nodded my head and took my info and left. I chased Tati and Donny down at their homes and found they barely remembered that night either. Donny was too stoned to even care what day it was. Tati had her hands full with kids and life. Nah, they'd give Rage no leads.

I rode back to Rage later after eating and grabbing a beer. The clubhouse was buzzing with the energy the guys emitted; I walked in and paused, skanks stopped and looked at me. Rage's three old ladies stopped and stared. I sneered at the skanks sending them warning looks and gave a curt nod to the old ladies.

Inwardly I snickered as even the brothers stopped and looked at me. I walked towards the inner sanctum and tilted my head towards Drake. He rose to his feet, kissed Phoenix on the top of her head and followed.

"I've a name, no idea where he is, but a witness firmly puts him in Hell's Rage. And puts him and Misty in the bar at the same time as Kayleigh the night she disappeared. The witness remembers Kayleigh looked upset." The door opened, and Ace walked in and leant back against it. I'd dithered over giving them this information, but I knew I'd find them before Rage did.

"What name?" Drake said, his voice low and ominous sounding.

"Thunder and Misty were both seen." Ace jolted.

"Thunder?" Ace sounded dumbstruck.

"Holy shit," Drake said.

"Thunder was forced from the MC when Drake took over Rage. He was one of a few of Bulldog's group that remained standing," Ace replied slowly. "For three years, asshole looked me in the face, knowing what he'd done."

"Semen was found inside Kayleigh and DNA under her nails. Find Thunder, get his DNA, and you'll have an answer."

"Anyone else?" Drake asked, searching my face. I shook my head, too soon for the rest. A little at a time, let the guilty assholes sweat.

"For now, no. Thunder and Misty are the two you need to track."

"Thank you," Ace mumbled. I saw burning in his eyes and was shocked to realise it was vengeance. Bastard. I nearly outed Ace then but kept my mouth shut with effort.

"You get Thunder and Misty. They'll give up whoever else was involved. Be prepared," I said, turning to Drake and ignoring Ace totally. "This goes deep, deeper than you realise. Brace," I warned Drake softly. Drake looked into my eyes, and I could see him trying to work out my secrets. Drake couldn't be protected from what was to come, neither could anyone else. With a sigh, I left the room.

"Artemis," Drake called as I walked across the forecourt to my bike. I stopped and turned to face him.

"You have more than you're letting on, darlin'."

"Yup," I said.

"You're not gonna share?"

"Nope, Drake, you ain't ready, one step at a time, one betrayal at a time. Wish I could spare you this."

"Can make you talk." Drake pushed. I shrugged off my jacket. Drake stepped back as I whipped off my tee and stood in front of him in a bra and jeans. I turned slightly in the light, making sure Drake could see my torso. Widened eyes told me he could see fine, so I began touching scars and giving explanations.

"Knife to the ribs, tried gutting me while I was tied to a pole, took him down with the knife still inside me. Always tie legs at the thighs if you're hanging someone from a hook. Two gunshot wounds, while rescuing a little girl, held her tight and got her the fuck out of there." I turned my back, and Drake made a low noise. A huge diagonal slash jagged from shoulder to waist.

"Machete, drug dealer in Detroit. Didn't appreciate I'd taken half his gang down and brought them in for the bounties on their heads." I spun in the opposite direction and faced Drake. A tattoo of an old-fashioned galleon covered my left ribs. I took his hand and ran it across the tattoo, so Drake felt the scarring under it.

"Held captive for four days and tortured. They began peeling off my skin, a slice at a time. Skin grafts replaced the skin I lost." I gazed into his eyes as I dragged my tee back on. Drake caught my hands and pulled the tee back up. He traced a scar that ran from hip to hip, his eyes questioning Drake looked at me.

"That one, Drake? You want the truth behind that one?" Drake nodded silently.

"Tied to a table and cut from hip to hip after being caught, government assignment. Can't discuss it, but I walked out of there with my guts slashed open and finished my mission. They had their hands inside me, Drake, when I made my move, and I didn't leave anyone breathing. I used rags to wrap around my open guts. Don't need to mention the raging infection that surfaced after that." Drake let go of my tee and looked at me.

"Think you can make me talk now? You haven't seen half the scars I carry or the ones inside. No one can make me talk. Because, you see this," I swished my hand at my body, "this is a shell, I get caught, get hurt, I shut down, go places no one can reach. I'm simply not there. Do what you want to my body because you can't touch me. No one will ever touch me again." Drake's eyes flashed, and I sensed his question before he asked it.

"Showtime is over, Drake. Good luck hunting Thunder and Misty. If I find more, I'll contact you. But I believe they'll have the answers you need."

"Owe you a marker."

"Don't need your marker because, by the time you clean house, you won't have much of an MC left." Plus despite my words, Drake and Rage would never get their hands on Thunder and Misty before me.

"You got a marker, woman and my thanks."

"Thanks, I'll take. I like Phoenix, admire what she does, and I like the fact you make her happy. So yeah, Drake, I'll take your thanks, your marker I don't need." Secure in the knowledge, I'd sown the seeds that would bring down the shit left inside of Rage, I got on my bike. Drake ran his hand through his hair as he watched me.

"You're a good guy Drake, great with Phoe, loyal to your MC, don't let loyalty blind you when the truth comes out. The truth will come out, and it'll make or break you. Don't let it break you. There's a young girl who thought the world of you for the way you acted the night you saved her. Don't let that girl down again," I muttered to him and rode off into the night. If I hadn't had been in a hurry, I'd have seen the look that crossed Drake's face. If I had, I'd have been worried.

"Need to call in a marker," Drake said to the man who answered the phone. He was in his home office at Reading Hall. Phoe was curled up in bed and waiting for him to join her.

"What do you need, man?" Dylan Hawthorne asked.

"I need information on a bounty hunter called Artemis." Drake heard a huff down the phone.

"Artemis is difficult to get a lock on. We've tried," Hawthorne replied. Dylan Hawthorne owned the premier private investigation company in Rapid City. His men were known to play it loose and fast to get the results they wanted.

"I've activated Antonio Ramirez, too; I want everythin' on her. Be needin' it quickly."

"Ramirez can run different searches from me, find out what bounties she's brought in. And what else Artemis is involved in," Hawthorne said agreeing.

Ramirez, Hawthorne, and Drake had crossed paths earlier this year when Phoenix was targeted by an insane fucker and her ex-husband. They stayed in touch because Miguel Santos had decided he'd an interest in Phoe. Santos was an extremely dangerous kind of crazy fucker, and he was still out there. He'd gone to ground, and no one could find him.

"No one knows shit about her," Dylan mused, "Artemis is good. Exceptionally good at what she does, but she's a loner. Hardcore."

"Woman's got body scarring, suspicious in the placement," Drake replied. "Says she got it during kidnap and rescue, but it strikes me as off."

"She ringin' your bell?" Hawthorne asked.

"More ways than one, look at links to Kayleigh Mitchell. I overheard a conversation. She was called Stace in it."

"You think there's a link?" Hawthorne asked, surprised.

"Not ruling anythin' out, man," Drake said and hung up the phone. Pre-occupied, Drake walked upstairs, where his wife waited.

I swung the bike into the garage and dismounted and entered the house through the side door. Two bodies launched in my direction, and I caught them before falling on my ass. I squeezed them both tightly and let them go to get to my feet.

"Mom! Mom! I made the little league team," my son yelled. Excited, he grabbed my hand and jumped up and down; I crouched and grabbed him in a tight hug. Falcon threw his arms around my neck and kissed my cheek.

"That's wonderful," I said, proud of my little man. My eyes drifted towards his sister, who was grinning as well. "Go on," I encouraged her.

"Won my three heats," Nova danced happily on the

spot. I grabbed her in a hug and tussled her hair. My kids were sporting, and in that, they took after me. Falcon was going to be tall. He was already nearly my height, and his body showed evidence he'd have his father's build.

Nova was my little darling, a vicious, bloodthirsty little darling who looked like a baby doll. She'd my body type, and it was obvious she'd be dainty. But Christ, Nova looked like her brother and, therefore, her father.

Falcon played baseball, ice hockey and was one of the best swimmers in his league. He'd been swimming since he was born. My brother Akemi had been teaching both of them mixed martial arts and ju-jitsu before they could walk. Nova, the same as Falcon, was into swimming and swam like a fish but did it for fun. Her thing was kicking the shit out of someone in a tournament. Nova had no mercy, only a desire to win and my determination and cut-throat philosophy, which made her unbeatable.

Nova flicked her hair back and grinned, showing me the trophies she'd won in this tournament. Usually, I didn't miss an event, but this shit with Rage had kept me away. There was a bustle, and Akemi and Mrs Humphries, my live-in housekeeper, entered the kitchen.

"Stacey," Mrs Humphries smiled. She opened the fridge and began pulling out food. Mrs Humphries idea of love was to feed someone to death, and my housekeeper was a damn good cook.

Akemi walked towards me, drew me into his arms, and kissed the top of my head before ruffling the kid's hair. Falcon took it in his neat little dude way, but Nova scrambled all over him, climbing him like a monkey.

"Home for a while?" Akemi asked.

"Yes, I've taken a two-week leave. Kids have finished their tournaments for a few weeks, so I thought we'd go away."

"That's a smashing idea, Stacy," Mrs Humphries said, frying bacon, steak and eggs at the stove.

"Thought we'd all go," I said, looking at Mrs Humphries and Akemi. They both looked shocked. "Oh, come on," I said laughing, "we are family, right?" I saw tears in Mrs Humphries eyes, and Akemi lost his usual stoic look.

"Where do you want to go?" I asked everyone sitting at the breakfast bar.

"Anywhere is fine with me, dear," Mrs Humphries said, turning back to breakfast. The kids began an immediate argument about where to go. Akemi raised his eyebrows and then jerked his head towards the office. I caught his non-verbal command and, excusing myself, went to my office.

"People are running searches on you; I've heard from Master Hoshi. He's blocking every effort, but something small may slip through." I rocked back on my heels, and my eyes narrowed.

"Poxy Drake Michaelson," I snapped at Akemi.

"Indeed, Master Hoshi is on it. None will meet fruition. But, power players of Rapid City have been utilised, Dylan Hawthorne and Detective Antonio Ramirez."

"Fuck, fuck, fuck."

"Master Hoshi is on it," Akemi repeated and drew me into his arms. "They may be the best, but no one is better than Master Hoshi." I heard running footsteps.

"Let's hope not," I said as the kids burst in laughing.

Later that night, I tucked the kids into bed and kissed them goodnight. They fell to sleep, worn out at last. After a hectic day of packing and booking flights and hotels, they were whacked. Nova had got her choice of destination after she pinned Falcon three times.

Leaving the night light on, I left their adjoining rooms and made my way downstairs to my office. Akemi sat there watching me, his elbows on his knees and his fingers pointed upwards, and he leant his chin on them.

"Artemis, are you sure you want to do this?" Akemi asked. I nodded. I dialled a number I learned off by heart, and a soft voice answered.

"Phoe, it's Artemis."

"Hey honey, how are you?" she asked.

"I'm good, but I've some bad news for you."

"Oh my god, Artemis, what's happened?" Phoe

exclaimed. I heard rustling behind her and a soft murmur from Drake. I narrowed my eyes and squared my shoulders.

"Did you a favour, one I didn't want to do when you asked me to get involved in Rage's business. Made it plain I didn't want to work with Rage, and you begged me to work with them.

Now they're looking into me. That's unforgivable. Rage and your husband's friends, Hawthorne, and Ramirez are running searches on me. You and I are both aware, I'm off-limits. As of now, I'm unavailable to you, and I won't be taking any calls from you ever again. Our business ends tonight."

"Honey, no!" Phoe exclaimed, shock colouring her voice. I felt a pang of guilt and then pushed it away.

"Goodbye," I said and hung up the phone. Akemi took the phone and snapped the phone in half before hugging me, and I left the room and headed to bed.

Phoe sat her ass on the bed and stared at her husband in undisguised shock. Drake walked over to her and crouched in front of her.

"Baby?"

"Artemis just cut me," Phoe whispered.

"What do you mean?" Drake asked although he'd a good idea.

"She's told me never to contact her again. Artemis

has cut the Trusts and me. Drake, you have any idea how much work Artemis did for the Trusts? How invaluable she is? Without her, we won't get half the leads we did!" Phoenix's voice began to rise.

"Baby," Drake began.

"No! Don't baby me! Artemis was my friend, I trusted her, and she trusted me. She did me this favour, and you blew it up into more than what it was. You went after Artemis, and now she's walked away. You cost me a friend."

"Artemis knows more than she is telling," Drake thundered. Phoe blinked at the evidence of his anger.

"So fucking what, you've leads follow them up. Find the truth on your own backs," Phoe finally shrieked at him.

"This is about Rage, you have no say in Rage, baby, and you know it," Drake roared back. Phoe's eyes narrowed on him.

"I see. So, you can mess with the Trusts and walk away, and it doesn't matter that our mission is saving lives. But God forbid that I know something or someone that can help Rage? Rage is more important than what I'm doing?" Drake spun around and narrowed his eyes.

"Think about what you sayin' baby. Nothing comes before Rage." Phoe paled at his words, and she stared at Drake in disbelief.

"Nothing?" Phoe asked, touching her stomach. Drake's eyes narrowed on her stomach and then Phoe as she paled even further.

"Don't fuckin' go there, woman," Drake snarled. Phoe shook her head.

"I think I said it plain enough. You don't give a toss that you've messed with the Trusts. You think my friend is hiding shit from you. And you didn't care who or what got hurt when you set your hounds on her," Phoe said weakly.

"I set my hounds on her as you put it, baby," Drake sneered. "Because that bitch knows more than what she said. Artemis knows more about Kayleigh than she let on. I want answers. Ace deserves answers."

"Yeah, at the cost of my friendship and my work." Drake ran his hands through his hair. Why couldn't Phoe see he had to protect the club, he had to get answers for his brother? Drake glanced at her and saw she was paler than ever, he felt a twinge of guilt, and then anger pushed it away.

"Goin' for a shower," he said and walked away. Phoe stared at him with her mouth open. Drake didn't care. Her husband knew what the Trusts meant to her, and he didn't give a damn. Phoe grabbed a bag and shoved clothing in it before he got out of the shower. Quickly, Phoe grabbed a piece of paper and wrote on it.

Phoe understood what Rage meant to him, and this Kayleigh thing had blown shit wide open. There was an undercurrent in Rage, and everyone was aware of it. She'd tried to be strong and give Drake and the

MC what they needed. But this shit with Artemis was the straw that broke the camel's back. Drake simply didn't care that he'd hurt the Trusts. Drake had just made Phoe's position in the grand scheme of Rage clear, and it was way at the bottom.

Phoe left the room at a run, tears sliding down her face. She snatched her car keys and purse, as she left the home they called theirs and got in her car. Drake exited the shower and walked into the bedroom.

"Phoe?" he called. Drake's gaze drifted to the open drawers, and he felt something twist in his gut. He turned to the walk-in closet and saw clothes scattered on the floor. A piece of paper lay on the bed, and Drake picked it up.

"Nothing means more to you than Rage, you said. Which means our child and me. You put your club before us, and not even your child means more to you than Rage. You don't respect my Trusts or me. I'm not your whore, Drake; I was meant to be your wife. Goodbye."

Drake read out loud and sank to the bed. Shock caroused through him as he realised his words and the impact on his wife. The woman who lit up his life and brought light to his darkness. Drake's pregnant wife, his child, who he'd never thought to have. He'd fucked up. Seriously fucked up. He'd wait for her to calm down and talk to her, explain that the club had to have answers.

Phoe had to understand what Rage was to him. He wouldn't let her leave him. She was his, and so was his kid. The woman just had to understand her place. He'd clear it up with her and sort this shit out. Drake loved her, and she knew that. Phoe just had to learn that if she had shit that could help the club, then he'd use that shit.

"Phoe?" Drake whispered into the dark night. There was no reply because his beautiful wife was gone.

Chapter Three.

21st October 2014.

Three weeks later, I sat on a gurney as a nurse tried to convince me to take an injection as she eyed the slash on my arm. I raised my eyebrows at her as she waved the needle in my direction again.

"Just stitch me up," I said, exasperated. I'd got cut bringing in a pimp. There'd been a sweet bounty on his head. Not too high a prize, but considering what he did to his girls, it'd been a pleasure.

He hadn't been a legal bounty, the brother of one of the girls was an underground player with pull. He'd taken offence that his little sister's boyfriend had forced her into prostitution. Hadn't liked the fact that the boyfriend/pimp had beaten and cut her to obey him. It had seriously been an absolute pleasure to bring the asshole in.

The idiot managed to cut me once, and that was an accident because he'd slipped on his fake tiger fur rug. The idiot now sat behind bars after I beat his ass. I was currently in North Dakota, sitting in a hospital in Grand Forks. My phone rang, and I saw the dirty look, the nurse gave it and me. Deliberately ignoring her, I whipped it out and hit connect.

"Artemis, don't hang up. It's Carmine; Ma's been shot." My body stiffened. What the fuck? Phoenix shot?

"Details," I snapped out.

"Things been volatile between Ma and Drake last three weeks. Real bad, she's not been home when Drake's been here, and he's started sleeping at the clubhouse. Yesterday Ma went to Rage, and someone shot her on the forecourt, Drake's lost it, and shit's hitting the fan. Ma's seriously hurt Artemis, she's been in surgery twice. Chance is kicking in so many doors the cops are involved," Carmine whispered.

I closed my eyes, and the image of Carmine hit my lids. A tall teen, now eighteen, who plays for the Cubs, Carmine was completely baseball mad. The second eldest of Phoenix's many kids. White father and black mother gave him beautiful mocha coloured skin. Phoenix adopted him four years ago when her feet hit the States. Carmine had been a street kid and struggling to look out for his street brothers and sister. Phoenix hadn't messed around and had adopted the lot of them.

"Okay," I said and snapped my phone shut. "You got five minutes to stitch me up, and then my ass hits the door." The nurse grunted.

I arrived at the command centre in Sioux Falls just under six hours later. Buzz got me a private flight home that was waiting for me by the time I hit the airport. The flight plan was pre-filed, and we took off twenty minutes after my arrival. My bike was at the airport, so I grabbed my rucksack and swung up on it.

The six hours I'd given Buzz meant he'd been busy. Akemi and Master Hoshi had been contacted, and their eyes and ears hit the ground. Buzz called in our hacker, who'd been on his day off. Nigel was crazy mad at computers. There wasn't an organisation he hadn't hacked into, yeah, including ones such as the FBI and NSA. I swung through our office door and strode into the computer room.

Nigel was drinking coffee and punching away at his systems, his eyes wide, and I saw he was on a caffeine high. He pointed towards Buzz, who was shuffling things around and on the phone.

"Angel and Kristoff are on the ground in RC. (Rapid City) Nigel's on the 'puters, and Akemi is chasing a lead," Buzz updated me. "Simone and Butch have an ETA of an hour."

"You pulled them in?" I asked, knowing the answer. Of course, he had, ex-military himself, what Phoenix did, meant a shitload to him. Buzz worked for me, but he'd two loyalties, his brothers in arms and us. And

Buzz's own history made it a no brainer.

We operated off the books. You didn't find us in a phone directory. We built a solid reputation up by word of mouth. I'd started this on my own, whatever you want to call this, a bounty hunting service, kidnap and rescue service, mercenaries, mayhem and murder. Whatever.

At first, it had been me alone, with Akemi taking my back when I needed it. Buzz came along next. I found him putting up a damn good fight outside a bar in Wyoming, trying to kick the shit out of six men. Brave Buzz might have been, but he was losing, and I intervened. That night he followed me, then he tracked me three nights later, and I hired him. Buzz was a paranoid nutcase, but his creativity with weapons was unsurpassed. He'd been a weapons specialist in the army, which explained his crazy skills.

Angel was one of Master Hoshi's little projects much the same as me, only he was more fucked in the head. Dangerously fucked, Angel had no line he wouldn't cross, apart from innocent women and children. Master Hoshi realised that and gave the man to me, so I kept him busy.

Kristoff was a career criminal and had been on the streets since he was six. He'd survived many things others wouldn't. Kristoff excelled at what he did, and we'd crossed paths a few times. When I realised he'd come to the attention of the cops, and they planned to nail him, I swooped instead. Buzz wiped everything on him, and Kristoff was clean.

Simone was my virtual twin. She thought like me, acted like me and had the same morals and ethics as me. We were, though, night and day in looks. Butch was the only one she'd work with and vice versa. Simone was another of Master Hoshi's projects.

If I thought Angel was certifiably insane, Butch wiped the floor with him. A big man who moved like a ghost, Butch had special force training. He'd been held hostage and tortured for two years by the Taliban. The minute he got free, he killed everyone in that camp in cold blood. Over forty men died. As a by your leave, Butch brought home six marine hostages, alive. Akemi found him and helped him channel his anger before it broke loose on an innocent population.

Nigel was a geek. He spoke computer and lived computer, and he didn't care who knew it. Wiry and slender, which disguised that Nigel was tough despite the fact he was a geek. Nigel and Buzz had hacked into every single system in the world. Those two together on a problem meant nothing was safe. Of course, the logical thing was to put them together, they earned good money, and Buzz liked money. His bitches liked money, and so he was onto a good thing with me.

I'd ended up running a business with people I paid a fuck load of money to. Master Hoshi sent his projects to me if they needed direction. Between us, we'd formed a company named Artemis. When people asked what Artemis looked like, they received varying stories. No one knew who Artemis was. No one knew whether I was male or female.

Artemis coasted the legal bounties which my guys hunted. When various people turn up claiming to be Artemis, well, that's why there were multiple descriptions of me. No one had a lock on the real Artemis.

My guys took ninety percent of the bounty money for their catches. The other ten percent paid Buzz, Nigel, and any equipment we needed. Artemis coasted the illegal bounties, and we took what we wanted. Every one of us had a shit load of money in our banks and hidden bank accounts. And we did, I repeat, what we wanted. Artemis was the best.

No one knew we'd a home base and offices. It wasn't known that Artemis comprised of more than one person. Suspected? Sure. But no one had proof. No one had contact with us outside our identity as anything other than Artemis. I know agencies and P.I's such as Hawthorne's investigated us. FBI, NSA, CIA, MI5 looked for us.

Thanks to the dynamic duo, they got shit on us, not even a photo. Anything electronic disappeared, including cop footage of us in their stations. Cops gave up bitching that their systems went haywire when Artemis entered their domain.

We'd earned our reputation of being ghosts. That's

all I wanted. Buried deep in layers upon layers of bullshit, we'd wiped our true identities. Every single one of us lived under aliases, and that's how we wanted it. Only one thing had ever slipped out. I'd been linked to an organisation known as Revenge. Sounds dramatic, right? It wasn't.

Less was known about Revenge than Artemis. It had only slipped out because someone Master Hoshi had taken in betrayed us. The traitor spoke to the cops, but we were three minutes too late in taking him out. To clarify, I didn't take him out. Revenge did. Rumours of Revenge went around the circuits. When the traitor's tale couldn't be confirmed, everyone dismissed Revenge as a fable as one of those bullshit stories made up to frighten people. No one knew it was real. Rumours of Revenge died a quick death. We made sure of that.

I eyed the whiteboard that Buzz scribbled on. Next to his handwriting was Nigel's with arrows and shit pointing at Buzz's stuff. I turned back to Buzz for the update he'd have. Buzz hung up the phone and looked into my eyes.

"Phoenix is stable but critical, but she may need further surgery." The snake that had been in my belly loosened. I may have cut her loose, but I still admired, respected and yeah, I cared about her.

"The baby?" I asked.

"Alive for now. It's being monitored closely."

"Guards?"

"Phoenix has Rage on her door, and Hawthorne's on the entrance to the ward. RCPD is showing a high presence. No one will get close. Someone of Phoe's status, RC, is lucky the fucking guard ain't been called out. The info we have comin' in isn't good, woman. Since you landed your bombshell on Rage, they have been turnin' Rapid City inside out. Kickin' in doors and upsettin' folk.

Word got back to various players, and Thunder acted. Angel is tryin' to track whether Thunder called in the warnin' hit or did the hit himself. Thunder's gone to ground with the whore of the year with him. Now RC has Hellfire rampaging through the city. It's a goddamn mess out there."

"Buzz, I'm going to shower and eat. I want answers when I get back," I muttered. Buzz nodded.

Half an hour later, I sat my ass on Buzz's desk, eating cold pizza as he informed me that Thunder had called in the hit. Fuckin' gangbangers, four guys Thunder hired, did the hit. One followed Phoe, the second and third shot at her, and the fourth drove the get-away car. I'd names, faces, and I'd places to be; I shifted towards the door.

"Get some sleep, then I want Thunder and Misty found. Boots on the street, I want them." The snake returned to my belly at the thought of them. Raping and torturing a teenage girl to death hadn't been enough for their black souls. No, they'd shot Phoe, who was pure goodness, an angel. A woman who did no harm.

I swung into my SUV and drove, fate had an appointment to keep. It was gonna be dirty and messy, and that's what I did. I excelled at dirty and messy.

Drake sat by his wife's bed and gazed at her still face. Thirty-six hours had passed since Phoe was shot on the forecourt of Rage. His wife, who should have been safe walking her ass across the land that Rage had bled for, hadn't been.

Phoe hadn't spoken to him for three weeks. Three weeks in which the emptiness inside him grew and turned bitter, Phoe had been right as much as it galled him. Drake hadn't considered the Trusts or his wife in his rush to get something on Artemis. He'd known what the hunter did for Phoe, and he'd ignored that. His arrogance shamed him now.

Emily informed him a week ago that Phoe was walking the streets in Houston, where Artemis had been tracking two brothers. They'd been marines, and both ended up on the streets, unable to cope with the PTSD they'd brought home. With Artemis gone, Phoe had taken on the task.

The Phoenix Trust had found one brother half dead. The PT feared the younger brother, a kid of just twenty-three, was dead. Phoe had been searching for him. Drake may have the death of a marine on his conscience. Jesus, a marine. Without Artemis, Emily informed him snottily, the job was more challenging and taking longer. The older brother faced a shit load of rehab and physio. If they'd been two days earlier finding him, it wouldn't have been so bad.

Drake had caused that. Drake had no choice but to accept responsibility for the pain and harm caused to the brothers. He'd no idea if they'd found the younger brother. He'd not even known his wife returned to RC until shots rang out across the forecourt. Drake watched in horror as Phoe was gunned down in front of his eyes. Drake sensed Carmine at his shoulder and looked up as his stepson squeezed his shoulder. The boy had flown in yesterday.

"I put in a call Drake. I had to," the teen said. Visibly Carmine swallowed as he gazed at the woman who'd given him a home, family, love and a life. Drake didn't ask who his stepson had called. Carmine could only have called one person. With Chance on the warpath already, it only left Artemis for Carmine to call.

Drake nodded and kept on holding her hand. His other hand rested on her stomach where for now, their child lived. It was too early for the baby to survive outside the womb. Drake knew it, and he prayed, he fuckin' prayed like never before, the thud of two heartbeats kept his own going. His wife's and his child's. If one stopped... no, Drake couldn't go there.

Chance was tearing apart RC. The underworld had fuckin' shit itself and hidden. Ramirez had been in to inform Drake, if Chance and Hellfire continued, Chance would be arrested. Drake shrugged, not the first time his cousin faced a cell. Several snitches had gone missing from their usual haunts, and Drake had no doubts Chance was behind the disappearances.

Carmine sat, his head between his hands. During the day, his siblings took turns visiting the room, Drake refused to leave. So they'd taken ten-minute visits, so everyone got a chance. The best doctors had been flown in, and so far, their mother held on to life. Carmine just needed Phoe to open her beautiful eyes and smile at him. God couldn't be so cruel that after giving him a mother, he'd take her away.

The door opened, and Micah entered; the teen looked shattered. He'd flown in on a red-eye yesterday morning, coming from Miami. Micah was apprenticing car designs under a famous streetcar designer in Miami. Drake studied Phoe's oldest child, the boy who'd become a man before he should have. Sometimes, Drake wondered if Micah sat on the fence, waiting for Drake to fuck up. Well, Drake had certainly fucked up this time.

Micah looked at his mother lying in bed, and his face twisted. His gaze drifted to his brother, and Micah grasped Carmine's shoulder and squeezed. He strolled to Drake and repeated the action. Drake's hand rose off Phoe's stomach and clasped his stepsons' hand.

"I want blood," Micah whispered, "I want blood, and I want oceans of it." Drake nodded.

Before entering the warehouse, I cased it and then walked in. Angel whistled, and I whistled back twice before following the sound. Angel stood on the first floor in the middle of the deserted building. Tied to a chair, beaten and bloody, was a pockmarked man. His skin was sallow and so scarred with acne pockmarks, he could have been a dot-to-dot puzzle.

I walked forward, allowing my motorbike booted clad feet to make a noise. The target lifted his head, and his eyes were dull. He spat blood, and it dripped down his chin and onto his stained and bloodied shirt.

"Part of a local gang, the Black Lords," Angel said in his low tones.

"Bastards signed their death warrant." The man looked up. He looked to be late twenties as he drew in a rattling breath.

"You're dead bitch." His head dropped, and I looked at Angel.

"Had playtime?" I asked. Angel grinned.

"Sure did."

"He'll survive the transport to Rage?"

"He'll live."

"Contact the Rage VP Ace, tell him I'm bringing in

four." I crouched next to the chair and grabbed the man's hair and forced his head up.

"You shot an innocent woman, Phoenix Michaelson, who only does good. You and your little gangbangers fucked up. See, Rage let you run around and play at being hard men. They're okay with that as long as you didn't fuck with Rage. You fucked with Rage.

You just wiped your pissant gang out. Michaelson's woman is in critical care, and he wants blood, so he'll have yours first. One by one, your members will fall, then Michaelson will work his way up until the streets bleed red. And they'll bleed, believe me." I slapped his face in a 'there, there' gesture and motioned for Angel to put him in the van. I'd a delivery to make.

"The other three?" Angel asked, walking beside me.

"Simone, Butch and Kristoff played. Buzz got inventive, but his target is still breathing," I replied. Angel nodded. His code of honour was shady, always would be, but innocents were off-limits. If an innocent needed taking out, Angel walked away. Wouldn't do it.

"They in the van?"

"Hogtied like presents on Christmas morning. Just bring your piece of shit to join them." Angel turned on his heel as I climbed inside the black van.

I watched as Angel slid the van door open and threw the body inside. The smell of fear penetrated every inch of the van; I didn't care. A woman lay fighting for her life and that of her unborn child, and I just didn't care. As Angel walked away, I saw him pull his phone from his pocket. Angel turned the corner of the warehouse and flipped me a salute, I was good to go.

Rage had sent directions to a clearing, Buzz acting the go-between, forwarded them to me. Bikes lined the clearing, and as I pulled the van into a space, I realised the entirety of Rage and Hellfire was present. Even the prospects, only Drake was missing. Ace strode forward, and I slid out of my seat and met him face to face. Chance stood tense; his hands clenched into fists.

Shadows moved behind him, and I took in Micah, Carmine, Jodie, Tye and Serenity. Rage had brought Phoe's children. Their choice, Chance and Drake, would have approved it; I searched their faces and decided not to create a scene. The kids knew what Rage was, knew what Chance and Drake were. They knew this wouldn't be pretty, and bodies would hit the ground. It was their decision. The kids were old enough to choose. Behind them, guarding them, stood Axel, Big Al, and Texas.

"Four inside. They belong to Black Lords," I said to Ace as he approached, observing his face carefully. It was blank, but a burning fury showed in his eyes. Ace nodded towards Lowrider and Manny, opened the van doors, and Chance climbed inside. Ace cocked an eyebrow at me at their condition. Chance stared at the four assholes I'd delivered and lifted his foot aiming a mighty kick at one.

"Appears they'd some trouble," Chance growled.

"Don't like their kind."

"You don't enjoy lots of shit," Ace replied.

"Nope."

"What do you want for this?"

"I'll speak to Drake." Ace shot a hand out and caught me by the arm. Chance turned that frightening glare on me. Ace beat him to the punch.

"You'll talk to me."

"You have three seconds to remove your hand Ace, or I remove it for you. I said I'll talk to Drake, and I meant Drake." Ace lowered his head to mine. I refused to give an inch.

"Drake is at his woman's bedside, praying her and their child to live. You'll talk to me." I let my lip curl.

"What I want, you can't give me. So back away, big boy, and let me walk, or they won't be the only ones lying bleeding."

"Ace," Apache said in a low tone. He'd walked to his son's side and now stood behind him. Ace stepped forward into my space, backed me against the van, and his arms came up to cage me in against it.

"Don't push me, Ace," I warned. Ace's gaze dropped to my mouth; yeah, my mouth. What the ever-loving fuck?

"What'll happen if I do, baby?" Ace murmured, oh that touched something deep inside me.

Narrowing my eyes at him and taking him by surprise, I slammed both hands on his chest, forcing him backwards. As he moved to counteract my move, I ducked under his arms and gained a few steps. I spun and faced him and crossed my arms against my chest. Ace took one step when the trees rustled, and Akemi stepped into the moonlight. Chance raised an eyebrow, still glowering at the four assholes in the van.

"Did you think I'd come alone?" I asked, sneering. Ace studied Akemi with as much interest as Akemi studied him. Silently, Akemi drifted towards me like a ghost and slid an arm around my waist. Ace's mouth tightened.

"Get them out, got things to do," Chance bit out. I heard movement behind me and looked up at Akemi. He gazed back at me, his face blank but a question in his eyes only I could see. Grimly forcing a half-smile to hit my lips, I shook my head. Akemi's eyes spoke back to me, and I gave him a full grin.

Bodies hit the ground hard, and we turned back to the van. We needed to get it a deep clean and get it put away until next time. As we turned back to the truck, Akemi paused and looked back over his shoulder. Akemi spoke to Chance.

"We don't like what happened. As Drake's old lady, Phoenix should have been off-limits, and she wasn't. If someone has a problem, don't bring an innocent into it. What happened was not a warning.

What follows will be a warning, though. Black Lords will cease to exist in a week, men, women, recruits, children. Black Lords will be gone. That's free, tell Drake, no charge for what's about to happen." Akemi delivered his words in his soft tone. Which made them only more deadly.

Akemi was right. Forty-eight hours later, twenty bodies hit the ground. Every male member of the gang was dead. Women who'd belonged to the gang disappeared or left town taking their babies with them. Families of those fallen left Rapid City fast; recruits decided against gang life. Black Lords ceased to exist, and the street gangs received a very stark warning.

Phoenix still lay in a coma, the woman remained fighting, and life stood still for her family. Rage ran the businesses, but life for Drake froze around the bed his wife lay in. It was now five days since the shooting, the door opened, and he looked up towards it. Micah, Carmine, Jodie, Tye and Serenity walked in, and Drake searched their faces. Chance marched in behind them. The nurse refused to argue with Chance, having done so before and lost.

"It's done. Last night," Micah mumbled. Drake nodded.

"You okay?" Drake asked, wrinkling his brow at the kids. They'd just done something he'd never have asked of them. Drake would never have dreamed of asking them. He'd tried to stop Jodie and Serenity going, but they'd insisted; Micah and Chance backed them. His daughters had bigger balls than most men. Chance nodded at Drake, reassuring him, his kids were fine.

"Yeah, Dad," Serenity replied and walked towards him and curled her body towards his and sank into his lap. Drake's stepdaughter lay her head on his shoulder as his body tightened. The other kid's eyes grew wide. His arms slowly came up around the girl, and Drake held her tight, burying his face in her hair. Chance's lips twitched, but he didn't say anything.

"We're okay," Carmine paused and then, as if trying the word out, said, "Dad." Drake felt his eyes sting.

His arms clenched around Serenity. He'd been in their life just over seven months. The first couple of months had been drama, chaos, and blood. The past few months had been sweet until the last three weeks. Drake loved these kids, they were a part of his beloved wife. What Drake hadn't known was they loved him back.

"Yeah, Dad, we're okay," Jodie said, walking to him and curling against his other side.

"Just dandy, Dad," Micah said. Drake felt that sting get worse, and a tear ran down his face. Acceptance from Micah, of all people, Chance nodded approval at the teen. Drake knew that Micah had wanted Phoe to get with Chance. Tye stood watching. Of the kids present, Tye was the most unapproachable. Tye nodded at Drake.

"We're good, Dad, Rage is good, we're good, and Mom will be good," Tye said. Drake swallowed the lump in his throat as he felt a faint movement against his hands. He looked to the bed and saw his wife's beautiful eyes watching him. A tear ran down her own cheek, Phoe tried to talk, and he moved quickly. Chance appeared at her other side, grasping Phoe's hand tightly.

"You got a breathing tube, baby. Don't fight it." The door slammed, and Micah rushed to get a doctor. The weight eased from Drake's chest that hadn't moved in a week. His wife was awake, alert, and by the tears in her eyes, aware. Chance's haunted look faded as Phoe's hand moved towards her stomach.

"Little Michaelson is alive, baby. Baby's a fighter just like its Mom," Drake muttered. At that, she closed her eyes as tears leaked out of them. Drake brushed them away and held her until the doctors arrived.

Four days later, Drake walked into the inner sanctum and sat his ass in a chair. His wife was still in hospital and recovering. Phoe was weak from three bullet wounds, but she was healing. The hospital had kept her while monitoring the baby for a few extra days. Tomorrow Phoe could go home, today he'd business to attend to. Texas and Ace sat in chairs, and Texas had a package in front of him.

"What's that?" Drake asked. Texas threw him the package, and he opened it.

Inside was a second envelope just as Texas had described, and on opening it, he found a CD. Frowning, he flipped it open and looked at the disc inside. Fish and Apache walked in and took a chair.

"Where's this come from?" Drake asked, confused.

"Found it. Look at the date. Bitch must have missed the mail that year, and I threw it in a drawer. Had a faint memory of doin' that shit, so went hunting and found me a prize," Texas rumbled. Fuck, Texas had found one of the disc's Misty had been keen to get her hands on. Drake put the disc into a CD player that was kept in the room.

They froze in their seats as a blood-curdling scream echoed through the room. Quickly, Drake turned the volume down, more screams sounded and then begging. Ace locked his jaw.

"Don't, please don't. No more Thunder, please, no more. I'm begging you. Stop!" The final word sounded on a scream. There was the sound of something hitting flesh and pain-filled cries.

"Ain't fuckin' no blood," Thunder's voice was heard. More cries, more sobs as they listened to Kayleigh being raped. Misty shouted over the screams, egging him on.

"Fuck her up, good Thunder," Misty yelled. A tick began in Ace's jaw.

"She's fuckin' tight. Ace never fucked her in the ass," Thunder grunted through his pants as he raped Kayleigh.

"Use the bottle, or let me use the bat on her again," Misty cried out excitedly. Bile rose in Ace's throat.

"You can fuck her with that after I'm done. I'd fuck her mouth, but she got no teeth left in it," Thunder laughed and then grunted again. Kayleigh's screams and cries faded.

"Fuckin' cunt is unconscious again," Misty sneered. "Gimme that bat, think she'd some fingers left intact." Sounds of the bat hitting flesh. Thunder and Misty speaking for a few minutes and then a sudden pain-filled scream.

"That's it, Misty fuck her good with that bat. I'm holding the cunt. She inn't going anywhere. Give it to her fuckin' good woman." A few minutes later, the soundtrack ended. Ace was looking at his feet, his shoulders tight. Drake gazed out of the window at his brothers lounging around. Fish cried silently, no shame in his tears as Apache paled. Texas leant over and threw up in a bin.

"You think she got a different CD each year?" Fish asked when he'd control again. That girl had been his daughter in everything but name and blood, to listen to that destroyed him. He'd never let his Marsha hear that.

"Would make sense. Misty wouldn't run from the same piece each year," Drake replied.

"Did we look under the floorboards?" Ace asked. His voice was raw, and Drake understood.

"Tore up the ones in the bedroom and living room."

"Tear them all up. Every fuckin' single one. Artemis said to look under the floorboards."

"On it," Apache said as he left the room. Minutes later, the MC rolled out, Ace remained standing as his father returned.

"Play it again," Ace whispered.

"Ace," Apache said, coming back.

"Play it again."

"Ace, you don't wanna…." Ace cut Fish off with a roar.

"Kayleigh lived that! She fuckin' lived it, play it again!" Drake hit play.

I looked out of the office window and watched as Nigel buried yet another search by Hawthorne's girl. Leila was persistent; I'd give her that. If Hawthorne hadn't got to Leila Gibson before me, I'd have recruited her. She was nearly as good as Nigel and Buzz but not as good.

Buzz smirked at me as he buried the trail her search had been heading for. I could imagine the girl smashing her head on the keyboard as it died a death, the same as the rest of her attempts.

"It's dead," Buzz confirmed. Hawthorne hadn't backed off the last few weeks, instead, his girl got more and more adventurous. Her efforts had highly entertained Nigel and Buzz. Leila was pitting herself against the best of the best. She wouldn't win. I got off my ass and glanced at the screens.

"Keep on it, Nigel," I said, patting his shoulder. Nigel grasped my hand and smiled back at me.

"Anything for you, my love," he grinned, and I strolled out of the door. Falcon and Nova had a tournament today, and I intended to be there. I drove home and got ready.

A long flowing skirt, a gypsy top and bangles at my wrist that covered my leather cuffs. Strappy sandals with thick soles hid the knives they carried. I threw a beige leather beaded choker on. Yeah, it held weapons as well and glancing at the clock, I moved my ass in a hurry. I left my hair down.

And now, I was Stacey Conway, mother of two and a widow. A widow whose husband had been prosperous, we lived in an upper-class area, and I drove a Mercedes. My hair was brown and hung down my back, and I wore brown contacts. I looked nothing like Artemis, who terrified the criminal elements. Just another suburban mother of two.

Akemi fell into step beside me, today was huge for Nova, and we'd both be there. Idly chatting about shit, we got in the car and drove to where my daughter was waiting to win her next tournament. Nova kicked ass and took the first gold, and Falcon took two golds and a silver. Nova then took two more golds. Then Nova took the competitor of the tournament award. It was a good day, a damn good day.

Leila's eyes narrowed as her computer pinged. She looked over, and her mouth dropped open; after four weeks, she'd a match. Leila scrambled to download it before whoever was blocking her acted. It just uploaded as they wiped her search. It didn't matter because she had it. Leila finally had it, and she left the control room running.

Drake sat in a chair at Hawthorne's and tapped his fingers on the table. Ace sat to his right, and Ramirez sat opposite him with a file in front of him.

"We have something," Dylan said, walking in. One of his men, Shane, walked beside him. Leila scurried in behind him and picked up a remote. Clicking on it, an image appeared on a screen. It was a dark picture of a Japanese man. He was tall and slender, his arm wrapped around Artemis. Both faced the camera.

"If Rock hadn't been quick to get the shot, we

wouldn't have anything," Leila said. "I've been running facial recognition and got shit until now." She clicked again, and a picture of a young girl and boy appeared on the screen. It was a newspaper report, and they were in the picture accompanying it. The two of them were dressed in Gi's, used for martial arts. The girl held a trophy above her head and three gold medals in her other hand.

"Meet Nova Conway," Dylan said. "Eleven years old and younger twin of Falcon Conway, Falcon was born ten minutes before his sister. Both Conway's are famous in the world of martial arts. They live with their widowed mother, and strangely, there's not a picture of her anywhere."

Drake sat up, paying attention as he studied the children. A slight frown creased his forehead, and he looked towards Ace. Jesus fuckin' Christ, the kids looked like him, a fuck load like him. A lead feeling sank into his gut, Ace seemed unaware of anything, and Drake swallowed his gut reaction. No one else seemed to be reacting to the likeness between Ace and the two children.

"Their father was Russell Conway, a self-made man who died in a tragic road accident before his children were born. Russell was married six months before his death to Stacy Meadows. Russell's only information is that he was Native American, owned his own business in investments, and there are absolutely no pictures of him anywhere.

Stacy owns her house outright, no mortgage, she drives a two-month-old Mercedes. There's nothing else, no credit, no pictures; she's a ghost. The kids go to an excellent public school, not drawing attention."

"Stace," Drake muttered. Ace nodded. Leila clicked the image of the newspaper again and closed in.

In the background, mixed among many other faces, was a couple. The guy had his arm around the waist of a brown-haired, small woman. As Leila clicked to enlarge the picture again, it grew a little fuzzy. She then superimposed the image of the Japanese man and Artemis over it.

"Facial recognition is seventy percent probable," Leila confirmed. Ramirez slid the file towards Drake.

"Did you know Kayleigh Mitchell had an older sister? It was hard, but I tracked a midwife who remembers Hannah Mitchell's birth. Their mother wanted her tubes tied but had been denied as she was only seventeen when Hannah Mitchell was born."

"Kayleigh never mentioned a sister," Ace denied shaking his head.

"Kayleigh may not have remembered her, but Hannah definitely didn't forget her. Hannah ran away when she turned sixteen; Kayleigh was four. Girl got her ass out and worked her way on a pole, getting an education paid for by that pole. Hannah became a doctor at a hospital. Once settled, she began searching for her sister. It was clear Hannah intended to bring Kayleigh to her and give her a better life."

"She failed," Ace said curtly.

"Yeah, she failed. Her mother had moved and married a piece of shit Adrian Cook, who disappeared in suspicious circumstances." Ramirez didn't look in Drake or Ace's direction. "Hannah Mitchell disappeared four weeks after Kayleigh Mitchell did. This is the only existing photo of Hannah Mitchell."

A photo slid across the table, and Ace drew in his breath. He knew that red curly hair, that button nose and pert mouth. Her frame was slender with full breasts, and she hugged a pole upside down.

"Hannah Mitchell is Artemis?" Ace questioned.

"Lookin' that way. Hannah discovered Kayleigh was murdered; I don't know how but she did. My guys will get more information. Hannah revamped her entire life and became a weapon of revenge."

"Got an address for Hannah Mitchell slash Stacy Conway?" Drake asked.

"Sure have." Ramirez slid a piece of paper across the table. Drake looked at Ace, and they both rose to their feet.

Chapter Four.

2nd November 2014

I sensed eyes on me before I even exited the van. I'd spotted Rage within seconds of pulling into my street. That was okay because I'd a fall-back plan; I always did. I don't know how they found me, but within two hours, I'd find out. Silently, I sent a text to Nigel and Buzz to get them on the exit plan and left the car. Casually, leaning against it, I watched as Ace got out and strolled in my direction.

"Gonna invite me in Artemis?" Ace asked smugly. My palm twitched to slap that look off his face.

"Sure, why not?" I replied and turned on my heel and opened the door. Akemi stood cooking at the stove, and the smell of curry filled the air.

"I see they got out of that van," Akemi grinned. "They've been sitting there three hours now." Akemi giving a time meant he'd alerted the offices, and they were packing. I nodded at him. Ace looked unsure of himself, not so smug, good. Neither of us was reacting the way Ace expected us to.

Akemi nodded once more, and it imparted the information that Mrs Humphries and the kids were long gone. This was good. They'd be in a safe room at Artemis with Simone and Butch protecting them. The fuck I'd let Ace near Nova and Falcon, I picked up a piece of cucumber and popped it into my mouth. Kristoff and Angel would be helping Buzz and Nigel pack the offices.

"What do you want?"

"Want the truth, Hannah," Ace said, playing his trump card. I sighed and shook my head.

"What's that line?" I asked Akemi, and I clicked my fingers, "you can't handle the truth!"

"Stop the bullshit," Ace snarled with a flash of temper.

"Always so impatient, Ace. Never learned, did you? Akemi honey, is that done?" Akemi turned to me and raised an eyebrow.

"Yeah."

"Go clean your weapons," I told Akemi, code for, get the kids and get to the safe house. Akemi left the kitchen, and seconds later, the back door slammed shut. Akemi's bike started up and swung out of the drive. The van followed a second later, and I grinned at Ace.

"Hope that van can go where a bike can." Akemi

would lose it within minutes.

I walked to the stove, dished up rice and several scoops of curry, and sat at the breakfast bar. Steadily, I ignored the dangerous vibes coming from Ace as I dug in and moaned. Akemi could make a curry.

"So, you think finding me means I'm backed into a corner," I spoke to Ace, who had his hips leant against one of the worktops. Ace gave a curt nod; I tutted at him.

"You're Kayleigh's sister."

"You know shit," I said and took another bite of the curry and rolled my eyes in pleasure.

"Fill me in. You found out Kayleigh died and started a revenge binge," Ace stated. I waggled my fork at him.

"Nuh, huh. What revenge binge? I've stayed well away from your fucking MC until now. *You dragged me in,*" I hissed. "You think you know shit, you don't. I do, however, know lots of shit."

"So fill me in," Ace repeated. I shook my head.

"By this time tomorrow, any trace of Stacy Conway and her two children will have disappeared, Akemi will be wiped from history. Do you think we haven't prepared for this?" I asked and took another bite. Green eyes narrowed on me.

"Come on now, Ace, we can move anywhere in the world in hours. New identities for my family, a sparkling new life. And we're both aware, I've a fuck load of money to set straight back up. Hell, I don't even have to take jobs. What I have in the bank I can live on for the rest of my life." I finished the curry and rose to my feet.

"You come into my home and tell me you think you have me." I dumped the plate in the sink and walked straight into Ace's space. "You've shit," I hissed at him. Ace blinked, and before I could move, his hands grabbed me. Ace pulled me into him, and his mouth descended on mine.

Fire lit deep within me as his lips touched mine. Without a thought, mine parted, and his tongue swept in. I've been kissed before, kissed when I was younger, but that was nothing compared to this kiss. The world erupted in flames, and my hands slid into Ace's hair, and I pulled his head closer. I wanted Ace to claim me, and his mouth did precisely that. Ace ended the kiss and raised his head. As he let go of me, I stumbled back, and my hands flew to my swollen mouth.

"What the fuck was that?" I yelled. My calm had gone, shot to pieces by a kiss that shouldn't have happened.

"Best way to shut you the fuck up," Ace said, but desire burned in his eyes.

"Fuck you," I spat. Ace moved fast, and I was in his arms again and his mouth on mine. This kiss was as smouldering hot as the first. Ace's hands slid around my waist and up my shirt. One hand cupped my breast, my nipple hardened under his casual flick, and

I moaned into Ace's mouth.

Of their own accord, my hands slid up his tee, and I touched warm silky skin. I ran my fingers across his back and pulled him into me. Ace's cock was hard, rigid against my stomach, and I moaned again into his mouth. Desire over-ruled any common sense I had.

Ace tore his mouth from me, bent his head and sucked my nipple through my blouse. I cried out and raked my nails down his back. Ace's head rose, and his eyes drilled into me. Oh my god, what the hell was I doing?

I tore myself from Ace's arms and moved as far away as I could get. Panting, I straightened my blouse and tried to regain my famous control. It wasn't there. Shuddering and struggling to regain my composure, I eyed Ace breathlessly.

"Could get used to that look, Hannah," Ace whispered from across the room.

"Never!" I spat. My body betrayed me, and I was beyond furious. How dare Ace affect me this way! Desire for that murderous bastard? What the ever-living fuck?

"Oh, believe me, baby, I'm gonna have my hands on you again, and the way you fuckin' respond, I'll be inside you in minutes."

"Keep dreaming."

"Baby, I'll dream of that kiss all fuckin' week. Never has it been so hot." That was my shot, I saw it, I went for it. Straight for his jugular.

"My sister not so hot?" I asked vindictively, and he shut down. Ace's eyes dulled and grew blank. His body locked and the vibes that came off of Ace made me want to drag those words back.

"Kayleigh was the most amazin', sweetest thing I'd ever seen. Innocence and wild rolled into one. She was my everythin'. Still is my everythin' but let's not pretend you've sisterly feelings for Kayleigh. You left Kayleigh when she was four; you were too late comin' back for her."

"Yeah, way too late, too late to save Kayleigh from the monster she loved. Kayleigh only ever had stars in her eyes when she looked at you. Fucking someone involved in her death, I'm *not* doing," I shouted. Ace moved again quicker than I thought and pinned me to the wall.

"Involved in her death?" Ace's voice dropped low and dangerous. "Involved in Kayleigh's fuckin' death? I searched for fuckin' months lookin' for her. Kayleigh destroyed me when she disappeared. I wasn't even aware Kayleigh was pregnant! I was involved in her death?" Ace roared.

"Kayleigh didn't know. She found out that day," I said stupidly.

"What?" Ace asked, his gaze raking me. Cover, oh shit, cover.

"She'd been feeling ill, visited the doctors that day, I tracked him and spoke to him. The doc told her she was pregnant that day. And I guess Kayleigh went to the bar to tell you." Ace stepped back, and he was a damned good actor, or he didn't know. Pain locked his body in place, and Ace bent over and folded his arms around his gut.

"Kayleigh found out that day?" Ace whispered so quietly I could barely hear him.

"Yeah."

"Keep fuckin' up with her," Ace said in the same voice.

"What do you mean?" I asked, drawn, into his pain despite myself.

"Blamed her for leavin' me, Kayleigh was rottin' in an unknown grave. I thought she couldn't hack what was goin' on at the club, and I blamed Kayleigh for being weak. I hated her for leaving me, fuckin' hated her.

My girl didn't leave me; Kayleigh was taken from me. Then I blamed Kayleigh for not tellin' me she was expecting, and she'd only just found out. I keep fuckin' up with her." Ace's eyes met mine, and they were so full of pain I wanted to reach out and take it away.

"Kayleigh deserved better than you," I snarled before I dwelled further on his pain. I had to stop this, push him away, keep him at arms-length.

"Yeah, she did. Kayleigh deserved a life full of laughter and happiness. A white picket fence and a yard full of flowers," Ace said, his eyes gazing past me and seeing something I couldn't.

"Well, she didn't get it," I growled. Ace looked back at me, but he wasn't seeing me. Ace was seeing her, Kayleigh. I'd never been so confused or conflicted.

"No, she didn't." Ace looked at me suddenly. "Black Lords. That wasn't Rage."

"Nope," I popped out.

"You did that in a week. Disbanded the entire gang."

"Clever girl ain't I to do that on my own."

"Did it for Drake," Ace kept pressing.

"I did it for Phoenix."

"No baby, you did it for Drake, because Drake couldn't do it himself, and the MC was in limbo. You acted before we did because you must have known we'd get to them. Rage weren't gonna let Black Lords walk free after what they did to Phoe."

"I did it for Phoenix," I reiterated.

"Liar."

"Takes one to know one, Ace," I sneered, his gaze raked my face.

"You did it for Phoenix. But also did it for Drake."

"So what if I did?" I shrugged.

"If you did it for Drake, he ain't involved in Kayleigh's murder," Ace summarised. Ah, that was where Ace was leading the conversation. I shrugged.

"So Drake, Fish, Apache and Texas wasn't involved. That's four brothers in the clear. Who was involved?"

"Honey, I'm sure you've that info."

"Who was fuckin' involved?" Ace thundered. I

shrugged and picked up a piece of bread and nibbled on it.

"Isn't it enough you fucked up her life, now you wanna fuck up mine?" I asked, my eyes narrowed.

"Don't wanna fuck up your life," Ace instantly denied.

"Then get the fuck out. You fucked Kayleigh's up, and you haven't got a hope in hell of fucking mine up," I snapped, arms wrapped around myself defensively.

"Don't wanna fuck it up, Hannah. I just want info, and I know you know." Ace's pain bit through me, touching my own pain, and I hated him. Ace had me off guard, and I flipped.

"Bastard, you were in on it!" I shrieked. Ace rocked back on his heels as shock crossed his face.

"What?" he whispered as the blood drained from his face.

"You were in on it!" I repeated, shrieking at him. "Those stupid assholes recorded it. Misty filmed everything because I've seen it. I'm well aware who was involved, Thunder and Misty named each of you. I listened to what they said, I saw what they did. Did you know Misty recorded it so she could watch over and over again, gloating she'd got rid of Kayleigh.

Do you know every time you fucked her that cunt watched parts again. But she didn't expect me. I got into her home, found and stole them. Then each year I sent her clips, letting her know someone had evidence on her and the rest of the cunts involved. I *know* you were involved," I screamed. Pain for the last eleven years uncoiled and lashed out, a monster unleashed. Ace stepped backwards one slow step at a time as I lashed at him with it.

"Thunder and Misty named everyone involved, and I fucking heard them. Kayleigh heard it, she knew you were done, and Kayleigh knew you gave the order! You stand next to Drake and pretend you're innocent. You're a goddamn fucking liar." Ace eyes burned, and he came at me. I moved just as quick and brought the stun gun I had at my waist out of hiding.

We grappled, and I zapped him, and Ace crashed to the floor. Ace looked at me as his body shook with shock. I kicked him hard in the ribs, and I crouched and got in Ace's face.

"I fucking know who was involved because you gave the order. By the time I'm done, Drake, your father, everyone will be aware. The MC will be clean of the scum who votes, gives orders, and follows through on the torture of a pregnant teenage girl. When I'm finished, Rage MC will finally be fucking clean," I hissed at him and rose to my feet. Furious, I allowed my monster to take over and aiming on purpose, I tasered his dick. Ace screamed, and his body shook uncontrollably. Stick his dick in Kayleigh's murderer? Scum.

"I'm just beginning, Ace," I sneered, and I ran from the kitchen and leapt on my bike. I skidded out of my drive and shot off. Drake and Apache raced out of the van, and they ran towards the house and disappeared inside. Just like Kayleigh Mitchell, it was time for Stacy Conway to die.

I jogged up the stairs to the offices. Buzz had seen me and lowered the security measures, so I'd get through the door. He grabbed hold of me and held me tight in his arms.

"Okay?" Buzz asked. I nodded and held on tight.

"You watched," I smiled at him.

"Of course, I did. Ain't stupid, not leavin' one of us hanging out there alone. Jesus, Artemis, a dick shot? That bastard won't walk for a week."

"Good, is everything done?"

"Cleared out an hour ago, honey, nothing's left, not even a scrap of paper," Buzz nodded.

"Meet you outside. There's a tracker on my bike," I mumbled. Buzz nodded and left the offices, and I walked through them, checking everything.

Buzz was right. The clean-up was done and dusted because we'd planned for this. We ran drills every few months, to ensure that we could move the offices within an hour of the alert going off. They'd had three hours, our planning and organisation worked. I walked over to my desk and sat. Opening my purse, I found a sheet of paper. With a grim smile, I pulled a pen from my purse and wrote a note.

I stood up and looked around my office, and then walked into the command centre. The usually busy room was empty, silent, dead, nothing but ghosts here. The smell of bleach overwhelmed me; it had been sprayed everywhere. Killing any fibre, fingerprint, or skin flake, we may have left behind. Artemis was closed for business. Swallowing a lump in my throat, I walked to the window and saw Drake's van pulling up. As I thought they'd a tracker on my bike or me.

A bitter smile briefly crossed my lips, and then I hit the escape panel and disappeared behind it. I walked down the dark hallway to a doorway. As I passed through, an EMP pulse hit me that'd kill any tracker on my body. Noiselessly, I slipped into a dark office and stripped off my clothing and dressed in jeans and a sweater. I pulled on boots and walked out. Two minutes later, I was on the back of Buzz's bike, and we headed to the forest where the cabins were.

Drake, Ace, and Apache walked slowly but with purpose up the stairs. Ace was limping, and in obvious pain. Drake was furious at what Hannah had done to his brother. Artemis's Lowrider was in the garage under the building. The three men had followed Artemis here. Drake was unsure whether to refer to her as Artemis or Hannah, but one thing was certain, he wanted to wring her neck for what she'd done to Ace.

They stopped where the tracker had died and,

without knocking, entered. The offices were dark, and Ace searched and found a light switch on the wall. Ace flipped the switch and looked at the barren reception area that met them.

"Hannah's gone," Ace said.

"Bitch has gone," Drake confirmed as he walked into an office and came out. Drake investigated another room with lots of sockets in the walls and stood in the doorway of a third office.

"Nothing here. This is wiped clean," Apache said thoughtfully. "The tracker's last signal is behind that wall." Apache pointed. Ace and Drake began looking for a hidden button, and Apache found it first. Apache hit it, and they watched as a section of the wall slid open.

"Who the fuck is she?" Drake asked, peering into the dark corridor that was revealed. "No one is this good without trainin'. What fuckin' trainin' has Artemis had?"

Apache disappeared down the corridor and came back minutes later. In his hand, he carried the clothes Hannah had been wearing, including the skirt Ace had slipped the tracker into. It was dead.

"Something hit me as I walked down, a pulse or something. Killed my fuckin' phone," Apache growled.

"An EMP pulse?" Drake asked. "Who the fuck is Artemis?"

"Artemis isn't working alone. There're at least two

men with her," Apache agreed.

"Buzz and Akemi," Drake nodded.

"There are more. Let's get real. It took Artemis two days to lay out twenty gangbangers. She couldn't have done that alone. It took Artemis five more days to wipe the Black Lords groupies from the face of the planet. We've spoken to a couple of the ex-recruits. They've described a woman who, unless Artemis can grow nine inches, isn't Artemis. Artemis is not a person; it's a group. Artemis is just the figurehead," Ace mused.

"You sayin' she fronts this group?" his father asked. Ace looked at him and nodded.

"Whoever Hannah Mitchell was, she is not that now. Eleven years ago, she found someone who took her and trained her. Trained that bitch hard, every day Hannah was training, specialist armed force trainin', I'm thinking seals or ranger. Hannah gotta have done that shit for at least two years."

"Why two years?" Drake asked.

"Because just over eight years ago, Artemis exploded on the scene. Kayleigh disappeared eleven years ago, a difference of three years. Hannah's been doin' this shit for eight years; it stands to reason she has others with her. Look at what Ramirez found. One day Hannah's on a bounty in Florida, next in Texas. No one can move that quick. No one can. There's more than one Artemis."

"See I'm not the only one who's confused what to

call her," Drake muttered as Apache switched to Hannah and then back to Artemis. Ace winced, and Apache looked sheepish.

"What are you saying Hannah is, son?" Apache asked.

"Hannah's a special mercenary, and she's not workin' alone. Hannah told me shit that she could only have happened if she was a merc. I've info of a mercenary group that did lots of shit abroad. Brought down Taliban strongholds, no survivors, those who'd tortured our men had a painful death. Group were the best of the best. Rescued shit loads of our armed forces." Drake replied, drawing the same conclusions.

"Well-funded. Fuckin' well-funded, Artemis doesn't bring in bounties for under twenty k. Ramirez found the group stepped out of that zone only seven times, and each case looked personal. Those that involved a kid, and each time she brought the kid back alive. Seven times the perp got dead. Ramirez says nothin' can be proved, but they think Artemis was behind the deaths. The incredibly fucked up painful deaths of the perpetrator," Drake concluded.

"Kayleigh," Ace whispered. "Get Ramirez to dig. Lay money those kids were fucked up."

"Four were, Ramirez says, the horror will keep the kids in therapy for years. But after each perp died, the kids received a visit from Aunt Alice. Same name, same description and after that, the kids slept. The kids didn't sleep beforehand, but after Aunt Alice visited, they slept, and they slept well."

"Get Hawthorne to trace the other three and talk to them, bettin' they had an Aunt Alice too. Ramirez would overstep his boundaries tracking those other kids," Apache said. Ace nodded.

"Hannah thinks I'm involved, says she's aware Fish, Texas, and Dad weren't. Hannah knew you weren't, which is why Black Lords paid. I couldn't get the thread of it, but I think Hannah thought she owed you somehow. This was her paying back the debt. But Hannah thinks I was involved, thinks I gave the fuckin' order," Ace turned to Drake.

"Did we find those CDs that Misty hid?" Drake asked, scratching his chin.

"No."

"Look under the floorboards," Drake muttered, remembering what Artemis had said to him. Drake tossed it over in his head.

"Brothers ripped up the living room and bedrooms. There was nothing."

"Just those four areas? Fuckin' rip it all up, expose the beams. Want that shithole gutted. Misty was a stupid cunt, but she wouldn't leave that shit lying around to be found fuckin' easy," Drake ordered. Apache nodded.

"Need to get back. Phoe's home and I don't wanna leave her too long," Ace looked at his brother. He spied a note on the reception desk and picked it up. Ace's mouth tightened and he showed it to Drake, on it was written, 'Time for payment has come.' They left the empty offices.

Drake watched as Phoe hauled her body out of the chair and winced. He hurried to her side and supported Phoe as she gained her feet. Phoe looked up at him and then dropped her eyes as she'd been doing ever since she'd come out of the coma. Everything was broken between them, he'd broken it, and Drake couldn't be more aware of it.

Phoe moved towards the couch, where she wanted to rest. Drake kept an arm around her waist as Phoe gingerly lowered herself and then curled up into a ball. He sat in front of her.

"We need to talk," Drake said, reaching out to stroke her hair. Phoe flinched back, and his hand froze and then dropped to his lap.

"Drake, you made our status clear. There's nothing to talk about. I come second to your club. The brothers and club come before your child and me. I understand exactly where I stand," Phoe told him bitterly. There was anger in her words, and Drake thought she was using anger to cover her pain. Drake bit back the angry words that sprang to his lips and took a deep breath.

"Phoe, you don't come second baby, Rage is about brothers Phoe. Old ladies don't get a say, that's what

I was tryin' to explain." Phoe's eyes gazed at the wall.

"I understood that clearly," Phoe said shortly.

"No, you didn't, not at all. You're my life, my heart and my soul. My everythin'."

"Yes, after the club and your brothers. Just once, I wanted to come first with a man. Be his everything," Phoe whispered, pain in her voice. Drake had destroyed her that night. Everything good between them had been laid to waste. And Phoe didn't trust him, and she certainly didn't trust him with her heart anymore. Then she straightened her shoulders, and Drake saw Phoe was readying for a fight. There was his wife, then again, he thought, gazing at Phoe's face, she might be bracing for a blow.

"I'll step down, black out the patch," Drake said firmly. Slowly Phoe absorbed his words.

"What?" Phoe whispered so faintly he thought she'd mouthed the word.

"I'll step down and black out my patch. The club doesn't come before you. I'm Rage, it's me, but I can't lose you or my kid. Won't be the same man, if that's what I gotta do, but I'll do it. For you and me, I'll do it, but I'll change; you ask that of me." Phoe laughed, and it was Drake's turn to pause. The laugh was so full of bitterness, so unlike his beautiful wife.

"I've never asked that of you. Never! All I wanted from you, Drake, was to be loved and cherished, the life I chose to live, valued and understood. Instead, you threw at me that what I did, what I loved, meant shit to you, Drake. You didn't care that getting Rage answers, you fucked over other people, harmed other people. All that mattered was Rage." Drake rocked back. Phoe rarely swore. There was a fire in Phoe's eyes, and Drake realised Phoe was coming at him swinging.

"Not all that matters. You and the kid's matter, the baby matters."

"Oh, we matter, Drake, just not enough to you. If you quit Rage, it'll be just another reason for you to push us apart. I can't live being second best to Rage and your brothers, and I can't live not even being second best. I'm way down in your list of priorities," Phoe said with such heartbroken sadness Drake's heart clenched. The fire in her eyes died, and Drake wanted it back.

"Listen carefully, Phoe, you're not second best to Rage or my brothers, and you'll always come first. I'll never let you walk or walk away from you woman, you're mine, always will be. Yeah, I handled the situation wrong. Was so focused on Ace, I didn't think of the implications for you and the Trusts. That doesn't mean you come after Rage.

I'll walk, baby, just say the word. Can live without the club, and my brothers, can't live without you or our kids. Can't imagine a future without you or our kids. Swear to you, if any shit comes up again, I won't drag the Trusts into it.

The club's male focused. Phoe, you got no voice in Rage or what we do. Hellfire is your club and voice. All you gotta understand is you'll be safe and protected. You let us do what we gotta, but I failed ya. Baby, you got shot because I wasn't at your back, and I fucked up. Fucked up with you, fucked up with the kids and fucked up with the Trusts. Won't fuck up again, Phoe, please forgive me, please don't stop loving me." Phoe gazed into Drake's eyes and saw he meant what he said.

Phoe wasn't sure how to feel. She was in so much pain from his betrayal, and yet she could see he suffered too. Should Phoe push past what hurt and anguish Drake had caused her and forgive him? Phoe had forgiven him once before. Was that to be the pattern of their relationship? Phoe looked into his eyes and swallowed. Drake would quit the club for her, but Drake wouldn't be the same man she fell in love with.

Phoe was furious with him as well. Drake had acted as if she'd caused this. He had, by being the stubborn pig-headed man Drake always was. Drake quit Rage? Ridiculous. Stupid man. Drake was Rage, but Drake had to recognise the importance of her job and calling. Phoe wanted to kick him in his shins but thought that may not be a good idea. Phoe settled for giving him the stink eye.

"Next time explain, it's okay being hard and protective but look what happened this time when you did. I don't want you to stand down and quit, and I just want to be loved. But I won't forgive a third time, Drake, twice now you've let me down, I won't be the fool constantly forgiving someone."

"Fuck baby, you've no idea how much you're loved. Swear it won't happen again," Drake said, taking her in his arms and kissing her. Phoe broke the kiss off and looked into his eyes. Drake let everything he felt show in them, and she settled into his arms. Drake loved her. He just fucked up.

I sat on my deck and stared at the sun, beginning to rise above the mountains. It was the early hours of the morning and our third morning here. We were in the middle of nowhere, and I could hear birds and animals snuffling in the treeline. Falcon and Nova adored the cabin and had settled in quicker than I could blink.

The cabins were our first fall-back. The funny thing was, they were an hour outside RC, up in the Black Hills. Hide in the open was what we'd been taught. Rage expected us to run for a different state. So we remained here as Sioux Falls was burned for us now.

If tracked, we'd four other places we could run to. As promised to Ace, Stacy Conway and her children ceased to exist. Since the age of seven, I'd told the kids that the job I did was dangerous and that we may just have to move one day. This hadn't affected their childhood because Akemi and I hadn't let it. Falcon and Nova had a full childhood and understood that mommy did what she had to. The last few days, they'd run through the trees surrounding us. Angel had taken them swimming in a small lake. Nigel and Buzz had set up on arrival, Simone and Butch chased a bounty.

Angel had taken himself off to a cabin within eyesight of our own and was crashing there. He'd claimed it as his own. Kristoff was in a third cabin again within sight of mine. The two guys were resting, although Angel had a bounty to hunt tomorrow. The entire area had been wired, and early warning devices set up. We'd installed cameras ages ago, and they were online and set to record at the first sign of movement.

So, for now, I relaxed, content in the early morning sun and sat with my feet up on the wooden rails that surrounded the front porch. Communications had been redirected from my old phone, which was now disconnected and sent to a new phone. Buzz had hidden the re-directions under a multitude of layers.

I thought back to last night's meeting where we'd agreed Artemis should continue, but I'd stay out of RC for now. No chance of running into Rage or Hawthorne's. We'd picked a go-between to take our bounties in. Buzz had decided it'd be him, and he'd be racking up a lot of air miles soon. Buzz was unknown and well trained, and no one could tail him. He delighted in getting out of office duties as he called them for a few months.

Rage hadn't stopped looking, and neither had Hawthorne's. Nigel threatened to hack Hawthorne's systems and crash them; I refused to let him do that for now. However, the idea hovered around my mind. Instead, Nigel had hacked their system and froze them for forty-eight hours with a warning attached. Nigel was satisfied with that!

Leila Gibson hadn't been able to crack the hack, and they'd received our warning loud and clear. Of course, looking at my symbol must've annoyed the hell out of Dylan Hawthorne. Cautiously, sipping my coffee, I looked up as footsteps thudded on the porch, and Nova landed in my lap. I laughed lightly and snuggled her up in my arms.

"My precious girl," I whispered in her hair. Nova tightened her arms around me and snuggled deeper. Together we sat there and watched the sun come up over the trees and light up the mountain.

Drake looked at Ace and Texas as they sat in their chairs. Fish kicked the door shut as he entered after Apache. Everyone looked pissed.

"Hannah did as she said. She's completely

disappeared, and there's no trace of Stacy Conway, Nova or Falcon Conway anywhere," Fish stated.

"Not surprised," Apache grunted, "Hannah's good."

"The house has gone up for sale through a third party that leads nowhere, and the bike and car has been sold for cash. The buyer showed up and disappeared before Hawthorne got a lock."

"Fuck me," Ace muttered.

"The furniture's gone, the house is a shell, this woman's a ghost. Nova and Falcon are simply listed as moving state, Ohio, but no trace of them there. No trace of them registering in a school; they're gone. Hannah's cell is dead, and we can't trace where her calls are being re-routed."

"Again, not surprised," Apache muttered. When Fish mentioned Falcon and Nova, Apache's gaze flicked to Ace and then Drake. Drake saw the burning question in Apache's eyes, but he'd no answer for his brother.

"We found the discs," Drake dropped the bombshell. "Hidden in the closet where Misty had tiled the floor. Phoe asked who the fuck tiles a closet, and it got me thinkin'. We have them, and I've listened. What Hannah said was true. You're named Ace." Ace sat up and stared at Drake in shock.

"I didn't…" he started.

"No doubt, brother," Drake cut him off.

"Not a single one," Fish supported Drake. Ace gave them a curt nod.

"That's somethin'," Ace muttered.

"The discs are cut short before anyone else is named. Still got no idea who was involved," Drake said softly. Drake was pissed because this was ripping Rage apart. Brothers were spying on fuckin' brothers. Artemis had warned him, and Drake hadn't listened.

"This shit is fucked up, brother lookin' at brother. Suspicions everywhere, no idea how Hannah found out what she has. But that woman is after revenge for her baby sister," Apache muttered.

"I wanna hear the discs," Ace said, and Drake shook his head.

"They're dark, brother, real dark, not gonna expose you to that."

"Already been exposed, I want Thunder found. Like yesterday, I want him fuckin' found. Wanna listen to what my girl suffered."

"These are worse."

"Not arguin' brother, get me the discs," Ace said firmly.

Ace and Drake were sat on stools at the clubhouse bar three days later when Dylan Hawthorne walked in. He'd a file in his hand, and walking over, he handed it to Drake. Drake dipped his head and opened it, and passed it to Ace, who read through it.

"Marker," Ace said, and Hawthorne nodded.

"I'll take it."

"Exhumation plans?" Drake asked.

"Already in motion, should have them in a couple of days, they'll come here. Do what you gotta do," Hawthorne said and walked back out.

Ace stood in front of a grave that had a wooden stick as a marker, a grave so overgrown no one would've known it was there. Kayleigh had lain here for eleven years, unloved, un-mourned, forgotten. It had taken longer than a few days; it took a week. Finally, they had the order to disinter the grave and bring Kayleigh to a grave of their choice with a proper marker.

Ramirez stood by Ace, watching as the crane began pulling up the dirt-covered, stained, cheap coffin. Drake, Apache, Fish, Slick, Mac, and Gunner stood with them, watching. Drake had banned the old ladies, saying it was too much for them. Marsha had pursed her lips and walked away, and Silvie had frozen him out for two days. Two gravediggers stood duty, watching and making sure the coffin was raised correctly.

The crane groaned, and one strap slipped, and they froze, then it recovered and carried on hauling the cheap coffin to the top. It reached the top and began swinging towards the racking placed on the ground for it to rest on. Halfway across, there was a snapping noise, and one strap gave way.

The two gravediggers leapt forward, attempting to either grab the coffin or balance it. But one fell, and the weight of the coffin sent the second man reeling. Ace watched with horrified eyes as the bottom end of the coffin hit the ground with a hard thud.

Then a second breaking noise echoed, and the lid of the coffin shattered on impact and fell forward. The release of the lid meant the corpse inside fell forward on top of the first gravedigger, scrambling to his feet.

He shrieked, no better word for it and shoved Kayleigh's corpse off him, scrambling backwards. Drake reacted instantly, moving his body in front of Ace and jerking his head downwards. Apache moved just as quickly and covered Ace's other side, his hand going to the back of Ace's neck and holding his son's head against Drake's shoulder.

"Fuck, shit, fuck," Fish shouted in a shocked voice.

"Jesus, who the hell is that!" Slick yelled equally loudly.

"Slick?" Drake questioned over his shoulder.

"That's not Kayleigh," Slick said, sounding both horrified and curious. Ace struggled to raise his head.

"Ace no," Apache muttered and looked over his shoulder, and his body tightened.

"What is it?" Ace asked.

"Ramirez check," Drake ordered, but the cop was moving. He heard a retch and then noise as Ramirez moved closer. Out of the corner of his eye, he saw a gravedigger moving swiftly away, hand over his mouth. Fantastic, the gravedigger had thrown up. Drake hoped it wasn't on the body.

"I don't think she's Kayleigh." Ace yanked free with everything he had and stared at the corpse lying on the ground. His own stomach heaved, and Ace took a couple of deep breaths and then, shoving past Drake, he moved closer.

Ramirez knelt near the corpse, one hand holding a handkerchief to his nose as he studied the corpse. The wizened features were familiar. It was a woman, eyes shut, thank God, although sunken. Ace looked at her hair, short red curly hair, a feeling hit him hard, and Ace bent over, gasping. Apache crouched near him, his hand on his back.

"Breathe, son, breathe."

"There're no wounds on her body to match what Kayleigh suffered," Ramirez said, confirming what Ace had realised. "Her neck has been broken."

"It's not Kayleigh," Ace forced out. Ace met Drake's eyes and saw Drake's held knowledge at the awareness in Ace's. Drake got it, he'd guessed, he'd fuckin' known, Ace's brother had doubt's the whole time. Ace felt fury well up, outrage at Artemis who'd played them and anger at Drake, his brother who'd suspected the truth.

"Brother?" Slick asked, confusion in his voice.

"Meet Hannah Mitchell," Ace forced out, glaring at

Drake. Slick and Apache rocked back. Fish stared at him and then Gunner and Mac, seeking answers they didn't have.

"She's got a broken neck," Ramirez confirmed, straightening up.

"Meet Hannah Mitchell," Ace repeated. And that sick feeling in his stomach intensified into a burning need to vomit.

"Who the fuck is Artemis?" Fish asked.

"Two guesses," Ramirez snapped. His mind making the connection and coming to the same conclusion Ace's had made a few minutes ago.

"You had suspicions," Ace bit out. Drake nodded.

"Artemis is Kayleigh?" Slick breathed, finally catching on.

"Artemis looks nothing like her," Fish denied.

"We saw the photos of her wounds. Kayleigh's had extensive plastic surgery, who's going to bet that she didn't make herself up like her sister? I bet that repaired most of the damage to her body too," Drake replied.

"We've seen her red and brown; bet she's using washout dyes or something, and contacts." Mac nodded.

"Holy shit, no wonder Artemis didn't want to get involved with us," Gunner said, shocked.

"Fuckin' Artemis," Ace ground out.

They heard pipes rev on the hill above them, and they looked up. Hair gleaming red in the sun and dressed in black from head to toe, a tiny figure sat on a Lowrider. Artemis looked straight at them, and they stayed motionless as she pointed a handgun straight at them. Ramirez's hand went to his hip, and he unhooked his own weapon.

Deliberately the gun took aim at Slick, Gunner, Ace, and Mac and made motions as if Artemis had shot the weapon. Then placing the gun in a shoulder holster, she put her foot to the bike and sped off.

Kayleigh Mitchell had just declared war, and they knew it.

Chapter Five.

18th November 2014

Three days later, Drake's phone rang, and he glanced at a blocked number. He showed the screen to Ace and then answered and hit the loudspeaker. They sat in the inner sanctum where they'd been discussing how to handle Artemis, who'd gone to ground.

"Yo," Drake said.

"Hi, how you doing, Drake?" Artemis asked softly.

"Pretty fucked up, Kayleigh," Drake replied and saw Ace's jaw clench.

"Yeah, that coffin breaking fucked things up a bit, didn't it?" Artemis laughed.

"Not thinkin' anything funny babe in that."

"Don't imagine you do," Artemis agreed.

"You declaring war, Kayleigh?"

"What do you reckon? It's time justice got served. You should've backed off when I gave you a chance, Drake," Artemis said breezily.

"You kill your sister?" Drake asked, and Artemis drew in a sharp intake of breath.

"Fuck no, Hannah died a week after Rage bastards beat the shit out of me. Poor Hannah had a car accident, and it's easy to make records disappear. Hannah hadn't done one thing for me when I was alive, so I thought my sister could help in death." Fuck, that was harsh. Ace winced.

"Want you to come in Kayleigh, I'll meet you anywhere. Your choice."

"Kayleigh Mitchell is dead, Drake, Rage MC killed her. Betrayed by those Kayleigh loved."

"You're Kayleigh Mitchell."

"No, I'm what was put back together of Kayleigh. Girl's got no resemblance to me. There's nothing of Kayleigh Mitchell left alive, Drake. If you're hoping to find that child somewhere inside me, forget it. Kayleigh's honestly dead and buried. Call me Frankenstein or Artestein," Artemis giggled. "Hannah's body may be in that grave, but Kayleigh was buried with her. Remember Drake, in Phoenix's office, I asked if you really wanted to do this?" Artemis asked curiously.

"Yeah."

"Told you it could mean the end of Rage, and you told me you wanted the club clean. And I said you weren't ready for the truth Drake."

"You did," Drake replied heavily and rubbed a hand across his face.

"I'm gonna make Rage clean, Drake," Artemis said and cut the connection.

"Ready the brothers, I'll contact Hawthorne and Ramirez. Artemis is coming for Rage, and RC will burn."

"Drake," Blaze hammered on his door. Drake rolled over and kissed his wife before getting out of bed and yanking his jeans on. Phoe mumbled and rolled back over, showing her naked body. Drake twitched a sheet over her and opened the door that Blaze continued to hammer on loudly.

"What the fuck, prospect?" Drake snarled at Blaze. The man wore boxers and looked pissed.

"Get out here now," Blaze demanded and walked away. Drake growled and followed Blaze to the rec room, where he stopped dead. Fuck! Drake set eyes on what had upset Blaze. On the wall to the left of the clubhouse doors dripped red paint, spelling out words.

"One, two Artemis is coming for you," Drake read aloud. What the hell?

"Freddie Krueger. Remember, Kayleigh was obsessed with those movies," Fish said, appearing at Drake's shoulder. Blaze's shouting had woken him, and he glared blearily at Blaze, rubbing his eyes.

"Jett had the door," Drake snapped out and headed back to the hallway to Jett's room. As he passed Gunner's door, Drake stopped. Written in dripping red paint was the word 'Eeny.' Drake kicked open the door, and Gunner lay bare-assed naked on his bed.

"Gunner," Drake roared. The man didn't twitch. Drake marched over, fear in his heart and put his fingers on Gunner's throat. Gunner's pulse was steady.

"What the fuck?" Fish asked.

"He's drugged. There's a needle mark."

"Drake!" Blaze shouted. Drake followed the shout to Manny's room. On his door was more paint saying 'Meeny.' Drake punched the door open and found Manny in a heap next to his bed. Fish checked for a pulse and nodded.

"Artemis must have surprised him," Fish muttered. Drake stomped to the next painted door. Jacked's, his brother, lay in the same condition as Jett and Gunner. His door said, 'Miny.' Jett's door was ajar, and Drake found his prospect drugged but healthy. No paint.

Drake stormed back to his hallway and punched through the connecting door. He saw now what he'd missed following Blaze. On Slick's door was 'Moe.' Drake's gut tensed, and he pushed in the door. To his relief, Slick lie in bed breathing. Drake tried to wake him and failed. Slick was drugged too.

Fish called from Mac's room. Drake looked at the

door and frowned, painted on the door was the word 'Catch.' Mac had stayed at his apartment last night.

"Get Hunter and get him over to Mac's," Drake ordered Blaze. Drake exchanged glances with Fish. The shit had hit the fan.

"I'll get Slate to Apache's; Ace spent last night with him," Fish strode away to wake the prospect. Pipes roared, and Drake heard Hunter ride out. Artemis hadn't touched the prospects apart from Jett, and that was because she'd wanted entry to the clubhouse.

Legs moving as fast as they could, Drake ran up the stairs to the next floor. Drake discovered 'A Murderer' on Lex's door. The brother wasn't in his room. Rock stumbled out half-awake, demanding an explanation. Drake brusquely gave Rock an answer and sent Rock to Lex's house on the other side of town. Ezra shoved his head out of his door, grumbling at the noise. Drake found 'By the' painted on Ace's door, Gid's had 'Toe' on his.

Artemis had stormed the clubhouse and marked the brothers for death, those she blamed for her torture. They all couldn't be involved, but which fuckers were guilty? Texas came storming up the stairs, his hair and eyes wild.

"Axel's gone," the man boomed. Drake rocked back against the wall and began to slide down it. He'd handle losing anyone, but Axel was the nearest thing Drake had left to a father. Not a chance in hell had Axel been involved in what happened to Kayleigh.

Axel's heart was too damn big. Drake glanced at Axel's door and didn't see a red mark on it. Fuck no, not Axel.

"No!" Drake croaked, and Texas frowned.

"What the fuck, brother?" Texas reached down and dragged Drake to his feet.

"She took Axel?" Drake ran his hands over his face.

"Who took Axel? Drake, what the fuck's going on?" Texas asked, confused. Drake pointed at the doors.

"Artemis came last night, marked those brothers she thinks are guilty. Axel's gone, you said."

"Shit, brother, no, I didn't realise. No, the fuckin' idiots went after his pain in the ass kids," Texas said, explaining more carefully to Drake. The colour came back into Drake's face as nausea faded.

"Artemis doesn't have Axel?" Texas gripped Drake's arm tight, reassuring him.

"No, brother. Need to get Axel back, before whatever shit his fuckwad kids have got into this time, kills him."

"Can't. Artemis drugged half the brothers, even took Jett out. Got Fish tryin' to wake 'em."

"Fuckin' Axel and his timing," Texas cursed, "who's not here?"

"Apache and Ace, Gid, Lex and Mac, you and Axel weren't here last night either. Marsha and Silvie are at home. Get Fish to call them. Remember Artemis said not just brothers at the club? I've no idea if she's targeting the old ladies. We'll deal with Artemis and then Axel's fuckwad kids," Drake muttered. Phoe came racing up the stairs, hair wild and dressed in one of his tee's.

"Half the brothers are drugged!" she exclaimed.

"You're going home and calling Liz. You and the kids locked down with Marsha and Silvie," Drake ordered. Reading Hall, their home, the safest place Drake could think of for the women. Take an army to get through the Hall's security. Phoe didn't argue, just nodded and raced back down the stairs.

"Artemis won't go after Phoe. She's proved that."

"Wanna risk Phoe, brother?" Drake asked slowly, and Texas shook his head. If Phoe got harmed, it wouldn't be just Rage riding out for revenge, Hellfire would tear up the world for her.

"Need to account for Mac, Gid, Apache, Ace and Lex," Drake said, running a hand across his face. His gut churned because Artemis wasn't making a statement. The bitch was making a move.

"Sent you a link. I suggest you get your brothers together. Payback starts today," Artemis said coldly an hour later and cut the line. Ace looked at him, eyes narrowed. Her last words worried him.

"Bitch's up to something," Drake's phone pinged with a text, and he opened it to find a website. Drake threw Texas the phone and called for his brothers.

Those who'd been drugged were awake, if barely. They slouched in chairs in the rec room and slowly made their way to the inner sanctum. Lex, Mac and Gid were still unaccounted for. Drake had Slate, Blaze and Hunter out searching for them. Jett was still messed up, but Drake knew the prospects were safe from Artemis.

As the website opened to a grey room, Lex and Mac walked in, relief hit Drake's gut. Only Gid was missing now, and Drake turned his attention back to the laptop. The scene opened, no distinguishing marks, just dark walls and one spotlight on a man sitting in a chair. A hood covered his head. He wore jeans and a white tee smeared with blood and a Rage cut.

"Fuck," Drake swore. His gut told him who sat there before Artemis strolled into view and whipped the hood off, Gid. The man bled from his nose and mouth, but other than that, Gid looked fine. Gid's hands were tied behind him, and his legs were tied to the chair bolted to the floor.

"Shit, that's Gid!" Ezra said, paling. Artemis looked at the camera and gave a slow smile. Artemis wore black head to toe, her hair tied back, she even wore black gloves on her hands.

"This is one-way, Drake; I see you logged in, and this is how it's gonna go. Gid here is gonna share what he's been up to, and Gid's been a very naughty boy." Artemis slapped him hard across the face, and

Gid spat blood at her. She laughed.

"Now, now Gid, you shouldn't spit at a lady," Artemis tutted at him and wiped it off her tee.

"Don't see no lady," Gid grunted.

"Hard or easy way, motherfucker?" Artemis hissed, grabbing Gid's face in a firm grip and tilting his head towards her.

"Fuck you," Gid cursed. Artemis grinned again.

"Today, you'll have it easy; show your brothers what a traitor you are. Let's see you spill your guts. I'll know if you turn the laptop off, Drake. If you do, you'll wish you never had. Anyone leaves the inner sanctum, I'll know. Test me if you don't believe me," Artemis said and pulled a needle from her pocket. She flicked the cap off and jammed it into Gid's arm. Gid cursed, and Artemis shot the serum into his arm.

"This is a special mixture of Sodium Pentothal, homemade. This beauty only takes a few minutes to kick in," Artemis told the camera, and Drake felt Ace twitch next to him. Gid's head sank to his chest, and he began cursing and then Gid fell quiet.

"Have you hidden Misty?" Artemis asked him.

"Yes," Gid replied. The air in the inner sanctum turned electric.

"Tell me why," Artemis ordered.

"The cunt knew I was involved and came to me and told me she'd spill everythin'. I took Misty and hid her as soon as we heard you were on the case," Gid slurred.

"Fuck me," Texas cursed, his hand squeezed Ace's shoulder.

"How were you involved?"

"Knew what Thunder and Misty were gonna do, was supposed to join them."

"Did you agree with what happened to Kayleigh?"

"Yes. Ace was too wrapped up in pussy, and we needed his head in the game. Distractin' Ace from what Bulldog wanted, bitch made Ace lean towards Drake's side." There was a harshly drawn breath.

"Was Ace involved?" Artemis asked, her voice turning dangerous.

"Thunder said Ace gave his blessing." Ace became dangerously still.

"And you kept this from Drake?"

"Yeah."

"Give me the names of those who *weren't* involved. Bet that's an easier list, Gid."

"Drake, Apache, Fish, Texas and Axel, anyone who joined after we fucked you up."

"Everyone else was involved?"

"Yeah, Thunder said we had to keep it to ourselves, couldn't risk Drake findin' out."

"And you think Kayleigh deserved it?"

"Yeah, wish I'd been in on it knowin' what I now know. But Ace fucked my plans for that. I'd have fucked you harder with that bottle." Gid's words became even more slurred.

"You want to die?" Artemis' voice dropped to

deadly.

"No. Gonna fuck you up, and this time I'll slice your throat."

"Turn this off, Drake, and I'll know, and I'll count you as guilty as him. You watch." Artemis turned to the camera and disappeared.

"Mac track this now," Drake ordered. Mac got his ass in the chair and began hammering at the laptop. Artemis re-appeared, and she'd a knife in one hand, which she placed on a small table he'd missed. A bat joined it, and knuckle dusters appeared on her hands.

"Can't track her. The signal's bouncing around the globe," Mac hissed at Drake.

"Okay," Drake said calmly, too calmly.

Methodically, Artemis began working Gid over. A few brothers turned their eyes away, unable to watch as Artemis took Gid apart. Beginning with fists and then the bat, ending with the knife. Gid begged, but Artemis didn't stop. Each time she stopped to change her weapon, Artemis asked him one question.

"Did you show Kayleigh mercy?" Then Artemis continued. Ace watched fixated as Gid, the man he'd called brother for over fifteen years, was beaten to a pulp and sliced to death. Two hours passed before Artemis stopped and looked at Gid. Taking off a glove, Artemis pushed her hair from her face. Gid breathed, but not for much longer. The man was a mess.

"You'll find Gid where Kayleigh died. Tick, tock,

who's next?" Artemis said, gazing at the camera and then cut the feed. Drake moved before Ace could and wrapped his arms around the man as Ace lost it.

"Who else was involved?" Ace roared, spittle flying from his lips. Ace strained against Drake, who locked him down.

"I'll let Ace loose. If you're involved, tell us now," Drake ordered.

"Artemis said Ace was involved," Ezra pointed out.

"Ace look like he was involved?" Drake spat back.

"Fuck's sake, what's happening to us?" Apache asked.

"Artemis gonna tear us apart, one by one, bitch wants vengeance," Mac said.

"You involved?" Ace roared and gained a step on Mac, even though Drake held him tight.

"Fuck no, loved that kid too, bro," Mac slammed his hands on the table.

"Gid didn't say my name. Artemis thinks I was involved in that," Slick said, and Ace's head shot in his direction. "Fuck, Kayleigh thought I agreed," Slick collapsed in a chair, and his head dropped in his hands. "Jesus, fuck, Christ, girl believes I gave my okay." Slick bent over and threw up. Lowrider and Jacked both darted back away from him as he emptied his stomach.

"Need to know who is at risk," Fish said.

"Ace, Mac, Slick, Manny, Gunner, Lex, Jacked are in her sights. Rock, Ezra, and Lowrider joined after

Kayleigh's murder. Someone needs to alert Axel and do it fast. The prospects are safe," Apache said instantly.

"Who's breathing and no longer Rage?"

"Sticks, and Prof are livin' from Bulldogs group. Smokey, Hammer, Archer, Breaker, and Iron are livin' but had nothin' to do with Rage since the fightin' started. They blacked their ink. Prince, Mad Dog, Skill and Mayhem, along with the rest, are in the ground. Can vouch for that. No idea where Thunder is, but you can bet Artemis knows," Texas said, eyeing Ace cautiously.

"You got a lock on it, brother?" Drake asked him. Ace nodded. Drake relaxed his arms, and 'Ace was in motion aiming for Jacked and Gunner. Drake slammed him face-first on the table and locked Ace back down.

"Talk now; you involved in this shit?" Drake ordered. Both guys shook their heads. Ace watched them with hate-filled eyes.

"Thunder bullshitted his way around this. Artemis trusts she's got the truth. She's gonna come gunnin' for blood," Lowrider said.

"My girl turned into that," Fish said, and sorrow filled his face.

"We know what Artemis is," Mac agreed.

"Ice in her veins, no fear of a kill or a messy kill as we just saw. Artemis is a cold-blooded killer. Ace, the girl you loved, she's dead. Artemis is not

Kayleigh," Apache said. His son turned his head on the table and looked at him.

"Kayleigh's in there somewhere," Ace hissed, hate writhed across his face. Deep inside, Apache winced and worried for his son. This was destroying Ace worse than the first time around. Apache tried to be gentle, but he didn't think Ace was hearing shit at the moment.

"No son, Kayleigh is dead, grieve her 'cause this Artemis? She's not going to stop until she puts everyone she believes responsible in a grave. We ain't going to let Artemis whack innocent brothers." Ace growled from deep within at his father's words.

"Anyone lays a finger on Artemis, and I'll put them in the grave next to Gid. Rage did enough damage."

"Can't let Artemis whack innocent brothers," Apache insisted, holding his son's gaze. Apache saw the animal in Ace, and he feared for the club and Artemis. If anyone put a finger on Artemis, Ace would bury them. They were caught between a rock and a hard place, either Artemis or Ace. Take your fuckin' pick because they both were cold stone killers.

"Every one of us got blood on our hands, Dad," Ace hissed. "May not be Kayleigh's, but we got blood on them." Ace struggled against Drake, who gripped him still bent over the table.

"Then we need to keep those in her sights here and keep them alive till we find her," Texas argued.

"Think that'll stop Artemis? Woman's got in once," Mac asked.

"Weren't ready for that. We are now," Texas replied.

"Do it, you lot are in lockdown, you leave here you better pray Artemis don't find you because she's just starting. Artemis got hate, vengeance and bloodlust on her side," Drake ordered, still holding Ace on the table. "Includes you, brother," Drake told Ace and waited for his VP to agree. Ace gave a reluctant nod, and Drake finally let him go. Ace slammed out of the inner sanctum before anyone could say a word.

"Apache, Texas on him," Fish ordered. They left instantly. Drake turned to Fish, Lex, Rock, and Lowrider.

"Fish, you and Lowrider go to where Kayleigh's body was found. Gid's going to be there. Bury the cunt. Rock, Ezra, find Misty before Artemis does." Boots slammed against the scuffed floor as they left the sanctum.

"You lot don't leave here, you don't move," Drake ordered, pointing at the brothers who were implicated. "Not even to the garage," he glared at them to enforce his words and left the room. Silence followed behind him.

I dragged Gid's heavy body out of the van and

rolled it into the grave that Akemi stood by. It was deep enough. I stood over him as I watched the man struggle for breath and counted his blood bubbles perversely. Akemi stood by my shoulder.

"You ready for this?" Akemi asked. I nodded. Akemi slipped an arm around my waist, and I leaned back against him and let him take my weight.

"You have that bitch?" I asked.

"Yeah."

"Let's get on with it." Akemi nodded once, and without a backwards look, we left Gid to die, struggling to breathe in his own blood.

"How the fuck she get in?" Drake roared at his brothers. Drake stared in disbelief at the second message Artemis had left. 'Three, four, better lock your doors.' Artemis was fucking with them. They'd used two planes of wood to secure the double doors last night that slotted into heavy iron latches. The bitch had got in and written the following line of Freddie Krueger's poem above them.

Stabbed in each door this morning had been a knife. Nothing else but a knife dripping red, Drake realised it was blood this time, Gid's blood. Hunter and Rock had both been drugged during their watch. The wood hadn't been disturbed on the doors, and Drake was furious. His fist slammed into a wall.

"Artemis is a ghost," Lex said. Rock raised his head, blinking to focus.

"Came from behind Hunter and me," Rock rumbled, struggling to form words. Hunter still snored on a couch. Drake shook his head.

"Find out how Artemis fuckin' got in," Ace ordered as brothers scattered. The room filled with dark vibes. Rage was being fucked with, and by a perp they couldn't lockdown. The woman was beyond dark. Half an hour later, they were still scratching their heads over her entry; nothing they found explained how Artemis entered the clubhouse. Hunter finally woke up but with no further information than Rock.

Drake's phone pinged. He looked and strode into the inner sanctum. Everyone was accounted for, which meant that Artemis had someone else. They took one look at his face, and his brothers entered the sanctum.

Mac typed in the link and set his shit going to track Artemis, and then they saw it wasn't needed. Sat in front of a hole in the ground and tied like Gid was Misty, who sobbed at the camera. The grave was where Hannah had lain buried, Misty's face was swollen, and blood dripped from her nose. The trees gave shade, and a light shone on her in the night's darkness. Drake frowned. If it was night, this was pre-recorded.

Artemis didn't say a word to them this time. She stood over Misty; hate written across her face.

Artemis tapped a bat against her leg as she watched Misty blubber and beg.

"Remember this bat, Misty? You raped me with it. Perhaps, I should fuck your dirty cunt with it, shove it up you, as you did me," Artemis sneered in Misty's face.

"No, please just let me go," Misty begged. Artemis leant into her face.

"Was fucking Ace worth it? Did he fuck you good? Ace make you scream? You'll scream soon, bitch, but it won't be from Ace's dick. We'll see if your bucket cunt can take a bat. That life you stole from Kayleigh Mitchell, you had eleven years of fuckin' her man. Hope he was worth it. Then again, Ace was always a good fuck. You know that now, don't you?" Someone audibly gulped, but Ace couldn't tear his eyes from the screen. He'd wanted Misty to pay, but he'd the feeling she was gonna do more than pay. Artemis had a fury burning in her eyes that was tangible.

"Let me go," Misty sobbed. Artemis backhanded her hard, and Misty's head snapped to the side.

"Like you let me go? Didn't I beg over and over? Shame you ain't pregnant; nothing would give me greater pleasure than to cut your fuckin' spawn out of you like you cut my kids. Remember them? They survived the same as I did. Beg as much as you want, I remember begging didn't get me anywhere," Artemis spat hatred, colouring her voice.

She began beating the living daylights out of

Misty and used the bat systematically to start smashing her bones one at a time. Artemis laughed every time Misty begged for mercy and hit her harder the next time. Ace watched as Artemis forced the bat into places it had once been shoved into Kayleigh. He tasted his brother's despair.

The sweet girl they had liked, loved and cared for had gone. In Kayleigh's place lived a cold-blooded monster who didn't blink at paying back shit in kind. Ace stood at Drake's side, and the man swallowed hard several times. He was just realising precisely what Artemis was capable of doing. Fuck, Ace didn't even think they'd seen half of what the woman had in her repertoire.

Artemis finally used her knife, slashing Misty where Misty had slashed Kayleigh. And then, gutting Misty like a fish, she cut Misty loose and kicked her into the grave. The camera cut out, and they sat there in silence, knowing this had just begun. Ace's head hit the table. Misty took several hours to die, alone and gutted and left in the dark like the piece of shit she was.

"Five, Six, grab your crucifix," Mac read. This line dripped down another wall above the bar, and Mac sniffed and smelt the copper of blood. Artemis was turning up the heat. A drawing of a cross was next to the line. Artemis had got in again, for three nights; there'd been silence from Artemis, and now there was this. Ace rounded up the brothers. They were accounted for.

"Artemis has got Preacher," Ace grunted, recognising the cross design.

"Yeah. That's the cross Preacher wore," Texas agreed. "He'd left the country. How the fuck did Artemis get him?"

"Preacher should've been safe," Fish said.

"Artemis not working alone, remember," Drake said and looked as his phone pinged. Drake winced and made his way to the inner sanctum. It was time for the horror movie Artemis insisted they watch. Gid and Misty died hard. Preacher died harder as he admitted he'd been the one who'd given Bulldog the idea. Nausea so deep, Ace didn't think it'd ever leave him. How many more of those Ace had called brothers had betrayed him and his old lady?

A week later, they stared at the line written on the last wall. 'Seven, eight, don't stay at the bar late.' Artemis was taking this Freddie Krueger thing to the extreme. With Preacher, she'd used a glove similar to Freddie's, which made Preacher scream each time she stabbed his body. Artemis should work for the movie's Ace decided. She didn't lack imagination.

"Who now?" Gunner asked.

"Prof or Sticks, they're the only two unaccounted. If it was Thunder, she'd want him last. Artemis will make sure Thunder is her swansong," Apache replied.

"Warned 'em. One of 'em didn't pay attention." Turned out Prof didn't pay attention. The idiot had been out drinking late at night; Hawthorne found the information for them. Didn't matter. The asshole died screaming after admitting he'd been the one to involve Misty. Prof had known how much Misty had hated Kayleigh and played on it. Prof took twelve hours to die. Artemis edited the video for them, cutting his unconscious periods out. Prof screamed for six hours.

"Nine, ten, never rest again," Slick read the message that had been pinned to his door. He'd known it was coming. Slick had prepared but hoped Kayleigh wouldn't taste the bitterness of guilt when the truth came out. Everything Kayleigh had suffered; she didn't need the guilt on top of it. Drake set guards on Slick. It wouldn't matter, Slick realised. Kayleigh was coming for him, no matter who stood in her way.

"Honey, I can't leave the clubhouse," Slick said into

the phone.

"Slick, there's someone outside the house," his sister whispered to him.

"Call the cops, honey, do it, do it now," Slick insisted.

"Okay." There was a faint noise and then a short scream. Slick bolted out of bed and dragged his clothes on before Artemis whispered down the phone to him.

"Tick tock, Slick, come alone to the address being texted to you, or she takes your punishment. I see one brother; she dies, and she'll die screaming. Akemi has an interesting playroom, and it needs a new guest." The phone died, and Slick got dressed and snuck out of the clubhouse.

Drake's phone pinged again, and he looked up pale. Ace was whiter than white, and Apache had tears in his eyes. Slick was missing, and Artemis had him. They knew it. Slick's sister had been found wandering in a road, and the police had been called. She'd been dosed with Rohypnol and remembered nothing. Artemis had now held Slick for eight hours.

Texas clicked the link, and it opened into the same room Gid was tortured in. Slick same as the four before him, was strapped to a chair. The same table held the implements that Artemis planned to use. He looked straight at the camera; he was unhurt for now. Slick's head snapped back as a punch came at his face.

"Want to play Ace? You for Slick." Artemis dragged Slick's head back, and he looked at the camera. Slick shook his head as best as he could.

"Jacked, wanna give your life for your brother? Mac? Gunner?" Artemis hissed, and at each name, Slick shook his head. Ace realised this was live, and he heard Mac frantically tapping on the keyboard, trying to track Artemis.

"They didn't do it, Kayleigh," Slick whispered.

"Liar!" Artemis spat, and Slick's head snapped back from two more blows.

"Not." Slick spat out blood. "Helped with your homework, you trusted me, you came to me with your problems, I was your brother," Slick told her. Artemis grabbed a bat and slammed it into his mid-drift.

"And you let them rape me with a bat, let them fuck with me a broken bottle. Let them cut my babies out of me," Ace sat up alert, babies? The file had only said one. Ace thought back to what Artemis said to Misty, and he hadn't picked up on it. A sick feeling hit him. Ace remembered the newspaper image, and a hollowness settled in his stomach. Falcon and Nova Conway.

Their mother, Stacy Conway, aka Artemis, aka Kayleigh Mitchell. Their father, a man no one had a picture of, their ages, eleven. Ace's eyes drifted to his father, and Ace saw the same knowledge in Apache's eyes. Falcon and Nova were his. The damn names gave it away. Kayleigh was still there; she'd honoured his lineage. Somewhere in Artemis, Kayleigh Mitchell lived. Ace had to reach her.

"I didn't, Ace didn't. No one left in Rage was part of it," Slick's voice grabbed his attention again.

"Fuckin' liar," Artemis screamed. They winced as the bat slammed into Slick with such force the chair bolts loosened.

"Give me the truth drug," Slick whispered, spitting out blood. Artemis was reaching for the knife.

"What?" Artemis stopped, her arm outstretched and turned back to face Slick.

"Loved you girl, like my own blood, I'd never, ever agree to that shit. If I'd known, I'd have come for you. Give me the Sodium Pentothal. Ask your questions."

"So you can fuck with my mind. It's not one hundred percent."

"Lift my shirt," Slick spat more blood. They could see his breathing struggling. Slick nodded his head towards his right pec. Artemis grabbed the knife and not being careful, slashed at Slick's tee in a downwards motion and ripped it open. A thin line of blood welled up.

Artemis gasped and stepped back in shock. She stood in front of Slick for a long time and stared at his chest, and then she moved. They saw what she'd seen, and then the camera went blank.

Around Slick's left pec was a tattoo, a forest of red, white, and purple roses surrounding a kneeling angel. Her wings glowed in a blueish white light, and the surrounding roses dripped red blood.

Her hair was straight and golden, and she wore a white tank top and a pair of blue jeans. She looked coyly up, and they recognised that face, Kayleigh's delicate features had been etched upon Slick for eternity.

Her hands lifted in prayer, and between them dangled a gold chain. Each end held a red heart, one with the name Ace and the other with Slick. Etched in amongst the roses was her name, spelt out in between the thorns.

"Did you know?" Ace asked Drake quietly. Ace's heart was breaking in more than one way. Slick loved the woman who planned to carve him up. No way would Slick have that tattoo if he'd not loved Kayleigh. A brother didn't randomly put a woman's name on them.

Ace wasn't worried that Slick had feelings for Kayleigh. Ace had claimed her, and the code between the brothers meant Slick would keep those feelings buried. Slick had done exactly that. Ace lifted his head impassively, not letting on to the turmoil of his emotions. Drake met his eyes knowingly. Fuckin' man knew everything, the only one worse than him was Axel.

"No, I didn't know until now. But I know what that tattoo means."

"Slick loves her," Ace stated baldly, "not as a sister."

"No idea brother," Ace gazed across to Fish and saw the truth in his eyes.

"Kayleigh only ever had eyes for you," Fish muttered.

"Fuck, he loved her," Ace whispered. "Artemis will kill him, and Slick loved her. All those years."

Chapter Six.

"Slick didn't stop looking for Kayleigh." Ace looked up and spied Dylan Hawthorne stood in the doorway to the inner sanctum. Minutes had passed since the laptop feed died. The last person they expected to see was Hawthorne. Hawthorne gazed at them with knowledge in his eyes.

"Huh?" Ace asked, rather stupidly. Drake made a flicking motion with his fingers, and brothers filed out.

"Slick kept a retainer with me, kept me searching for any leads on Kayleigh. Continued doing so for the last ten years. Slick didn't want Kayleigh for himself but for Ace. Slick needed you whole again," Hawthorne said, shutting the door behind him.

"Bad timing, Dylan," Drake said.

"Bodies are hittin' the floor, bodies linked to Rage. Ramirez is putting two and two together, and his next stop is here. Ramirez is clean, he won't dirty for Rage, but he's tryin' to keep things quiet. Someone's

on the warpath and cleanin' up, can guess who,
Artemis is marked by the police."

"Shit," Fish whispered.

"Rage got a brother missing. Guess Gid's gone back
home, I suppose, must have a family emergency. Ex
Rage members are turning up like extras in a slasher
film. Got a second brother whose sister was running
barefoot down a highway. So I'm guessing Slick got
a family emergency too. But you got a cunt in a grave
that was meant to have held Kayleigh Mitchell.

That cunt has been beaten with a bat and slashed
with a broken bottle. Had a knife taken to her, exact
wounds as Kayleigh Mitchell. Don't need to be a
genius to work that out. Ramirez is holding off the
big guns but make no mistake, Artemis is marked.
Call her off."

"Can't," Drake said shortly.

"Better bring me up to speed," Hawthorne said.
Hawthorne's eyes stared at Drake.

"Can't," Drake said again.

"Stood by you when Phoenix was taken, didn't
know your woman well, Drake. You and I had
differences, but I kept a man on Phoe. Ramirez on the
scene, and he let Ace go in after Phoenix and not
himself. No bullshit, Drake, we've your back and
Rage is neck-deep in shit.

I'll get a shovel and start shovellin' but gotta know
what I'm fuckin' shovelling. Rage got a brother in the
hands of a killer the fuckin' CIA would love to

recruit. Drake bring me up to fuckin' speed," Hawthorne thundered the last. Drake rose to his feet and studied the man in front of him.

"You're not wrong. You've covered my back, took my back, and Phoe is alive because of you and Ace. No doubtin' that, but this is club business. Friend of mine or not, you're not Rage."

"Goes beyond Rage when we've a killer the likes of Artemis on the warpath. A path that's lined with bloody bodies, and Gid is dead. Saw the ground assholes laying in. Artemis now has her hands on a man I respect and call a friend.

Rage ain't aware, but Hawthorne's kept digging, two organisations cropped up. We think we've tracked Artemis to both. First, is a group called Revenge. The organisation is a fuckin' ghost, only ever been one mention of it. The informant was freakin' terrified.

If Artemis comes from these people, there's no stopping her, you get me? These people can make a fuckin' seal shit his pants and cry for his momma like a bitch. The name of the organisation says everything, Revenge. Artemis waited and hate built. She's gonna bring down anyone who gets in her way.

Now, not sure if for years Artemis been kept leashed or the fact you called her in on this, unleashed her. But Artemis is *unleashed.* Woman will bring a shitstorm down on my town that there's no fuckin' chance of stoppin', and then Artemis will disappear.

Completely disappear."

"Revenge?" Ace asked.

"No one knows shit about it. No one knows where Revenge is based, who runs it, who's in it, what their mission is. And trust me, they've a mission. It's not known how many members, what trainin' they have, nothin'. Can't get a lock on Revenge, can't prove it exists.

Rumours consist of an organisation that takes a victim and trains them fuckin' hard. At least two years training, and the victims get their revenge. It's often bloody and messy, but again no fuckin' proof they belong to Revenge. For each victim, it's personal. Once they got what they want, they disappear. Tell me who that sounds like?

No morals, no rules or governin' in either group, and only one man ever spoke of Revenge. Took a bullet minutes after he opened his trap. Authorities couldn't find shit, so the assholes thought it was bullshit made up to deflect from his crimes."

"Artemis is linked to Revenge?" Ace asked.

"No fuckin' proof anyone's linked to it. All we got is one man's testimony, and minutes after he spoke his last word, his brains were blown out. No proof Revenge exists at all."

"Shit," Drake muttered.

"Got a second organisation, this is your girl, I got no doubts, little proof but no doubts. I've heard of a merc team going into zones that not even God would.

Drake, you've heard of these guys. You set me on their tail, and I've got better info now.

They've brought out hostages alive, cost a fuck load, and there are no contact details for them. This organisation contacts you, tell you the price of business and then calls back in twelve hours. Say yes, they go in, say no, they don't bother with a further call, and your person is dead. Rumour was they're called Rescue, but I'm thinkin' that's a smokescreen for Artemis. Artemis ain't one woman. She's got a group behind her.

With what Artemis told you, there's little doubt she belongs to this team. Artemis has been places that the fuckin' devil would baulk at going. The fuckin' devil turns a blind eye to this 'cause even for him, it's dark. They're ghosts, no trace is found, they make the drop-off, and if you don't pay, they'll get paid one way or another.

Telling you, knowing what Artemis is capable of, and what your girl did in a week when Phoenix took her hit. It would not shit me to find Artemis belongs to both organisations. I'm ninety percent sure on the merc team, seventy on Revenge."

"You can't find anythin' on Artemis direct?" Ace asked.

"Your girl is so dark; Artemis makes the night look like daylight."

"Not good, not fuckin' good," Apache muttered.

"Understatement. Lock your brother's here for

safety? Artemis will take this place and walk away whistling. Rocket launcher, bomb, stealth entry, you won't know Artemis is here." Hawthorne leaned forward to emphasise his point.

"Experienced that. Artemis broke into the clubhouse five times now. Each time guards never saw Artemis coming and ended up drugged. Can't find an entry point," Ace informed Hawthorne.

"I want to know what shit Rage is in, and how big a shovel Hawthorne's need, and how we take Rage's back. 'Cause I'm telling ya, I'm taking Rage's back, and so are my men."

Drake sat back in his chair and considered the options. If what Hawthorne was saying was true, they were fucked. He'd never heard of Revenge, if it and it was a huge if, Artemis belonged to one or both organisations, Rage was neck deep. Drake couldn't envisage a way out without further bloodshed.

Drake had learned about Rescue, who dared complicated rescue and recovery. Bringing out hostages from dangerous places, and he'd assumed Artemis was part of that. Revenge was darker than Rescue, Drake assumed, based on Artemis's scarring, that she ran or belonged to Rescue. What if Artemis was linked to both? His brothers were up the creek without a paddle.

Drake trusted his brothers, they'd one snake, and his gut told him there was a second at least. Another brother who Drake trusted was a piece of shit. Drake

had known them years, and Gid had rocked him.
Which other brother or brothers would rock his trust?
Rage was reacting and not thinking. When Rage
started thinking, shit would hit the fan, family had
turned on family, and that couldn't be forgotten or
forgiven.

"Take a seat," Drake said. "Once you up to speed,
do what you can to bury Artemis. Bury anythin' that
leads to her, and we'll handle it." Drake got a chin
lift, and Hawthorne sat.

I traced the tattoo with a fingertip, soft brown eyes
watched warily. I traced the roses one by one and
then traced the letters of Kayleigh's name. A nail slid
around the angel, and the hearts and I remained
kneeling, looking up into a face I'd once loved as a
brother. Kayleigh had died horrifically. The girl I'd
once been, no longer existed. It was hard, I'd
Kayleigh's memories and pain, but she wasn't me any
longer. It was similar to being two separate identities
in one body, but I dominated it. Not that I had
multiple personalities, I just had Kayleigh's
memories.

"Talk," I whispered to Slick.

"Fell in love with you when you got that first A in
your maths test and jumped all over the place like a
fuckin' rabbit girl. Kayleigh, you were jailbait then,

and only one man held your eyes but didn't stop me lovin' you with everythin' I had.

Was always at your shit. Think I wanted to sit through concerts and shit at a school? Couldn't have you but couldn't let you go either." I rocked back on my heels and placed my hands on Slick's thighs. They were solid and firm. I touched him with a nail and traced it upwards towards his crotch.

"Love?"

"No, Kayleigh," Slick said as I paused just before I hit Slick's cock.

"Kayleigh is dead Slick, your brothers tortured and killed her. Kayleigh's man took her murderess to his bed and fucked Misty like he fucked Kayleigh. Ace gave the order."

"Ace didn't give the order."

"Still fucked Misty, want to know how many men I fucked since Ace? None."

"Kayleigh," Slick whispered brokenly.

"See getting fucked with a bottle and bat, well shits not pretty down there or inside. Surgery does wonders, but not sure if I can be fucked, so I never bothered. But I'm wondering, just looking at you."

"Fuckin' slit my throat because not touching you, girl. You weren't meant to be mine. And this is far worse than anythin' you can imagine."

"I don't know; I can imagine a lot," I whispered. Slowly I trailed my nail up Slick's chest and stopped short of his nipple.

"Kayleigh," Slick whispered, tortured.

"I like how that sounds, Slick; I enjoy knowing you get to share my pain. Wanting someone I couldn't have. Jailbait be fucked; if I'd have been yours, would that have happened to me?" I leaned forward and kissed Slick's chest.

"Can't answer that girl," Slick whispered back at me. I slid my other hand forward and cupped his cock, Slick was hard, damn hard, and I felt a twinge inside me.

"Inked me on you, Slick."

"Wherever I travelled, you was comin' with me," Slick whispered again. I sat back and studied him.

"Why did you want to kill me?"

"Never did baby, needed you to live, needed your beauty."

"Why didn't you tell on Thunder and the others?"

"Didn't fuckin' know. If I'd 'a known, I'd have put a bullet in them."

"Who else is involved?"

"No one, I don't think my brothers were involved. Bulldog's brothers got ended. They may have been involved."

"Want me?"

"Fuck, yes." I leaned forward and touched my mouth to his. Slick groaned and then moved his head to one side.

"You're Ace's, baby, always was and always will be. There's been no one else for either of ya."

"But Ace fucked Misty, I can fuck you. Wouldn't you enjoy that?"

"Love nothin' more than you under me, wet, desperate, panting, but it's wrong. I'm not Ace."

"Who else was involved?"

"Don't know, didn't know Gid was involved, fucked us all up seein' Gid betrayed brothers like that. Gid. The man was dark but not that dark."

"Tell me why Ace wanted to kill me," I kissed Slick's throat and licked him. Straddling Slick, his cock bit into me. I ground my pelvis against Slick's cock, and he hissed.

"Brother didn't. Ace broke when you disappeared. Thought it was the shit at the club that made you run, had to lock Ace down."

"When did you lock Ace down?"

"When we got the file. Man lost it, totally gone, not there, not thinkin', like an animal roarin' pain." I got off Slick, and he looked into my eyes again.

"Let him go, Akemi. Slick's telling the truth," I said, shattered. I'd slipped him the serum before starting the shit I did, and I felt dirty. In Slick's eyes, he showed he didn't blame me, but I was dirty. Something I hadn't been for years, not since I woke up and looked into Master Hoshi's gentle eyes.

Akemi stepped out of the shadows and injected Slick again. We waited for his head to drop and cleaned Slick up and then carted him to the van. Carefully we drove Slick to Rage. Akemi drove up, lights off and then cautiously got Slick out of the truck.

We laid Slick gently on the forecourt. Then once we were both back in the van, Akemi hit the full beam of the headlights, lighting up the forecourt and clubhouse. Akemi hit the horn twice, and then we drove away.

Ace ran hard, harder than he'd ever run when he saw the figure laid on the ground. He hit his knees as he dived to the ground where Slick lay motionless. Drake hit the ground seconds after Ace. Frantically, Ace checked for a pulse, and he gave a loud sigh of relief when he found one.

"Get doc," Drake snapped at Hunter as Drake lifted his fallen brother into his arms. Ace took his back, and they got Slick into the clubhouse, where Slick opened his eyes for a few seconds. Slick caught Ace's gaze and held it.

"Didn't betray you, brother. Held off against her," Slick muttered and then fell silent again as his eyes closed.

"What?" Mac asked. Ace shrugged, but Ace knew somehow whatever Artemis had done to Slick deeply affected Ace's brother. Ace hated her for that split second, hated Artemis made a good man hurt. Phoenix and Marsha came skidding in from the back and flung themselves in Slick's direction. Silvie was already there, Slick's head on her lap as Silvie stroked his hair and murmured to Slick.

As soon as the shit had hit with Gid, Drake had ordered the skanks off-site and kept the three old ladies safe at the clubhouse. Phoenix had insisted Artemis wasn't a threat to her, but Drake was taking no chances, not with Drake's precious wife and kids. Hawthorne's had been busy for the last few days.

Doc Gibson checked out Slick and told them to let Slick sleep it off. He'd been sedated, and Slick had no further injuries. Doc had strapped Slick's ribs in case they were broken. But apart from bruising to his face and torso, Slick was okay physically. Ace guessed that Artemis had done a number on the man's head.

Ace looked as he received a text, and his body locked as he read an address, time, and nothing else. He slipped his phone back into his pocket and avoided everyone's gaze as Ace kept watch with his brothers waiting for Slick to wake up.

Ace walked into the abandoned warehouse and looked around. He was alert and wasn't surprised when Akemi appeared out of thin air and patted him down. Akemi gave a nod, and a woman came forward; she wasn't Artemis. Ace's gaze narrowed on her, and he wondered what her relationship was with

Artemis. Their impression that Artemis was more than one person was correct.

She jerked her head, and Ace followed her as she led the way up the steps to a second level, and Ace saw two chairs. Sat in one with legs outstretched and crossed, and arms folded against her chest was Artemis. She looked at him, and Ace inwardly flinched at the coldness in her expression.

"Sit," Artemis said. Her face turned impassive, and Artemis watched as Ace walked across and sat.

"Talk," I said, looking at Ace. His face was ravaged, and Ace allowed his emotions to show. Pain and betrayal were the foremost expressions on his face. Ace reached out a hand to touch me, and Angel pushed his hand away. Kristoff and Butch appeared from behind, and they took my back. Simone was to my right and Akemi to my left.

"Wasn't involved," Ace said.

"Hard to believe," I said, striving for calm. I wanted to scream and rail at Ace, but that wouldn't solve anything.

"I didn't. Shit, Kayleigh, you really think I'd do that to you?"

"Misty, you fucked her."

"Yeah, I shoved my dick in her and came. She didn't get off with me once. I never put the effort in," Ace snapped, leaning forward. Anger crossed Ace's face.

"You did so repeatedly," I bit back, those actions

alone, damned Ace.

"Fucked Misty every few months. Misty was a cunt that I shoved my dick into nothing else," Ace hit back.

"You kiss her?" I asked. I was hurting bad, so bad, but I hid that from Ace.

"Never," Ace said adamantly.

"Yeah," I drawled softly. Ace looked at me and saw disbelief written across my face. "No woman will let you just fuck her, Ace. You put some effort in with Misty. Otherwise, for the last eleven years, you couldn't have kept shoving your dick in. Guess how many lovers I've had?"

"Loved you so much," Ace said brokenly.

"Don't know about that. I know, I loved you, I'd my babies ripped from my gaping stomach for loving you. Everything done to me, that hurt the most, the cunt you fucked, didn't mind trying to kill your kids.

Except they're my kids too, and Falcon and Nova fought for life. Falcon was flatline when they brought him in. Doctors worked on Falcon for hours before he stabilised enough. Falcon died several more times," I lashed out, allowing my pain to roughen my voice.

"Nova and Falcon are mine," Ace stated, his voice mirroring my pain.

"No, they're mine. You're just a sperm donor who decided to get rid of them. When did you realise I was pregnant?"

"I didn't. Realised you'd put on weight, we were

eating a fuck load that summer, thought it was that."
Ace held my stare.

"Still shoved your dick in the cunt that tried to kill
your kids." I controlled the startled jump my body
gave as Ace shoved to his feet. The chair flew
backwards, and he leaned towards me.

"I shoved my dick in the cunt that tried to kill my
kids. You think that don't haunt me? We talked about
kids; you, and me, dreamed of that house with a big
yard and it bein' full of kids. Think I'd kill my
babes?" Ace roared. I blinked as a memory hit me of
us in bed, eating chicken and laughing about making
the most of it. Because when we'd kid's, we wouldn't
get many chances to do that. My eyes glazed, and
Ace saw and sat.

"Wanted kids, wanted 'em so bad with you, could
taste it. Blond-haired, blue-eyed baby girls and dark-
haired, green-eyed boys. We lay in bed night after
night talkin' that shit through. I'd kill my babes?
Even if I wanted you gone, I'd have taken my kids
first, made sure they'd survive before gettin' shot of
you. That alone should tell you, I wasn't fuckin'
involved."

"Ace is right, daughter, the man wasn't," a gentle
voice spoke from the shadows. I looked up as Master
Hoshi appeared, and he was looking directly at Ace
and me. I stared at the man who'd been my father for
eleven years. My mentor, my children's grandfather
and for the first two years of my meeting him, Master

Hoshi been my damned nemesis.

"Master," I said, rising to my feet and bowing. Master Hoshi bowed back, and I studied him.

Late fifties, possibly early sixties, he was lean and trim. His frame held wiry muscle, but he'd beaten my ass a load of times. Master Hoshi was dressed in an expensive black suit and wore a silk grey shirt under it. I could see the gold chain from his pocket watch crossing his right breast.

Master Hoshi wasn't much above five foot four, face lightly lined, and his head shaved bald as it had been the whole time I'd known him. He stood straight, and his demeanour, as usual, was projected calm. Master Hoshi was patient and had a face that anyone who met him would trust. Brown eyes looked deep into mine, and I saw love for me. I'd always been the closest of his students, apart from Akemi.

"The man speaks the truth. We've one who knows more of the truth," Master Hoshi said, his voice becoming harder. "My daughter deserves the truth."

"You do?" Ace asked. Looking at him, Master Hoshi held a hand up in Ace's face. Angel, who'd disappeared, appeared out of the shadows carrying a body over his shoulder. Angel slung it none too gently on the floor, and it rolled over, and I frowned as I recognised Sticks laying there unconscious. I'd been searching for Sticks, and Master Hoshi had him.

"Fuck, Sticks?" Ace whispered in horror.

"Wake him up," Master Hoshi ordered Angel, who

withdrew a case from his pocket and pulled a needle out. Angel jabbed it in Sticks, and a few seconds later, Sticks' body jolted. Eyes opened and then grew wide as Sticks realised he was surrounded, and then Sticks spied Ace. The blood drained from his face, and I recognised Stick's guilt then.

"Start talking," Ace demanded.

"Brother."

"Ain't no brother of mine," Ace spat.

"Tell our present company what you told me," Master Hoshi said. He dragged a chair over and sat on it, facing Sticks.

"You're gonna kill me," Sticks muttered. Master Hoshi shook his head.

"I give my word I will not kill you." I looked towards Master Hoshi as I caught his phrasing. My gaze flew back to Sticks.

"Bulldog guessed early that Drake was making moves. Bulldog realised that if he took Ace from Drake, Drake's foundation would shudder and probably crumble. To get Ace, Bulldog decided to take out Kayleigh. Bulldog didn't wanna lose the club. Rage was Drake's legacy. He wasn't going to let Drake have that."

"Bulldog ordered Kayleigh's death to rock Drake?" Ace whispered, and I caught the dangerous edge to his voice.

"Yeah, Bulldog ordered it. We followed orders," the man said beseechingly.

"And you didn't think it was wrong to do so."
Stick's gaze shot to my face, and I rocked back as a
memory hit me with the speed of a train.

"Oh my god, you were there. You raped me too," I
whispered. And Sticks lost whatever blood he'd left
in his face. I'd hadn't remembered seeing him, either
forgotten or blocked it. Sticks hadn't been there the
whole time, but he'd raped me before the bottle, and
he'd anally raped me.

"Keep talking," Master Hoshi said before Ace
reacted.

"Bulldog got Thunder in on it, Thunder was
whacked, he'd do anything. Misty joined willingly,
bitch hated Kayleigh with a passion, wanted Ace."
That blow hit Ace hard. "They got Gid who wanted in
your pants and me on board. The others followed. It
was orders," Sticks wailed. I began shaking, and Ace
was doing the same.

"Orders?" I screamed at Sticks, "raping and
torturing a teenager was orders?" Sticks dropped his
head.

"Who else? Who fuckin' else?" Ace roared.

"Apart from Thunder and Jacked, I'm the last,"
Sticks cried.

"Not Mac, Gunner, or Slick, not anyone else?" I
asked, leaning forward. Akemi stepped behind me
and laid a hand on my back. Akemi's warmth and
strength flowed through me.

"Lock Jacked down," Ace said and then flipped his

phone shut. I hadn't even realised Ace had pulled his phone out.

"No one else, no one, I swear."

"Why torture me like that? Why?" I screamed at Sticks. Everything came boiling out of me, and I kicked him in his face and then bent over Sticks dragging him up. "How could you bastards do that to a teenage girl? A pregnant teenage girl? What sort of evil were you?" A hand gripped my arm, and glancing at the hand, I saw the gold ring that said RH on it. That hand had held me so many times. I let Sticks go and stepped back, and Master Hoshi retook his seat.

"Wouldn't put out for anyone else, and most of the MC wanted in Kayleigh's pants. Don't see why a fuckin' prospect got her, but you were on the ground, and I was gonna get me some. I could look at Ace and know I'd had you, and I'd one over him." Sticks proved his stupidity as he sneered at Ace, who was motionless.

"You got off on it?" I asked Sticks. Sticks nodded, remembering Master Hoshi had said he wouldn't kill him.

"Why did Misty name innocents?" Ace asked. I wanted the answer to that too.

"Should'a heard her scream when we said you agreed. Pain, pure pain, Thunder got off on it. Misty wanted her to die thinkin' you'd done this to her."

"But Slick, Mac, the others?"

"Hurt you deeper, didn't it? Cried buckets when we said their names, rammed it into your head over and over. You cried more from that than the fact we fucked your virgin ass," Sticks sneered. Yeah, Sticks was way beyond stupid.

"Tortured Kayleigh because Bulldog wanted Drake to fail?" Ace asked.

"Yeah. Liked the money we got, don't see why the MC couldn't remain the way it was. Us taking you out meant we took Drake out, meant MC didn't change."

"Yeah, 'cept it did, you didn't take me out. Kayleigh's body never turned up, so your plans got fucked. You tried to kill my kids," Ace whispered so softly that Sticks scrambled back on his ass. Even I felt a twinge of fear at Ace's tone. "Tried to kill the woman I loved, raped and tortured her, you cut up my old lady. Tossed my babes aside like garbage."

"Never cut Kayleigh, just fucked her back and front," Sticks kept piling it on.

"And you rapin' her back and front were okay?" Ace said. Ace turned away from Sticks and looked at Master Hoshi. "We done?" Master Hoshi rose to his feet and flicked an imaginary piece of lintel from his suit.

"Yes. My daughter has her answers and the truth." Master Hoshi walked to me and kissed my forehead, and then disappeared into the shadows. Sticks moved to get up, and Ace kicked him back and placed his boot on Stick's throat. Ace looked into the shadows.

"He said you wouldn't kill me," Sticks squeaked.

"No, Master Hoshi said he wouldn't kill you," I told him. "He said nothing about us not killing you."

"You hear it?" Ace asked. I watched as Drake walked forward, Apache and Slick at his back. Texas and Fish with them, from behind them came Dylan Hawthorne and several of his men. Behind me, Kristoff and Butch appeared. I hadn't even noticed they'd gone.

"Clocked 'em walking in," Kristoff said into the silence. People moved, apart from Ace, who remained with his boot on Stick's throat. Rage took one side of Sticks, and Artemis took my side.

"Ezra is locking Jacked down," Drake said and looked at me. The pain in Drake's face took my ability to breathe away. It was naked.

"You got fucked up because I tried to get the MC clean," Drake said bitterly and struggled to meet my eyes.

"I got fucked up because Bulldog was a sick bastard." Instantly, I denied Drake his guilt. What happened was not Drake's fault. Drake didn't need the guilt. I looked at my people and then at Rage. "Guessing you want this one." Drake nodded.

"You've got this," Dylan Hawthorne said and waved a hand. He and his men disappeared.

I looked at Ace, whom I'd loved with a passion so many years ago and spent twice that time hating him.

Ace was broken. I could see that now, he'd been broken for years, just existing, and this had broken Ace further. Ace didn't have a Master Hoshi, but Ace had Rage. He'd make it. I gave a finger signal, and my people faded away; I looked at Rage and then disappeared too.

"Artemis, wait," Drake called. I heard him, but Drake didn't know that; I kept walking. I reached the limo sitting outside idling and opened the door, and climbed in. Then I laid my head on Master Hoshi's lap and let the tears fall.

Chapter Seven.

8th December 2014

A week later, I sat in Akemi's SUV and studied my nails. I wasn't sure what I was doing was right, but I owed Ace and Rage this. Although now I was here, second thoughts were creeping in. I looked in the mirror at Nova and Falcon, who both patiently watched.

"Mom, take your time," Falcon said, and I smiled at my son. So like his father, this wasn't a bad thing, and I knew that now. As Falcon's mother, I'd never held it against him. What mother would? The twins' father was a good guy, and that sank deep within me. Nova gave me big eyes, solemn and serious.

"If you're not ready, Mom, turn the car around," Nova said, but she stared out of the car window.

Five days ago, I'd sat the twins down and gave them a very child-friendly version of the truth. They knew I thought their father had been involved in an attack on me, and I'd hidden us to protect them. The twins had the truth, and their father was innocent, so now we sat here, on Rage.

I took five calming breaths and put the car into gear and drove onto the forecourt. Parking near the front of the clubhouse, I checked the time. Eight o'clock at night, Ace should be in the clubhouse, the garages and parts store was shut, and so was the shop. Reluctantly, I got out, and the kids climbed out behind me. As usual, I placed myself in front of Falcon and Nova, Akemi at their back and walked to the clubhouse door.

Greedily, gulping another deep breath, I jumped as a small hand touched my back, Falcon. I reached behind and squeezed Falcon's hand tight. Nova moved behind me to stand by Falcon's side. The kids knew the drill; I always entered first. I pushed open the clubhouse door and stopped as noise hit from every direction.

Phoenix and Drake sat on a sofa, her in his lap and wrapped around him, Phoe's head on Drake's chest. Brothers stood at the bar, the pool table that had been there before I'd hit Rage, was occupied by Fish and Marsha. Silvie leaned closer to Apache and made a face at him. Texas was hollering at a Blaze who looked as pissed as Texas, and my gaze settled on Ace. I heard a loud gasp and guessed Marsha had seen me. A cue hit the floor.

Drake stared over and stilled, and so did Phoenix. Drake's calm mood changed to alert and hit the club instantly, and brothers began stopping and looking up. Ace turned from the bar where he'd been sitting with a bottle of beer in hand.

Ace still drank Coors. Why that mattered, I didn't know. It was something I randomly noted, a distraction from the feelings swamping me. His body tightened, and my presence hit home. I stepped inside and moved to the right, and the kids came through the doorway.

Ace's gaze flew straight to the twins, and pain, wariness, shock and worse than that, disbelieving hope crossed his face. He stared at the kids as they gazed straight back at Ace, no question who their father was. Falcon tilted his head, and Nova wrinkled her nose.

Ace's face softened, and then he was up and moving fast across the floor. Nova and Falcon remained still as their father reached them, landing on his knees. Without hesitation, Ace dragged the twins into his arms. Ace wrapped them both in a hug and buried his head between them.

Falcon remained standing still, but Nova, my beautiful girl, shyly lifted her arms and wrapped them around her father's neck. There was a muffled sob, but we couldn't move our eyes away from the scene in front of us. Falcon lifted a hand and put it on his father's neck, and Ace held on tighter. Tears choked the back of my throat, and arms came from behind. I leant back, knowing Akemi was there, as always, at my back.

They remained standing there for a few minutes, with everyone watching them. Akemi and I were ready to move to protect the kids when Apache hit the huddle. He fell to his knees as well, and Apache's strong arms hugged the three figures. A memory of Apache holding me tight surfaced, and I remembered how safe those arms were. Ace lifted his head with tears running down his cheeks and leaned on his father's shoulder for a few seconds.

Nova reached up a little hand and wiped tears from Ace's face. Nova studied one on her finger and wiped it away. Ace broke into a wondrous smile and wrapped his arms around his father and kids again.

"Righted a wrong woman," a voice whispered in my ear, and to my surprise, Drake was there. I looked up and saw approval in his eyes, and that warmth hit my stomach. I gave Drake a half-smile. Akemi tightened his arms.

"Meet Uncle Akemi," Nova said into the silence. Ace looked up and saw Akemi with his arms around me. Something crossed Ace's face and disappeared quickly.

"Uncle Akemi meet our Dad," Nova said with a grin. That burrowed into Ace and me at the same time.

"Uncle Akemi was there when we were born. He's

like Mom's big brother, only I think Uncle Akemi gets into more shit." My eyes narrowed. "Sorry, more trouble than Mom does," Falcon said.

"Yeah, Mom says she's going to get grandpa Hoshi to put Uncle Akemi up for adoption. Like that will happen," Nova chipped in, and Akemi grinned at his girl.

"Grandpa Hoshi will have trouble doing that," Akemi chuckled.

"Grandpa Hoshi is a kickass badass," Falcon said, his eyes narrowing, and he turned to Ace. "Mom says you're a kickass badass too." Falcon looked to his dad to confirm that.

"If your Mom says so, it must be true," Ace finally spoke.

"Don't say badass," I muttered, and Drake squeezed my hip.

"I'm grandpa Apache," Apache said. Nova studied him.

"Hi, I can see that," Nova replied, and I rolled my eyes. Apache grinned.

"Yo, I'm Uncle Drake, and that's your Aunt Phoenix," Drake snapped his fingers.

"You're not Native American," Falcon announced.

"Nope. But in an MC, we're all brothers, which makes every one of these your uncles. Every single one of them," Drake replied, pointing at Rage, seeing Ace was still struggling.

"Well shit, er, sugar," Falcon corrected at another

eye glare from me. Ace chuckled, it sounded rusty, and Falcon grinned.

"Mom doesn't like us cussing; she says not until we're sixteen," Falcon shared.

"Your mom had a potty mouth herself at your age," Fish said, coming forward. Marsha lurked behind him, and they seemed hesitant.

"Nova, Falcon, this is Grandpa Fish and Grandma Marsha. They raised me," I informed the kids. A strangled sob from Marsha echoed, and then she was there, hands latching onto Nova's face and twisting it one way and then another.

"She's so pretty, you're so pretty," Marsha said, quiet tears rolling down her cheeks.

"You're pretty, too," Nova said magnanimously.

"Precious babies," Marsha said and gathered the twins in her arms. Fish wrapped his arms around the three of them, and Ace and Apache stood up. Ace looked at me, and there was hope in his eyes that this meant what Ace thought it meant.

"Need a beer," I said. Ace nodded and bellowed across the room to a prospect. Ace got close as Drake, Phoe, Fish, Marsha and Apache made a fuss of the kids.

"Thank you," Ace whispered.

"Punished you for too long, and I correct my mistakes," I whispered back. Green eyes flared, but Ace nodded and held a hand out to Akemi. Akemi released me and took his hand.

"Thank you for watching out for them," Ace muttered to Akemi, his voice hoarse with emotion. Akemi gave a sharp nod.

"Artemis is the little sister I never…." Akemi broke off, and it was my turn to search Akemi's face and make sure my brother was okay. Akemi swallowed hard and nodded towards the bar.

"Got beer?" Akemi asked when he'd control of his voice again. Ace nodded, and Akemi walked in that direction.

"There's a story there," Ace drawled.

"That's Akemi's story. None of us shares each other's stories," I told Ace bluntly, and Ace's eyes narrowed, and I realised my slip. Ace didn't push.

"Thank you," Ace whispered again.

"Go spend time with your kids," I moved to join Akemi. Ace's hand reached out and snatched mine.

"Need to find time to talk."

"Not tonight Ace, this is taking enough out of me."

Ace gave another nod and moved towards the kids. One by one, brothers were coming forward and introducing themselves. The twins looked to be in heaven. They'd always wanted a big family, Akemi and Master Hoshi and Mrs Humphries was not enough. The kids had a huge family now. Ace had his arms around both kids when someone else wasn't hugging them half to death.

I spied Slick standing to one side of the bar and slowly approached, shame on my face. Slick watched warily as I stopped two steps in front of him. Shit was awkward between us now, it never had been, but I'd caused this. Trouble was, I'd no idea how to fix it because I'd punished an innocent man.

"Artemis," Slick finally said.

"Slick, I'm so…" Slick cut me off mid-sentence.

"Don't!" Slick looked at me and dropped his head and studied his boots. I waited.

"What you did to me, girl, I'll not ever forget. Forgive you, understand where you were comin' from but can't forget. Those few minutes, I could have given in and taken what you offered. Betrayed a brother." Slick stopped and lifted his head, eyes blazing into mine and full of hurt.

"I thought…" I began, and Slick cut me off again. "Loved you with everythin' I have. You took that and tarnished it, dirtied it up, nearly made me betray my brother. That I don't forgive, you took something from me, and you can't ever give it back, girl. Time will tell."

"Give you all the time you need, Slick," I whispered, genuinely meaning it.

"You do that, and maybe one day we'll be okay again," Slick said and walked away towards the back rooms. I dropped my head and, turning, saw Drake's gaze on me. Drake's face was thoughtful, and he shook his head. Give Slick time, Drake was saying silently. I nodded.

Texas had called in a pizza order, and a prospect

had run out to get soft drinks and snacks from a local shop. There was a happy vibe in the clubhouse, brothers celebrating, but I picked up an undercurrent. I got Apache to one side and asked what was wrong. Apache gave me a look that said not tonight. Tonight was about being happy.

Phoenix whispered something to Drake, gazing at me. I was going to ask Drake what was wrong when Marsha collared me and began firing questions. Marsha wanted to know everything. In Marsha's eyes, I saw fear and worry over what I'd endured and survived. Out of sheer kindness and the fact Marsha had raised me, I kept most of the dark from her.

Marsha and Fish had seen enough dark. Although I saw in Fish's stare, they didn't need mine, and that he knew more than I was telling Marsha. Marsha took what I gave her, and when she pried for more, Fish distracted her. Ace led the kids from group to group, with Apache never far from Ace's side and Silvie never far from his.

I zoomed in on Silvie as I recognised her. We hadn't been close, but even back then, I was aware Silvie had strong feelings for Apache. Silvie had been young then, too, eighteen or nineteen. By his body manner, Apache hadn't acted on Silvie's feelings. In Silvie's eyes, I caught a look of love that was quickly hidden. And my heart sank. For over a decade, she'd loved that man, and Apache wasted it.

A hand touched my waist, and glancing up, I saw

Ace stood there. Ace's face was blank, and I looked for the kids and saw them with cues in hand playing pool with Gunner and Rock. Ace's hand clenched on my waist, and I picked up his non-verbal cue and shook my head. His hand clenched again, and I gazed at the kids.

"They're fine. Need to talk, now," Ace muttered.

With a sigh, I allowed Ace to lead me from the room. Ace wouldn't back down once he set his mind to something. Ace led me to his room and shut the door behind him. The room hadn't changed, a single bed, a chest of drawers and a bedside table. Nothing else.

"Ace." That was as far as I got before Ace's mouth slammed on mine.

Ace pushed me against the door as one of his hands cupped the back of my head so he could deepen the kiss. His other hand remained on my hip, holding me tight. Ace broke off the kiss.

His stunning eyes were a storm of emotion, and Ace swallowed. Ace gently ran his fingers through my hair, and his mouth hit mine again. He pulled me closer to him and pressed me into his body. Ace's cock hardened against my body, and I gasped into his mouth.

That one gasp sent electricity shooting through both of us, and Ace hooked his hands under my ass like he used to do in the old days. I wrapped my legs around his waist, damp between my legs. In two strides, Ace had us on the bed, and he was lifting my top as I scrabbled to get his off. I needed to feel Ace, needed Ace with a burning passion, I thought I'd combust from.

With a pissed off growl, Ace gave up trying to pull my top off and ripped it down the middle. Ace gazed at my bared breasts in their black satin bra and groaned. I gave a cry of protest as I'd got his tee halfway off, and he moved one arm and yanked the tee over his head.

My hands ran across his back, touching smooth flesh and rigid muscles. I ran them down to his ass and grabbed hold. Ace was no longer a boy but a prime example of male masculinity. Ace thrust against me, and I shifted to meet him. Hands scrabbled at my belt, and I slapped them away and undid it and my buttons. Ace's hand thrust between us roughly.

"Christ, baby, this will be fast," Ace rasped, and his hands were at his own jeans. He shrugged them off and yanked mine to my knees and knelt beside me.

"Ace," I cried out with a hint of fear. With effort, Ace dragged his eyes back to my face, and I saw his face in sharp relief. Ace was barely holding onto control.

"I haven't, don't know if I can," I said, confused, trying to tell Ace that I'd not had sex since being cut up.

Ace's face gentled, and he ran his finger down my

face and dropped his head between my legs. The second Ace's tongue hit me there, I squirmed wildly. Oh God, yes, this is what I'd missed. Ace always knew how to deliver this. My hands clenched in his hair, holding Ace in place, and I thrust against his tongue.

A finger thrust inside gently, and I clamped around him. There was no pain, just slightly uncomfortable. Oh god, I could do this, I could so fuck Ace, he felt so good. I gasped as Ace twirled his finger inside and added a second. Ace stretched me, strain showing on his face as he wrestled for control.

"Baby, you're soaked," Ace whispered, and I felt him deep within. I moved my hips upwards to meet his tongue, and he smiled and gave me what I demanded. Ace stretched me further with two fingers as his thumb hit my clit in just the right spot. I cried out as an orgasm hit hard.

As I was still riding it, Ace moved and slipped slowly inside. Ace bit his lip, forcing control when he wanted to take. I shifted, trying to get away, Ace was large, and this time there was pain. Ace held on and kissed me, wet and long, and while doing so, inch by inch, he slipped in. Ace stayed still, allowing me to get used to his size and girth. My eyes widened when he was fully rooted.

"You're so tight," Ace rasped and began to move, and I knew nothing but Ace.

I laid on Ace's chest, damp with sweat and our body fluids. My hand idly played with his nipple, and his hand held my ass tight. Somehow during our lovemaking, we'd shed the rest of our clothes.

"I'm not her," I said against his chest, "she died; Kayleigh died."

"No, Kayleigh's there somewhere. I've seen glimpses. All I ever needed was you, Kayleigh or Artemis; it's you," Ace mused. Ace shifted and moved onto his side and turned my body, so I lay on my side, facing him.

"If you think I can be Kayleigh again, I can't."

"Only need you, woman. You feel it; what's between us, it never died."

"Sex," I told Ace bluntly. To my surprise, Ace began to laugh. His laugh sounded rusty as if unused to it. He was beautiful when he laughed, and I watched with a dazed expression on my face. Ace traced my mouth with a finger.

"Sex is the least of it, baby, but we do have good sex." I glared.

"We can't do this again. I have my life, Ace. You have yours. I won't stop doing what I do." Ace frowned, and I bit my lip.

"Did I ask you to stop, woman? Christ, you took out an entire street gang, hunted criminals, caught your...." Ace broke off, and pain blossomed in his eyes.

"Caught those who left me for dead," I whispered. Ace gave a curt nod.

"Just want what you can give."

"Don't have shit to give; everything I have goes into the twins."

"Liar," Ace said, tapping my nose; I bristled. Ace grinned, and I blinked dazedly again at that grin. The damn man was oh so sexy! Ace was not going to get away with dazzling me!

"You have Master Hoshi as a father, Akemi as your brother. Guess you've others working for you. Don't tell me, woman, that you won't walk through fire for them." I shook my head, and Ace's eyes narrowed, and I changed to a nod. I would; I'd not stop to get one of my guys safe. Maim, torture, kill, I'd do that in a blink of an eye if Angel, Kristoff or any of them needed me.

"We bonded," I grumbled.

"So did we, you're shovin' your head in the sand," Ace said bluntly. "I didn't live Artemis, did nothing but exist, if not for Dad...."

"Don't say it," I said, putting my hand over his mouth; I couldn't bear to hear that. A week ago, I'd have handed Ace the gun and watched laughing while Ace did it. Now I couldn't bear the thought of Ace ending it.

"Dad didn't deserve that," Ace whispered, looking into my eyes. He saw my pain at the thought of him ending it. "I died with Kayleigh. Shit, baby, I fucked; I didn't prepare them; it was a hole I fucked to get rid of the edge. Forgot love and the finer points of it, and I didn't have relationships. That died with you, and now you're here in my bed, naked, sated. Not givin' you up again."

"Your fear of me doing what I do will come between us," I said. This was a point I thought would cause contention, and I was scrabbling for something to use as a barrier. Ace was too open. Too willing to pick up where we'd left off, Ace wanted to put everything behind us and start anew.

"I can't go backwards. Ace, I managed without you for so long, hated you for so long. Took a huge step tonight towards righting the wrong done to you. But for us to go further than this, it was an itch we scratched." Stubbornness flared in his eyes, and a cunning look crossed Ace's face.

"Okay," Ace said and gave my ass one last squeeze and rose from the bed. Drool collected in my mouth, and I swallowed hard. Tanned silky skin, thickly muscled thighs, hard abs, ink on his arms, back and chest, Ace was a picture of masculine hotness. Bastard gave me a knowing look, bent, and picked his jeans up. I audibly gulped at the sight of his tight muscled ass. Ace pulled them up and shrugged his tee back on.

"Clean tees are in the second drawer, ripped your top," he said. He came to stand over me, a wall of sexy muscle. Ace gave me a smile and bent and kissed me. Just as it turned hot, Ace pulled away and gave me a wink. "You know where I am when you want that itch scratched," Ace grinned. And I watched open-mouthed as he walked out of the room. No, Ace didn't fucking walk, Ace strutted in his, I got myself some, strut!

Pissed, I leapt up from the bed and dressed. My top was beyond recovery. I rummaged through the drawers and pulled on a plain black top. Under my breath, I cursed the cocky man and left the room, imagining the ways I'd make Ace beg. Methods that included handcuffs, torment, and lots and lots of sex.

I hit the rec room and searched for the kids. They were now playing air hockey with Akemi and Fish, and by the looks, on their faces, they were cheating. Nova had such a look of innocence, I could see Akemi shaking his head at her. Ace was standing near them, arm slung casually over Falcon's shoulder as Falcon watched Nova take Fish apart.

Ace glanced over, and a smug, self-satisfied look crossed his face, and I wanted to punch it off him. Giving Ace the dead eye, I heard a snicker and found Apache watching us.

"What are you laughing at?" I demanded, annoyed.

"Think you'll get away from Ace?" Apache asked, smiling.

"Kayleigh is dead," I told him. For God's sake, these people needed to realise that. I wasn't her!

"Maybe," Apache said, "maybe she's being resurrected." I shook my head.

"Kayleigh's dead," I hissed.

"If she's dead, why the need to keep insisting she is?"

"Because you keep looking for Kayleigh." I turned to Apache and stared deep into his eyes. "She's dead. Let her rest," I snarled and strode over to the kids to tell them it was time to leave. To their credit, both kids got ready at once. They said goodbyes and hugged their grandfather and father and walked out to the car. Ace grabbed my hand as I went to follow.

"It's not over, Artemis," Ace said in a growl. I looked at him and shrugged.

"Scratched my itch, Ace. Thanks," I replied, digging deep for a cold tone. Ace grinned, and I sent him a death stare.

"Whatever, baby. See you soon." The smug bastard turned on his heel and walked away. Akemi glanced over and got in the car and drove home.

The phone kept ringing incessantly, and I sat up glaring at it. I read a number I didn't recognise and growled as I connected the call.

"Artemis?" a voice asked. Actually, it stated more than asked.

"What?" I sniped, annoyed at being woken up.

"We haven't yet met, but I believe you're aware of who I am. My name is Miguel Santos, and we've business to do." I woke up. Literally, woke up hearing that name. I waited and listened to the silence on the phone and realised Santos was waiting for me to ask how he'd got my number. This was my private line, and Santos was flexing muscle by ringing it.

"We do?" I asked, thoughts racing. Santos was well known in Rapid City and most of the surrounding towns. Drug running, guns, and pussy, I was aware of, and I'd suspicions he'd homegrown terrorist connections. Almost certain the bastard was human trafficking.

"We've a mutual acquaintance."

"I don't see how that affects me."

"I have Thunder," Santos stated calmly, and I stilled. Shit, I wanted Thunder and wanted him bad now I was about to find out how bad I wanted him.

"And?"

"Well, I believe you want Thunder, you and Rage are both looking for him, and I have him."

"Whoop de do," I muttered. Santos laughed.

"I'm willing to make a deal if you're interested."

"What do you want?"

"There's a man running extremely far away. He's stolen something from me, and I want it back. I'm prepared to give you Thunder for this man. Fetch me a man called Pen Thera, and I'll give you Thunder," Santos said and disconnected. I hadn't agreed to the deal, and I was now annoyed that Santos thought he could flex his muscle around me.

As badly as I wanted Thunder, I guessed the minute I brought Thera to Santos, Santos would add my name to his list of associates. And I'd no intention of being that person. I climbed out of bed and checked the windows and doors before waking up Buzz. Buzz met me in the office we'd set up, and I told Buzz about the call. What Santos hadn't realised was that every call to anyone in Artemis was recorded, private or not.

Buzz dragged up the file and opened it, listening. Buzz tapped his finger on his chin and watched my face as Santos mentioned Thunder.

"No dice," Buzz said firmly. He coughed and cleared his throat. Buzz's hand went to the drawers, and he pulled out one of the energy drinks he kept there. I'd long ago learned to trust Buzz's gut feelings, and I sensed Buzz was having one of them now.

"Agreed but need information on Thera. Who Thera is, what links he had to Santos, what this item Santos has lost is. Need to know Thera's background, history, family, everything. Get Nigel on the task," I said, sitting on the edge of Buzz's desk.

"Simone and Butch are on jobs, then vacation, as is Angel. Kristoff is heading back tomorrow," Buzz said, his mind already working towards solving the Thera problem.

"Didn't Kristoff have the Theakston job to do next?"
I asked, looking at our wipe boards.

"Yeah, but Angel can pick that up."

"Tell Angel to pick up Theakston, and I'll put
Kristoff on this. Tell Kris I'll match the bounty on
Theakston. I want Thera yesterday," I said, rubbing
my brow. Buzz nodded and picked up the phone to
tell Nigel to get his ass into work.

I sat at the table that was doubling as a conference
table. Akemi had taken the kids to see Rage while I
stayed back with Buzz, Nigel, and Kristoff. Three
days had passed since Santos woke me in the middle
of the night. Kristoff was grinning manically, and
Buzz and Nigel looked shattered.

"Talk," I said.

"Pen Thera, Caucasian, age twenty-eight, mother
dead, father a drunk and still kicking around in
downtown Rapid City. Thera's father is a serious
bum. Abused the wife and kids, Thera has two sisters,
both whores and one hooked on drugs. Thera is the
abnormality; got himself educated, got a decent
home, no wife, kids, or steady girlfriend.

Lives with a dog, an attack trained German
shepherd, got money in the bank, the tune of sixty
thou. Seems to be his earnings and some carefully
thought-out investments. Drives a new car, black

Mercedes, no criminal record, no juvie time, nothing, Thera's as clean as a whistle."

"What the hell does Santos want with Pen Thera?"

"Oh, Santos is gagging for him. Thera witnessed a murder, and he identified one of Santos's top lieutenants, Chill, as the shooter. Thera identified Chill and did a bunk with the woman the victim was murdered over. Sister of a guy who owed Santos big bucks, the brother met with Chill, and Chill insisted on taking the girl as part of the payback.

Brother objected, had a familial feeling for the girl and took shots to the head. Thera watched from across the street in his car. Did a U-turn, pulled up next to the screaming girl, yelled at her to get in. Drove to RCPD, where they both gave a statement.

Chill got bail, and Thera went into hiding with the girl. This isn't provided by RCPD. Thera is hiding himself and the girl, and no one can get a trace. No one's seen them. They call the police every day for thirty seconds, and that's it, the only confirmation they're alive.

Santos made two attempts on the girl and Thera while under police protection. Thera decided he'd handle his own safety better than the locals, took the girl with him. Santos wants them both dead. One, so Santos can prove he takes care of his men, two, he can show no one gets away, and three dead men tell no tales, is a powerful lesson."

I sat back and blinked. While I had no qualms

accepting bounties on evil men and women, I never brought in an innocent. Thera was innocent, and I wasn't going after him, however, I wouldn't put my neck out for Thera either.

"There's more," Kristoff said, and I looked at him, not liking Kristoff's tone. "Santos has put the word out on the street, he's got you as his personal hunter now. Word is you're after Thera, and everyone knows who the fuck you are Artemis. People know you don't stop until you get your man. Thera is running fucking scared.

Word must've got back to him. It's all over the streets that Santos has something you want, and he's brought you to heel." My mouth opened and closed. I struggled for a few moments to find the words. Now I'd put my neck out for Thera!

"Santos made a huge mistake. No one brings me to heel," I said calmly. I looked at Kristoff, who grinned like a maniac. "Pick up Thera and put him and the girl into a safe house. Guard them, Kris, with your life. I want them alive to testify."

"Court is in four weeks," Nigel broke in.

"Get them there, Kris and keep them alive. Buzz, we have any locations for Santos?" Buzz smiled with unholy glee in his eyes.

"I'll call Simone and Butch, get them to cancel their vacation. Fuck, this will be a vacation for them," Nigel hissed in laughter as he picked up the phone.

Chapter Eight.

18th December 2014

On Thursday at six o'clock in the evening three days later, a warehouse belonging to Santos Holdings blew itself sky-high. Several million dollars of expensive stock was destroyed in it.

At a quarter past six on the other side of Rapid City, an apartment block blew up from the bottom upwards. Luckily, someone had hit the fire alarm, and the apartment block was empty when it lit up the skyline. The men who rented the apartments weren't nice. It belonged to Miguel Santos.

At half-past six in Spearfish, a house that had been under investigation for drug running mysteriously blew up. No causalities were recorded. Funny enough, the authorities noted it belonged to a Miguel Santos.

By six forty, various police forces were scrambling, and communication lines, although slow, were beginning to open, and information flowed.

At a quarter to seven, several containers blew up in Deadwood and firemen and police reported they contained weapons. A kindly tip-off informed them of that fact, and they stayed well back out of range of any bullets getting hot and firing. The containers were on a piece of land registered to Santos Holdings.

At seven o'clock, a second smaller warehouse caught fire, sending around five million dollars of drugs into flames. Sturgis Police found Miguel Santos was the owner of the warehouse.

At five minutes past seven, Rapid City and local towns braced. Calls went out, ten minutes later, to a house on fire suspected of prostitution and money laundering. And three million dollars in cash burnt itself into the ground. Police didn't even bother looking for the owner. Miguel Santos owned it.

At seven twenty, everyone around Rapid City and the surrounding towns kept a watchful eye on everyone and everything around them. Therefore they didn't miss it when the offices that Santos owned in Rapid City, blew themselves sky-high in flames that could be seen for miles. The miracle was, the damage was only limited to the Santos holdings.

All attending police officers reported a burning bow and arrow set into the pavement at each of the explosions. Ramirez and his colleagues knew in

Rapid City, a message had been sent and war declared.

I picked up the phone and didn't speak as I listened to the angry breathing. It was hard to suppress a grin. Santos was freaking fuming.

"Are you fucking insane?" Santos snapped at last.

"That is a matter of public opinion. But yes, as far as you're concerned, I'm insane," I said agreeably.

"I'll fucking kill you, skin you alive and make you eat your entrails," Santos hissed.

"Ah, how melodramatic. I've been threatened by that before, a little archaic, but if it rings your bells."

"This is war!"

"Really? You declared war when you tried to get me to hunt an innocent man and hand him over. You declared war when you put it on the streets, I worked for you, and you held my leash. That's a declaration of war. This was my reply; you've no idea where I am, who I am, who I work with. You know nothing about me. However, I know a shit load about you, buddy. So back off, or I escalate," I growled.

"Your kids enjoy having a mother?" I gave him silence for a few seconds and then calmly and slowly began rattling off addresses. I started with his son, then his mother, next his two sisters, his three younger brothers and finished with Santos's aunts and uncles and nieces and nephews, his cousins. I finally ended with business legal and not so legal that we'd found so far. Silence met me.

"You will not touch my son," Santos hissed.

"You will not touch my children," I hissed back. Silence met me again.

"Between us, no innocents," Santos snarled.

"No associates either," I said, and I hung up on him as an answer. Akemi had taken the children to Rage again and returned with a message that Ace needed to speak to me. I shook my head. Akemi told me Drake had demanded to talk to me too, and I shook my head again.

This war was going to escalate and escalate quick. For now, I'd the upper hand, I'd made sure of that. Santos would hit back, Rage could be caught in the crossfire, Phoenix already had paid a high price. No more. If Santos came for me, asshole came for me, and I'd be ready.

On Christmas eve, Ace paced the inner sanctum. Tomorrow was Christmas Day, and Akemi was bringing the kids to Apache's home at two o'clock. To add to that, Artemis was letting Ace have the twins overnight for the first time. Ace was excited about that but worried about his woman.

His gaze slid to Hawthorne, who was updating

Drake on the situation that was hitting the streets. Artemis had declared war on Santos, and Ace was worried. No scratch that; Ace was fucking terrified. His and Drake's requests to see or speak to her had been denied by Akemi.

Akemi diligently brought the twins every day for a couple of hours. Still, all Ace got was a grunt when he asked about Artemis. Artemis had fired her warning shots a week ago, and Santos had fired back, but his shot missed by a mile. Artemis responded by tipping the police off on a movement, which led to the arrest of three of Santos's men and a shipment of arms. It'd be funny if it wasn't Ace's woman involved.

Santos scrambled, changing schedules and movements, and Artemis responded again by burning another whorehouse and a strip joint. Blood hadn't been spilt, but it was only a matter of time considering how hard Artemis was gunning for Santos. Artemis was a ghost, and Santos had put a seven-figure bounty on the streets for information that led to her.

A few had tried and had been intercepted by either Rage or Hawthorne's. The information they had was shit; it led nowhere. Ramirez was strangely quiet on the whole matter, and the cop was staying out of their business for now. Everyone knew eventually he'd have to get involved.

Ace figured it was one of those situations where

you were damned if you did and damned if you didn't. Artemis was taking out illegal places, illegal shipments, and drugs, and so on. No one had yet been hurt. Yet, in the eyes of the law, Artemis was committing crimes, Ace could understand why Ramirez was stalling. Artemis was single-handedly, taking out Santos's criminal empire.

Something Ace knew the police and feds had been chasing for ages. Yet this tiny slip of a woman was taking on one of the biggest and nastiest crime lords in South Dakota. And kicking his ass while doing so. Artemis had cost him millions, sheer millions and showed no sign of slowing. Which meant Santos was cornered and fighting back, which meant people could get hurt. Namely, Ace's girl.

"Artemis can't be found; she's not been seen. Santos will change tactics; blood will be split," Hawthorne said.

"Not hers," Drake mused.

"No, if he can't find Artemis, Santos will go after those he knows Artemis had contact with."

"The twins." Fear clutched at Ace's heart at the thought of the twins in danger.

"Protected, that's the word on the streets. No one touches the kids. They're safe. Artemis has something powerful on Santos that ensured the kids are safe. Can't get a bead on what Artemis has, but it's powerful."

"Sounds like our girl," Apache mused. Ace shot

Apache a sharp glare.

"Artemis is in danger again, Dad."

"I know, son, but Artemis has firepower I don't think we can match. Not even we can provide the power Artemis has at her back. Artemis is a weapon in herself," Apache replied thoughtfully.

"Could decimate this entire city. She's capable of it," Hawthorne said and pushed a file he'd been toying with at them.

"What's that?" Ace asked, stopping his pacing and looked at the file.

"Some information I think you need. What we talked about before was mild." On that note, Hawthorne stood up and left the inner sanctum. Drake pushed the file at Ace. Ace picked it up and flipped it open and began to read.

The day after Boxing Day, I looked across at Simone, who was idly cutting her nails with a sharp blade. I could have rolled my eyes at the pretentious action and sniped but held my tongue. Simone and Butch had flown in a few hours ago and were up to date. We'd a few jobs, which I'd sent Kristoff and Angel out to complete. First was a bounty we'd a lead on, and the second, a rescue.

Nigel was working the data side with them, and I was receiving hourly updates on their status. Angel had a more dangerous job with the rescue; it was a woman whose husband was a real estate mogul. Our information had led to the facts her brother was severely in debt to the darker side of Rapid City. The asshole had kidnapped his own sister for the ransom to get debtors off his back. His brother-in-law, the sister's husband, had called the Artemis line for help. Poor guy didn't have a clue who he'd really called.

Nigel was keeping in constant contact with Angel and updating me every two hours. I wasn't as worried about Kristoff bringing in a drug dealer bounty out in Ohio, but Nigel kept tabs on him.

The war escalated between Santos and me, with me firing more direct shots than Santos. I ordered my people to check in more frequently. Master Hoshi called in once a day. Akemi refused to leave the twins side, sleeping in the same room.

Buzz and Nigel didn't leave the cabins, so they were safe enough. Our security had been triply checked, and we'd get an early warning if we needed it. Multiple escape routes had been planned. If attacked, it'd be costly and bloody while we escaped free and fell back to Camp Two. Those maniacs you read about and see on TV where they rig their camp? That was Buzz; attackers would be dead before they made the second circle of defence.

Simone and Butch had finished their case, and Nigel informed them of the stunts I'd been pulling. They hustled their asses back to Rapid City to partake in the fun, as Simone put it. Simone loved chaos, Butch revelled in creating it, and they were good partners to have for this.

Butch entered the room and crossed to Simone, dragged a chair out next to her and sank into it. Butch leant towards Simone and then moved back. That was all the emotion he'd show, but he was relaxed and yet alert.

"Santos is scrabbling. The seven-figure sum on you just doubled," Butch said with a grim smile.

"Santos doesn't understand it's not just me," I said. I believed that Santos thought I worked alone.

"His info which is fed by us, makes him believe it's only you. Santos is scratching his fuckin' head tryin' to work out how you timed those bombs to go off. No timer was discovered at any site, and Santos and the police are troubled," Butch confirmed.

"Yet Santos is operating under the mistaken belief I work alone. I don't understand how on earth the asshole thinks I can be in all those places and yet operating alone?"

"Fuck knows, the man is a prick. But I don't think we should underestimate him. Santos wouldn't be where he is today if he was stupid. And he's stayed out of police hands. For years law enforcement has watched Santos, and he escapes each time," Butch said.

"There's no whisper of anyone being linked to you. Santos is literally scratching his head," Simone confirmed. I felt a bump of unease. "I think Butch is right. There is no whisper of you working with anyone, yet it's obvious you must be working with someone. Not even Akemi is mentioned in relation to you, yet Akemi is the one you've been seen with. Santos is holding his cards close to his chest, or he's clueless."

"We'll go with holding his cards close to his chest. Akemi's on guard, I got a feeling," I broke off. My trouble bump was pinging, Santos was up to something, I'd yet to discover what.

"One of those feelings?" Butch asked. Butch had learnt not to ignore my gut.

"Go back out and keep digging, see what his next move is. Santos won't back down. Santos still has Thunder, and we've a lead on that," Buzz said, rising to his feet. I gave Buzz a nod and left the room to sort through two case files that had landed on my desk.

Ace cornered Akemi as soon as Akemi dropped off the twins. The man watched Ace march towards him with purpose in his stride. Ace's face was as blank as Akemi's, but Akemi could sense the emotion raging behind the expression.

"Where's Artemis?" Ace muttered, looking over his shoulder at the twins entering the clubhouse.

"Safe," Akemi replied. He realised this man worried about his sister. Akemi knew the man was deeply in love with Artemis, and he'd never stopped loving her.

"Where?"

"I cannot tell you," Akemi said regretfully.

"Need to see her, know she's okay. Tell her, tell Artemis it's killin' me, I need to know," Ace said, allowing some of his emotion to leak. Akemi gave him a sharp nod.

"As always, I'll pass your message on." Ace gave him a chin lift and stalked back to the clubhouse, pissed off anger in every line of his body.

"Tell Artemis we have her back. We've taken several people off the streets who thought they'd information on her. They had shit," Ace growled over his shoulder.

"I will do, Tomodachi," Akemi promised.

Ace felt a small hand grasp his dick hard and then a mouth pressed against his. Barely awake, he responded to the demanding kiss, and his hands grabbed Artemis's ass. Artemis nipped his lip as Ace tried to take over the kiss and forced his arms above his head. Artemis moved before Ace was fully awake, and he found his hands tied above his head.

Ace's eyes narrowed, and Artemis dropped kisses down his throat and to his chest, and she kept working his dick. Ace was rock hard in her hand. Artemis held him in a tight grip and traced kisses back up his chest. Ace realised she was naked, and then she sank herself down onto his straining dick.

Ace pulled against the ropes tying him to the bed, but she'd tied them fast.

An hour later, I'd untied Ace and was sprawled on his chest, sweaty and tired. Ace stroked my hair with one hand, and his other held me to his chest.

"Wow," I muttered. I couldn't move; I felt boneless and relaxed and sated. Ace dropped a kiss on my head.

"Hi, baby," Ace whispered, and I began to laugh.

"Hey, Ace," I whispered back.

"How you doin'?" Ace asked. I dropped a kiss on his chest.

"Far better now."

"This shit with Santos…." I put a finger over his lips.

"No, Ace, you've no voice in what my team does. Stay out of my business," I told him. This is what I worried about, that Ace would try to control me.

"Need to know you're safe."

"Of course, I am. Santos has yet to hit me anywhere, and meanwhile, I've cost him millions. Asshole has no chance against Akemi or me."

"Or the rest of your people?" Ace asked, his tone curious and eyes searching mine. I decided to give him something.

"Or against the rest of my people," I confirmed.

Ace's body relaxed, and I hadn't realised he'd been so tense.

"At least you've someone at your back," Ace muttered. I lifted myself up onto his chest.

"Ace, I'm not alone, I've my people, and there're more I can call upon if I need to. Although Rapid City will quickly resemble a war zone if I made those calls. They ain't all stable," I stressed to him. Ace's beautiful eyes stared into mine. Worry and doubt in them.

"Know that. Hawthorne thinks he found stuff on you." I stiffened. There shouldn't be information on me for public consumption, nothing on any of us. If so, Master Hoshi had a leak.

"On me?"

"You're not named. Hawthorne looked for a pattern, and his girl found one. It's nothing conclusive, a merc team. One who does daring rescues, like the one in Belize, which took out a mercenary camp holding two young teens' hostage. A team infiltrated them and killed every single one of them, rescuing the two girls." Yeah, that had been me, Akemi, Angel, Butch and Simone.

"Really?" I asked, dissembling.

"A lone assassin who took out a high-ranking Isis general. A second lone assassin stormed a clubhouse where women and children were held hostage by a religious fanatic. Disarmed the bombs and brought down the fucker.

A team who went into Afghan after four soldiers, who were being held hostage in a camp of fifty terrorists, and killed everyone, rescuing the hostages. A second similar incident in Afghan and a third which took out a weapon depo. And a lone merc who boarded a ship being held by pirates and brought them low. Rescuing over one hundred hostages," Ace stopped speaking and looked at me.

"A woman on a rescue in Germany and was shot in her back but picked herself up and killed the shooter and then rescued a royal baby." Ace's hand slid up my back and hovered over a bullet wound between my shoulders. I looked at him. Some of those missions were mine and my teams. Some weren't, but I'd knowledge of them, I couldn't tell Ace.

"Seems a lot of rumours abounding," I whispered.

"You're better trained than a seal or marine or even delta force," Ace muttered. I gave Ace a slight nod, wanting to reassure him.

"Do what I need to, Ace. It's been over ten years. I won't stop being who I am."

"You're Kayleigh Mitchell," Ace muttered. I shook my head and got up off him. Quickly, I dragged on my clothes and looked at Ace.

"I'm Artemis, Ace. Please start getting your head around that. Kayleigh Mitchell died on the operating table and never came back. Please," I begged, sitting on the bed next to Ace and grasping his hand.

"Please understand that Kayleigh's dead; I'm what

arose from her ashes. Ace, you need to mourn Kayleigh; now the truth is out, but don't search for Kayleigh in me. Stop looking for Kayleigh in me. If you can't stop, we can't see each other. I can give you this. I enjoy this, don't want more."

"Sex?"

"Yeah, and our kids. Don't ask me for more." I stroked Ace's face, and then like the ghost I was, I left his room.

Ace lay back on his bed, confused. Artemis hadn't admitted to any of the missions, but he'd seen recognition of all of them. He'd touched the bullet wound between Artemis's shoulders. Ace guessed that Master Hoshi had found and trained her. They'd pieced together that information; Akemi played a part too. Whoever the rest of her team were, Rage was clueless.

Ace was beginning to believe that whatever this was that Master Hoshi had built far extended beyond Artemis and her team. No matter how deep they dug, they came up with little evidence. But stories abounded in Italy, France, the UK, Germany, and several other countries of teams like Artemis's.

Ace believed Master Hoshi had removed every scar possible from Artemis's body. Those left were ones she'd earned since. The wicked machete slash across her back, the scar on her stomach, Artemis kept them for a reason.

Ace suspected that whatever Master Hoshi had built, it was worldwide. Not limited to Japan and America. Rage and Hawthorne suspected Master Hoshi was behind Revenge. From Revenge, teams had formed who were behind these stories, Artemis ran the American team. The woman he loved was part of something huge, and Ace didn't understand what it was. The question now remained, could Ace live with it and take what she'd give him?

I ran across the path and burst into the office. I'd received the SOS from Buzz while on my morning run, and I'd stopped jogging and sprinted the whole way back. Buzz was looking worried.

"Who?" I asked, seeing Butch and Simone moving and Nigel with an earpiece.

"Angel, the job was a setup. Santos has him. Info coming in now," Buzz said, gathering paper together.

"How the fuck did we miss a setup?" I snarled.

"Seems the money owed to Santos was genuine, and they used it to trap you, instead, they got Angel. We've a call coming in from Santos now." Buzz threw me a phone, and I hit answer.

"Hello?" I said calmly, although sweat dripped down my back.

"Well, it seems I set a trap to catch a whale, and I caught a minnow instead," Santos gloated.

"Not sure I enjoy being called a whale but carry on," I said, keeping my voice calm. Santos grunted, and then a wheeze echoed on the line.

"Hear that? Wonder what it takes to make your man cry out?" Angel would never cry out. Never.

"My man?" I asked, aiming for confusion.

"The job was aimed at you, and lo-and-behold, this asshole walks into my trap. You've an hour to turn yourself in at my new offices, or I chop parts off your boy." Santos hung up.

"Word is out on the street. Santos has someone you work with, in his clutches," Nigel said, hanging up the phone.

"Ready to move," Butch said, snapping a knife into its holder.

"How far out is Kristoff?" I asked.

"Not in the state," Buzz confirmed.

"Akemi?"

"Here," Akemi said from behind, dressed in dark mottled clothing and armed to the teeth. Akemi's Katana was slung across his back. I began stripping out of my shorts and tee and pulling on combat gear, arming myself. I turned to Buzz.

"Tracker?"

"It's active. Angel is here." Buzz pointed at a map on his computer screen, and I saw the tiny red dot remaining static. Not Santos's new offices, but somewhere remote near the edge of Rapid City.

"Give me directions on the way. Buzz guard the twins," I ordered and left the cabin ahead of everyone else.

"Santos has one of the Artemis people," Hawthorne said urgently as he strode into the clubhouse. Apache looked up and nodded his head.

"Do we know who?" Apache asked, walking into the inner sanctum. Hawthorne close on his heels.

"No. Only info is it's not her or Akemi; word has reached RCPD, they're organising. This is gonna get messy. The woman will create rivers of blood."

"Any leads on where?" Drake asked, catching the end of the conversation.

"Fuckin' none. Santos is promising a video of him taking Artemis out," Hawthorne cursed. "Usual places are empty. Santos has taken this guy off the grid, and we can't get a track on where."

"It'll be heavily defended. Got a lock on Santos's people?" Apache asked, his brow furrowing.

"I've every ear to the ground I can get. Get your brothers out there," Hawthorne said, and Drake nodded as he replied.

"Mine are mobilised. Why you think no one's here? Got word half an hour ago."

"Artemis is gonna go after him," Hawthorne said.

Drake nodded in agreement. "It'll be a trap," he stated the obvious.

"Oh, Artemis will trigger it; she'll walk right in and go in firing," Drake mused. Drake's phone rang, and he picked it up.

"Brother, got word of a large gathering in an abandoned warehouse on Mount Rushmore Rd, near Carton Blvd. An informant has seen groups of armed people entering," Texas said. "We're heading there." Drake rose to his feet.

"You hear that?" Drake asked Apache and Hawthorne. They nodded and followed Drake out.

I looked at the abandoned warehouse and saw movement on the roof. Counted three people, and I spied a fourth hiding. Akemi was drifting through the surrounding trees, looking for ground guards. Akemi signalled six. I listened to him mutter directions to Simone and then silence. Minutes later, Akemi whispered he'd taken care of four of them.

Simone, a minute after Akemi, whispered she had taken care of hers. The fact there was no noise meant they'd had slit their throats. Easy enough to keep quiet. I signalled Butch, who was waiting for me, and Butch took aim and fired the first two shots; Akemi fired the next two.

The shots were silenced so no one would be alerted

inside. Four targets went down. We split up and headed in the directions we'd chosen; I planned to go in the front but not directly.

Silently, creeping up towards the front door, a shadow outside the poorly lit open door in front of me moved. I took aim and shot through the broken window, and the body fell. Silencers on our weapons meant the only sound was a soft whuff as I fired, and then the body hit the floor. I peeked around the open door and drew my head back just as quick.

I glanced towards the trees surrounding us, and Akemi signed that there was three waiting for me. Going in low and firing, I hit two before I'd finished entering. I dropped into a roll and aimed at the third who was firing.

A sharp sting in my arm, and Akemi dropped the fucker with a headshot. I clicked twice on the microphone that was collared to my throat, signalling I was clear. A shadow entered behind me, and Simone had joined the fight and headed left. I waited, and Akemi appeared from the shadows giving me the all-clear. Butch followed Simone.

Akemi and I moved right, finding two more guards. I took the first from behind. My hand slammed across his mouth before he could call out. My knife slit his throat as his hands moved to pull mine away. He sagged against my body, forcing me a step backwards, and I allowed his body to drop. Amateur move trying to remove my hands, duh.

I sank back into the shadows and heard a slight scuffle, and then Akemi was behind me. Akemi, having taken care of the second guard as I knew he would. Remaining hidden, we watched two more of Santos's soldiers walk past and taking aim, I threw a knife in the back of one's neck. Perfect throw.

He staggered, and his companion turned and took my second knife in his throat. They both made gurgling noises and hit the ground. Akemi rolled his eyes at me, and I grinned. Two clicks on the radio, and Butch's voice came low into my earpiece.

"Ground floor and perimeter clear on the South and West sides. Holding position." I gave a click back as an acknowledgement and kept heading inwards. Once we had secured the North and east side of the bottom floor of the warehouse, I headed upstairs. Akemi on my heels. I signalled Akemi to go left again, and we made our rounds. I encountered five more of Santos's men, and five more fell.

"First floor clear, minimal resistance. Heading up to the second floor," I whispered into the mic. Three sets of a single click returned. Akemi passed me by, his Katana held in position and dripping with blood. Akemi slammed a hand up and pointed at the floor, and we saw a tripwire.

Santos had set either traps or alarm's up. I followed the wire and saw it tied to a sawn-off shotgun, traps then. Akemi whispered into his mic, warning Simone and Butch, and we carried on. Together we dodged several more tripwires and took out three more men. It astounded me that Santos would throw away lives so easily.

Shots were fired and then silence. A man's groan echoed through the warehouse, and I clicked once and received the okay back. It wasn't Butch groaning.

"Artemis come out," Santos shouted. I motioned to Akemi to go right, and I made my way left, keeping to the shadows.

Sounds of a scuffle reached my ears, and then a second man groaned and then a high-pitched yelp. Akemi clicked, and I relaxed. I crept forward, and, hiding behind a half-demolished wall, I saw Angel hanging from chains in the ceiling. Angel's arms were tied taut above his head and his feet weren't touching the ground.

I took stock, Angel's face was bruised, and blood dripped from his cheek. His shirt had been ripped open, and I could see bruising to his torso. Angel's head hung limply, but I saw a finger tap a sequence, and I knew Angel was awake and alert. Angel's legs hung loosely, not tied. Shit, Santos was a thick prick.

To either side of him stood two men, both armed with shotguns aimed at Angel. A man stood behind Angel with a third shotgun aimed at him. Santos sat dressed impeccably on a chair in front of him.

"Status," I whispered into the mic.

"In position back," Simone whispered back.

"Position left," Butch replied.

"In position right," Akemi whispered.

"Affirmative," I confirmed and then strode forward into the bright light that lit the centre of the warehouse. Angel twitched his fingers three times, and I waited as three more men came out of the shadows.

"Six men? I'm insulted," I told Santos, my guns and knives holstered. My arms hung by my sides. A guy held a camera and began filming.

"There's more bitch," Santos sneered.

"Not anymore." I grinned back. Santos frowned and then nodded to one of his guys, who lifted a radio to his mouth and spoke into it. Silence met him; he demanded an answer and again received none. He radioed a second man, no response, and I grinned.

"They're dead," I informed Santos. Santos lifted his gaze to me, and I saw doubt cross his face.

"There are thirty-three men out there," the guy with the radio muttered, paling. He lifted a gun in my direction.

"Was. Now there are thirty-three corpses." I looked over as Santos began to clap. The sound echoed through the vastness of the warehouse.

"We could have been a force together," Santos said, secure that he was safe.

"Never. I'd never work with scum like you," I said. Santos's eyes narrowed.

"Not now, certainly. You attempted to make a fool of me, and you cost me a lot of money. It is a shame it came to this," Santos said, looking over his shoulder, and I stared at the man filming us. I sent him a terrifying grin, and the man blanched.

"Your mistake was attempting to send me after an innocent man. When have I brought in an innocent? You've paid with money, goods, your reputation and now the lives of your men." I turned my gaze to those watching. "Give you one chance, leave now or die. It matters little either way to me," I said with a chill in my voice.

"You're outgunned. Remove your balaclava Artemis, as I wish to see the face of the woman I'm about to kill," Santos sneered, and I sighed and then looked at the asshole.

"Was outgunned by thirty-three assholes, and yet here I stand. Let my man leave; it's your last chance. You can see my face when I'm dead. Of course, you'll be dead before me." Santos threw his head back and laughed, and as Santos did, I sliced at my throat and moved.

Knives flew out of the darkness, and three men fell. The fourth stumbled back towards Angel, who lifted his legs and snapped them around the man's throat. The man gasped and clutched at Angel's legs, but to no avail, Angel had a lock on him. He choked the man out and let him drop to the ground. The cameraman dropped the camera and fled.

I dived at Santos and knocked him out of the chair, trusting the others to watch my back. The asshole got a punch off at my face, and it connected. My head snapped back, and I sprang and head-butted him, Santos howled, and one hand flew towards his face. His second hand shoved at my ribs, and I felt a slice down them. Santos had a knife jammed in and was pulling it downwards.

I leant forward, dislodging the knife and kneed him in the balls at the same time. I put my elbow up as his hand with the knife flew towards my face, despite him screaming in pain. With a twist, I blocked his arm and jabbed Santos in the throat. Santos began choking, fight over. I rolled off him and leapt to my feet and kicked Santos in the head as Angel heaved himself up the chains and unhooked himself.

"Took your time," Angel muttered, bent over. Angel straightened painfully and walked over to Santos. He unleashed a mighty kick which lifted the man off the floor and made him roll. Pissed as hell, Angel stamped on Santos's knee, causing the man to scream and choke again.

"Got here as soon as I could," I said, putting my hand on his shoulder and making Angel stop. I ran my hands over his body, searching for any life-threatening wounds. Angel stood still and let me complete my check. I patted his cheek, and he gave me a wink.

Santos and one of his men were crawling away, Santos still choking. The guy turned, and I spied a machine gun and dived out of the way as the gun opened fire. My intention was to draw the fire away from Angel who couldn't move as fast. Out of the corner of my eye, Akemi took Angel down and covered his body. I rolled and kept rolling as bullets hit the gravel near me, and I pulled my weapon.

The gun stopped firing, and I looked up and saw Santos and his one remaining soldier had fled. I wavered for a minute whether to give chase but tossed the idea away. We'd discovered several traps. Who was to say there wasn't more? They'd move quicker than me knowing where traps were, and Angel was my priority now.

Butch had hold of Angel, Angel's arm slung around his neck, Angel was suffering. My check had found broken ribs for a start, not life-threatening but painful for him. Yeah, my man was a priority. Santos would pay in blood after tonight.

"Get Angel out of here," I said. Simone led the way, and Butch followed.

"You're hit," Akemi said. I breathed through the pain in my ribs caused by the knife and needed to check the wound.

"Not bleeding out yet, let's move, as I don't want my blood on the floor."

"Knife?" Akemi said, striding over and shoving a pressure bandage over the wound. He looked for a blood trail and found it. Akemi pulled bleach and began destroying it.

"And a bullet graze."

"Lucky shot," Akemi said with a small smile. Akemi deftly slapped a second pressure bandage on my arm.

"Fuckin' was," I agreed as Akemi finished destroying mine and Angel's blood trails.

"Hmm. Let's get you and Angel home." As we approached the exit, sirens screeched into the yard of the warehouse. We sank back into the shadows as police exited vehicles and approached the building, weapons drawn. Akemi and I faded backwards, looking for another exit.

We heard pipe bikes, and I looked up as I saw Rage pull into the yard. Drake got off his bike, and I saw four of the MC behind him.

"Head for the trees," I said to Akemi, pointing at a broken window on the far side of the warehouse. The police entered the front, so the back was uncovered. We headed there at speed.

We clambered out, being careful not to cut ourselves on glass shards. The police come into the warehouse as we slipped into the tree line. The SUV hadn't been in the yard. Butch and Simone had got Angel away from the police cleanly.

A figure stepped out in front of us, and Akemi raised his gun. With a groan, I pulled the balaclava from my head. Lowrider regarded us, lowered his weapon, and then cocked his head in the direction of the tree's indicating for us to follow. We ran through the trees and hit a clearing, and found Jett waiting beside two bikes.

"Get on," Lowrider told Akemi, and Akemi swung up behind Jett. Lowrider threw a leg over his own bike, and I climbed up behind him. I wrapped my arms around him as he kicked the bike stand and roared away. I clung to his back as he weaved through the back roads and straight to Rage. There was our SUV, Butch standing beside it in the darkness.

"Go," Lowrider said to Akemi, "Artemis stays."

"Not happening," Akemi replied. Lowrider and Jett squared up to him.

"Artemis is staying. My brother will want to see her."

"Artemis is injured and needs medical care. We're taking her with us," Butch said, and his loose body went tense. His gun was in his hand, and a quick glance showed Lowrider was similarly armed. Jett watched him with careful eyes, his body also tense.

"I'm going with them. We've medical training," I told Lowrider. Lowrider prepared to argue, and then bikes roared into the forecourt, and the argument became moot. Butch and Simone disappeared into the darkness of the SUV, and Akemi materialised at my side.

"What the fuck were you thinkin'?" Ace roared, swinging his leg over his bike and stalking towards me.

"It's got shit to do with you," I snarled back. Blood

loss was making me dizzy and tetchy.

"You took on Santos without backup," I made a pfftting noise.

"Had back up, now move. Need to get stitches." Ace drew back, looking at me and then saw the cut shirt and the bloody arm.

"You're hurt? You got shot?" Ace asked and then grabbed me by the other arm. Akemi plastered himself to my back, fire in his eyes.

"Take your hands off my sister," Akemi growled, a threat in his voice. Ace ignored him.

"Yeah, took a bullet. Gotta stitch it up, let me go to get this shit fixed up," I told Ace, not liking the worry I saw in his eyes.

"This stops. We got kids; you stop this shit now. No more," Ace demanded, and I allowed sadness to cross my face.

"This is what I do Ace, something you just don't understand, this is me. This is why we won't work," I told Ace. I pushed past him as Butch gunned the engine, and Akemi and I were in the SUV before Rage could react. Ace's burning gaze followed me, and I allowed one tear to fall before leaving the man I loved behind.

Chapter Nine.

Drake sat with his arms around his pregnant wife and resting his chin on Phoe's shoulder. Phoe stood between his legs and was watching Ace. Hell, Drake was watching his brother too. Ace had returned to the sullen man he'd been before this shit with Artemis had started.

They'd tried to find Artemis, but as usual, she was a ghost. No one had seen hide or hair of Artemis since that night. The police had found numerous bodies scattered at the warehouse but no perpetrator. RCPD had no direct leads leading them to Artemis and had no grounds for a warrant. Somehow, Drake believed, Ramirez had taken his back or Artemis's back. Drake would never, ever ask Ramirez to compromise his principles, and Drake swore he'd never ask Ramirez if he had. But there was that niggling feeling; Ramirez may have compromised himself.

Drake knew of the events that had happened on his forecourt and knew Ace had fucked up. The problem was Ace couldn't tell Artemis he'd fucked up, that he'd lost his mind, worrying that night. Akemi brought the twins but refused to be engaged in conversation unless it concerned Falcon and Nova. Akemi remained respectful, as was his way, but the guy wouldn't get involved.

The twins said nothing, although they'd been asked. Nova, being Nova, asked if they were being forced to take sides. At the denials Nova received, she replied that her loyalties were with her mother. No one should put her and Falcon in the middle. After that, they left the kids alone.

It was quiet on the streets, but not for Santos. Police began receiving tip-offs and evidence, and they'd started dismantling Santos's empire. Rage, Hawthorne's and RCPD knew the information came from Artemis, but it was solid and allowed the police to move fast when they needed to.

Instead of blowing shit up, Artemis was now playing informant and hacker. Drake shook his head. Artemis was undoubtedly in a league of her own. Wearily, Drake compared her to the girl she'd been and found very few similarities. Kayleigh had winced at the sight of blood, and puke made her heave too.

Kayleigh would never have told Ace to go fuck himself. Nor would Kayleigh have gone against Ace if it was something Ace was passionate about.

Kayleigh didn't have the stamina or physical fitness she had now. She'd been more prone to laughter and happiness back then.

Yeah, Drake had a hard time reconciling the girl she'd been to who Artemis was now. Out of Rage, Drake understood what Artemis meant when she said Kayleigh was dead. Kayleigh was gone, buried, murdered, and Artemis was an entirely different personality from Kayleigh. It was just damn confusing. Drake looked up from his contemplations as the door opened, and Slate stuck his head in.

"Drake, someone here to see you. Say's it's important?" Drake frowned. He'd shut the clubhouse tonight because Drake wanted time with his brothers and old ladies. No skanks, no biker bunnies, no hangers-on. Just family.

"Tell them to come back," Drake snapped at the prospect, pissed that his family time was being interrupted.

"Think you'll want to see him," Slate said firmly. Drake liked the prospect, saw good things in Slate's future but the prospect needed to follow orders.

"Tell him to come back," Drake snarled this time, and Slate turned on his heel. Drake watched as seconds later, the door opened, and a small Japanese man entered.

"How rude when I came this distance to speak with you." Master Hoshi said calmly. He flicked an imaginary piece off fluff of his suit sleeve. Drake frowned.

"What are you doin' here?" Drake asked, "where's my prospect?"

"The charming young man is taking a short nap; I wish to speak with you and Ace."

"Can't see much to discuss, especially if you've hurt my prospect." Drake tilted his head to Lex, who left the clubhouse.

"The prospect merely sleeps. I wished no harm." Master Hoshi's tone left no doubt he could have caused harm if he so wished.

"Yet you put Slate to sleep," Phoenix spoke up. Master Hoshi turned and studied her, and Drake stepped between them.

"Yes, my dear child, I put the prospect to sleep, a simple nerve pinch. Slate, was it? Will awake furious at being forced to sleep by a far older and smaller man than himself. Slate's pride will be damaged, no doubt. Yes, yes, I see why my daughter went to war for Phoenix. Your wife is beautiful," Master Hoshi said, looking Drake in his eyes, "inside and out." Drake nodded curtly.

"What do you want?" Drake asked as Master Hoshi let the silence fall as he looked around. Master Hoshi dragged his eyes back to the irate man.

"World peace, harmony for all living things, innocents to never experience the dark side of life, but that's unlikely," the old man said. "I wish to talk to you and the man who aims to be my son." Master

Hoshi spun on his heel and regarded Ace, who'd moved silently up behind him. Ace stopped moving and folded his arms across his chest.

"Why?" Ace asked.

"My daughter suffers pain again. Is it not the duty of a father to stop a child's pain? Come, come," Master Hoshi said, clapping his hands and moving swiftly towards the inner sanctum. "Just you two if you please," Master Hoshi flung over his shoulder. Drake met Ace's eyes, and Ace shrugged. What the fuck? They followed the quirky man into the inner sanctum and found Master Hoshi had settled himself into Fish's chair at Drakes left-hand side.

Drake and Ace settled in their chairs and turned their attention towards the wiry man. Master Hoshi fussed at his suit pants, took out a small box, hit a button, and then looked at them.

"This will short out any electrical listening devices and block recordings. Only you may hear this. If someone else hears or is told, I shall take care of the problem," Master Hoshi warned in a soft voice.

"Stop the spy shit and get on with it," Ace said, unimpressed.

"If Artemis spoke of whence she came, Artemis faces death. Akemi or I would have to deliver it due to her position in our ranks. I may speak; I make the rules and may break them. I choose to do so now to help my daughter.

It began many years ago when I was visiting an

old friend in the hospital when a young girl was brought in as I left. It was intriguing because she'd two babes with her, both of whom were rushed into the theatre before I understood what was happening. The extent of Artemis's injuries meant I knew a grave and serious injustice had been committed, and so I remained.

Artemis had been viciously assaulted. No woman should ever suffer such horror. She flatlined several times while I waited, and survival appeared hopeless. The doctors thought to give up, but I'd power and used it to keep doctors working on Artemis and the children. They survived, and I became a regular visitor.

With my money and power, I ensured Artemis and the two babes received the best medical care there was out there. Artemis was put back together like Frankenstein with one difference. I can wipe the scars on her flesh away with a good plastic surgeon, but I can't wipe away the scars on her psyche.

I covered every base. We recorded Kayleigh as dead, another Jane Doe. No name was given, and records wiped from existence. The babes I registered as dead and paid or cajoled those in the know to stay silent. The fact they have done so is because they fear death. I brought in my medical people to treat Artemis and her babes.

Akemi and I took the hate and the violence choking Artemis and honed it. I informed her it was possible to get justice and live. Artemis grasped the offer with two hands, and I trained her for two-and-a-half years. She became a weapon forged in hate and revenge. She trained twelve, sixteen hours a day with little time off except time allowed to bond with the children. Artemis drove her own training with a dedication that even Akemi didn't show.

Many years ago, I found myself in a similar position, a victim of betrayal and lust. My father taught me the old ways. I took my revenge against those who had betrayed me, and then I encountered a man a while later. Hurt and betrayed, same as I was, I trained him, and he took his revenge. So my idea grew, why should evil escape punishment for their crime? It often leaves their victims in the dirt, but not those I found. They got their justice or revenge," Master Hoshi paused and looked at Ace.

"I find myself thirsty. Perhaps a cold drink will help? Rarely do I talk so much about such things anymore," Master Hoshi asked politely. Ace left and returned with a bottle of water.

"Didn't think you'd want a beer or cola," Ace said, giving it to Master Hoshi.

"I drink beer," Master Hoshi said, opening his bottle and drinking.

"Make a note," Drake said wryly.

"Over many years, the people I collected got their justice and then needed direction. I offered them guidance, same as I gave Artemis advice. My daughter, though, was different. Artemis saw revenge as her and the twins surviving. She didn't want blood at first. Artemis and my son became close and together began raising my grandchildren.

Artemis is special. Incredibly unique, and so is my son. Everything Artemis felt for you she honed and used on missions. Yes, your information is half right. She did many missions, men died, she has countless deaths on her soul and is covered head to toe in blood.

The girl brutalised so terribly is dead, and a hunter arose from Kayleigh Mitchell's ashes. Artemis is stunning, is she not? For years Artemis did what she wanted, ran her own team. There are others, as you surmised. Artemis is strong, so strong that I send her the ones who'd had revenge and yet can't be risked to live in the world. She takes them and utilises them.

When I pass from this world, Akemi and Artemis will run the organisation. They know the future and embrace it. Akemi and Artemis will continue to aid victims. They will continue to seek those downtrodden, used and broken and remake them into something beautiful and strong, the same as I did with them.

Yet my daughter, with her hate and disgust, never once came here for actual revenge. Artemis stayed away until Rage MC called her. Artemis didn't want to return here, she wanted the past to remain dead, but she had to face this. This was her last test, the last obstacle, and I fear I forced an agreement on this.

What we thought was, was not. Artemis got beaten and brutalised again, although this time it was mentally and emotionally. Artemis decided actual revenge was needed. Her soul cried for blood and sought it out. Until we found out the truth amongst the deceptions. Artemis should have broken again then, shattered in the fire of real betrayal and hurt, but she did not. She moved to make peace.

Artemis is a difficult woman. One cannot merely control her; she needs aim and motivation. I am skilled at aiming Artemis where she needs to be. Artemis will not leave this life because she cannot leave this life. There's something none of you realised." Master Hoshi broke off to take a drink.

"What did we miss?" Ace asked, leaning forward.

"Artemis has a monster. Every negative emotion Artemis suffered created a monster, although she appears to have it under control. However, I look, and I see the beast; it rages, the terrified child I first met has gone, consumed by the monster. I did not create that monster; Artemis did, but I helped guide the beast into a position Artemis can control.

If left unchecked, Artemis is capable of raining blood and chaos where she walks. The missions let her monster out and feed it until it is glutted. The beast knows what it is to be alone, violated, scared, left for dead, and her monster will not let that happen again. Artemis would kill without reason or rhythm until she is put down. What Artemis does now allows her to control her monster."

"Monsters can be gentle and find love," Ace said, leaning forward.

"Indeed, even a monster can find and fall in love. A beast by one perception is an angel by another's. A child rescued perceives an angel come to save her, a hero who walked through fire to protect them from nightmares. The perpetrator creating the hell sees a real-life monster coming for him. Artemis is both.

Understand, killing does not faze my daughter. The killing will never disturb my daughter. Artemis will not shy from it, nor will she ever hesitate. Artemis will not take an innocent's life. That is the control we have taught her. But she can give those who are guilty, a bloody and horrible death and feed the greedy monster. Artemis excels at justice and being a nightmare to those who are guilty.

Your friend Hawthorne did not lie when he informed you she would take this clubhouse and everyone in it before you even knew Artemis was coming. You'd awaken to feel the whisper of her knife as it slit your throat, and she'd watch as you bled to death.

I gave Artemis two-and-a-half years of training. For the next nine years, she sought her own further training. Artemis continued training with Akemi and myself as well. I do not think you understand the weapon Artemis is. A navy seal is a child compared to her, a marine is nothing, a ranger irrelevant, there's no comparison for what Artemis and my organisation are."

"You're Revenge, the organisation, there's only been one mention of." Master Hoshi nodded at Drake.

"You killed anyone who mentioned it," Ace said.

"I killed those who sought to betray. There is a difference. Which is why my daughter cannot speak of these things."

"Why now?" Drake asked, sitting back.

"Artemis will walk into a terrorist base alone and take out the fifty members before she stops. Even if her target is secure, Artemis will remain and kill those who are still alive. Why? Because she can, because Artemis needs to and wants to. Do you understand what I am telling you?

She loves you, she doesn't recognise it, but she does. Or perhaps, being as perverse as she is, maybe Artemis knows she is in love with you. And chooses not to feed that love. That is unhealthy. Artemis feeds the monster, and Artemis needs to feed love too. By telling Artemis she can't be who she is, it means you feed the beast. Instead of accepting Artemis for the wonderful woman she is, you tried to change her.

Her monster revelled in that, gave it something to fight, to rage against. It began smothering the feelings Artemis had for Ace. It burns bright now and needs to smother love, so Artemis indulges."

"What do you mean?" Ace asked, confused.

"My grandchildren have a father now. If Artemis dies, they remain having a parent. That is, if Akemi doesn't take Falcon and Nova. This means that one of the things that kept the monster in control is gone. Falcon and Nova have a parent if Artemis dies. This, in the past, stopped Artemis from taking stupid risks, from burning the entire village.

Now you have challenged the monster by telling Artemis she cannot be who she is. This means it's tearing her apart; you've hurt Artemis by not seeing what and who she is. You have told Artemis, the man she loves, she is not good enough for you, that she is expendable."

"What of your own part in this? You created that monster. You helped hone it," Ace shot back, annoyed at the accusation.

"I did not create the monster, those that tortured, abused and violated Artemis created that monster. I taught her to hone and control it. Artemis could have become an embittered, hateful psychopath if not for my training, and I have seen it happen. Artemis would've possibly sunk into the dark, with no light in her life. Falcon and Nova, taught hate and without question, the amazing children they are, destroyed," Master Hoshi denied.

"You trained Artemis," Ace insisted.

"Yes, I did, and I trained Artemis to survive. Taught her to ensure Artemis never became as helpless as she did that horrible day. I ensured Artemis would survive anything; I gave her monster a focus, real bad guys she chased after. That kept the monster sated, and Artemis did not look to feed it elsewhere. By challenging Artemis, the monster rages out of control. I see Artemis losing her grip with each day that passes.

You have a choice, Ace. You can continue to deny who Artemis is, and you can continue to look for the girl you loved and who is dead. If you choose that, leave Artemis alone. Do not keep sending messages through Akemi. Let Artemis go because Kayleigh Mitchell died on that road, died in the operating theatre. Kayleigh is dead, mourn lost love but let Artemis go and revel in the joy of your children.

Your second choice is harder and much more difficult. Accept Artemis for who she is now. Love Artemis, if possible for you to do so, I find Artemis easy to love. Maybe you will find the same. If you can love her, love Artemis for what and who she is, do not tell her to stop being herself. You support and celebrate the life she has with you.

I cannot tell you more about her missions. Artemis can tell you of her missions as an Artemis operative. But Artemis cannot speak of Revenge or Revenge missions. Artemis utters one word, she signs her death warrant, which will pain me greatly. I cannot make an exception for my daughter and not anyone else. I hope I am clear. There will be aspects of Artemis's life she cannot and will not discuss with you." Master Hoshi rose to his feet.

"Seen Kayleigh inside Artemis, just little bits," Ace mumbled.

"See parts of Akemi in you, does not make you Akemi," Master Hoshi said, watching Ace.

"That's true," Ace mused.

"Make a choice and stick to it Ace, let Artemis go or hold her tight. Although at the moment, Artemis is ornery as Santos escaped. While she is single-mindedly dismantling the Santos operation, Artemis and the monster are occupied. Artemis still seeks Thunder, and the man Jacked, who I understand escaped. Artemis will find her final vengeance. The question is, will you be at Artemis's side? The man who beat his old president and sliced the patch off his bare skin and then put a bullet in his head.

Oh yes, Ace, I watched you and this MC for many years, ensuring no threat came near my child. I know your secrets as you now know a few of mine. An exchange of information is always acceptable, is it not? By the way, this device has killed any bugs Artemis or myself may have placed." Master Hoshi gave Ace a shit-eating grin and then left the inner sanctum. Ace watched as Master Hoshi bowed over Phoe's hand and then left as quietly as he came. Slate's eyes burned into Master Hoshi as he watched him leave.

"This is Artemis," I said into my phone. The number wasn't familiar, and I'd a suspicion it was Santos. For the last two weeks, I'd taken apart the criminal enterprise, and Santos was hurting.

"This is Romeo Santos," a rich voice said down the phone. I sat up and dragged my covers up with me.

"What do you want?" I asked.

"I want to sue for a parley, a meeting between just you and myself. Miguel, well, father overstepped, and I wish to make amends. I have three gifts for you if we can call a ceasefire. If you wish to send one of your operatives to an address that I'll text you, you'll receive one of those gifts," Romeo crooned down the phone. I wrinkled my nose.

"A gift?"

"Yes, an immediate one. The other two you'll receive if you'll agree to a ceasefire until we can arrange a meeting. Father no longer is running things."

"That doesn't mean shit to me."

"It will when we meet up Artemis, give you my word." I paused for a few seconds and then agreed to meet if I liked the first gift. Romeo said goodbye and cut our connection. Seconds later, an address hit my inbox and rising from the bed, I dressed and crept from my room. Akemi waited outside, and I cocked an eyebrow, and Akemi gave a small smile.

"Heard your phone. Buzz and Angel are home, let's

go," Akemi said in a low voice. He looked at my raised eyebrows. "What, you think I will let you walk into a potential situation without backup?" Akemi asked as his long legs began to stride away. I'd have kicked his ass for that, but instead, I meandered after him.

Akemi drove to an abandoned house, not one of Santos's, from what we could determine. Quietly moving, we both entered, searching for any traps. On discovering none, we made our way through, searching for this mysterious gift. Akemi halted abruptly in front of me, gazing in a bedroom and then stepped to one side.

"Well," I exclaimed with a bitter laugh, "didn't expect that." Akemi pulled a phone out and dialled Drake. He answered sleepily on the third ring.

"Drake, sending you an address. There's something here that belongs to you," Akemi told Drake the address and disconnected. Forty minutes later, bike pipes roared, and then a few minutes later, Drake walked towards me with Fish and Ace. Ace's eyes flew straight to me and checked me from head to toe before Ace smiled, seeing I was okay.

Ace confused me a little, but I turned away and gave Drake and Fish a nod before pointing into the shadows of the room.

"Jacked," Drake growled.

"Jacked's yours. I want Thunder and Santos, but Jacked's yours," I told Drake, whose eyes glistened with anger and spite.

"Fuck yeah, Jacked's ours," Drake agreed. In the shadows, Jacked's eyes widened and then Jacked began shaking his head. Jacked began screeching against the gag in his mouth.

"Make it hurt, make it painful and make Jacked bleed. Like I did," I told Drake and then turned on my heel. Ace's hand snaked out and grabbed my arm, and I tensed.

"Need to talk, Master Hoshi paid a visit," Ace blurted as I started to pull away. I stopped, and my own eyes widened this time. Master Hoshi can only have gone to see Ace for one reason.

"Master Hoshi did?" I asked, looking over my shoulder at Akemi, who watched me expressionlessly. Akemi knew, I realised and glared. So, Akemi and Master Hoshi were colluding behind my back. I wasn't happy. Akemi saw my expression, and his implacable face grinned, and then Akemi walked away. Aware I resembled an angry puppy, I followed him.

"I'll call," I tossed at Ace.

"Do not start," Akemi sniped as I got into the SUV, still glaring.

"You and Master Hoshi are interfering," I snapped at Akemi. Anger was building slowly.

"Yes," Akemi said. My mouth dropped open in surprise as Akemi admitted it.

"You're going to admit it?"

"Of course. I'm not hiding it; neither is Father." Akemi spun a left, and I slid across my seat a little. I pushed my way back into the middle.

"You've no right. Either of you," I snarled.

"We've every right, you're family, and you love Ace." I opened my mouth to snap out an instant denial and then shut it. Akemi was correct on a couple of things, though admitting he was right stuck in my throat.

We were family; we'd made that family eleven years ago. Maybe an odd family, but family didn't mean blood, not to me. It meant people who I let into my life and trusted and loved them. Thunder and Misty had taught me a hard lesson in love.

Master Hoshi and Akemi had taught me a gentler one. They'd burrowed their way into my heart without warning, and I loved them as a brother and father. The twins were their family as they were Uncle and Grandfather. The twin's family had grown tenfold, but I knew that Akemi and Master Hoshi would always hold their special place.

As much as Akemi galled me, he was right as well. I loved Ace. I think deep under the hate and bitterness I always had. It was a bitter pill to swallow, and I'd tried to destroy that love with hate, and yet I think I'd buried it instead. I'd honoured Ace's heritage with the naming of Nova and Falcon.

The twins understood a hell of a lot about their ancestors and where they'd come from. Ace's side held a richness of legend and history. My side held nothing apart from being trailer trash, so I'd encouraged studies in their heritage. So in being brutally honest, I hadn't wiped Ace from my life as I'd hoped.

"You had no right to interfere," I muttered mulishly. Akemi gave a short laugh and concentrated on getting us home.

"Where you off to, brother?" Drake asked as Ace walked towards his bike.

"Meetin' Artemis. At the bar."

"Got hope?"

"Got somethin', dunno what yet. She's meetin' me, that counts for something," Ace drawled his eyes on his bike. He glanced up towards the wall, and his gaze narrowed on two figures.

"Ace?" Drake asked.

"They're back, brother," Ace tilted his head towards the figures who stood in the shadows. One a boy of approximately sixteen and one in his younger teens.

"Keep seein' them, fifth time they have been around lookin' this month," Drake agreed.

"We got names?" Ace asked as he studied the kids.

"Yeah, not happy with who they belong to."

"Hit me," Ace wondered if he should approach the boys.

"Rio Valden's kids," Drake said and Ace raised his eyebrows at the name.

"Valden, Spearfish's best tattoo artist Valden? Egotistical asshole Valden?" Ace asked.

"Yeah. I'll see what they want. You get going, Ace," Drake said, watching the boys watching him.

"Can stay."

"Get gone. I'll deal with them." Drake shoved Ace towards his bike, and with one last look over at the boys, Ace climbed on his bike and rode out. Drake cocked his finger at the kids and then pointed at his feet. The two boys discussed something furiously, and then the taller one approached.

"What you need, boys?" Drake asked.

"Wanna join. Prospect."

"Name?"

"Jonas, my brother is Zac," Drake studied the boy.

"How old are you, lad?" Jonas straightened his shoulders.

"Eighteen." Drake let out a laugh, then he gave the boy a stern glare.

"Want to be Rage? The first rule is don't fuckin' lie to a brother or your Prez. Wanna try that one again." Jonas dropped his gaze and toed the forecourt.

"Fifteen, sixteen in seven months." Drake's lips pursed. He sensed the kids were in trouble.

"Rage don't take no prospect under the age of eighteen, boy. Need help with somethin'?" Jonas's shoulders snapped back. Fuck, this kid had pride.

"Can take care of Zac and me." Before Drake could ask or move, Jonas ran back to his brother, tugged him behind him, and they disappeared into the shadows. Drake cursed out loud. He'd been too slow to catch the kid, and his gut told him the kids were in danger. Drake pulled his phone and dialled Chance. Hellfire was based in Spearfish. Why the kids applied to Rage and not Hellfire, Drake didn't know, but he'd get his cousin to keep an eye on them. He'd heard enough shit about Rio Valden.

"So," I said, staring across the table at Ace.

"So?" Ace replied, I'd called him as I promised, and we'd arranged to meet at the bar. The bar was busy, and the noise level hid our conversation from curious ears. I looked in Drake, Fish, and Lowrider's direction. Lowrider grinned and tossed back a drink.

"What do you want, Ace?"

"You. Everything," Ace said shortly, making me choke on the sip of water I'd just taken. Well, Ace wasn't beating around the bush.

"Well, according to you, I have to stop what I'm doing. Won't do that, I won't be micromanaged, nor will I quit something I enjoy doing."

"Was wrong." Damn that man, I thought as I choked a second time. Ace admitted he was wrong? That was new! Ace never admitted he was wrong in the past.

"You were wrong?" I said, wiping tears from my eyes.

"Yes. Master Hoshi told me part of your history and told me part of the background you can't speak of. Got a better understanding, and a better understanding, of what I desire, that's you. Not a lost love." Ace stretched his arms above his head, making his biceps tighten, and my eyes went to them of their own accord. Ace gave me a smug grin. Two can play that game, I leant forward, and my boobs pushed together and Ace's eyes dropped.

"We have sex between us, Ace."

"Oh yeah, babe, we've sex all right. I was wrong in so many instances when this started; I wanted revenge for Kayleigh. It blinded me, then I found out Kayleigh didn't die, that she lived in you."

"I'm not fucking Kayleigh."

"Let me finish," Ace snapped back, and I nodded. "You weren't the Kayleigh I remembered. My girl never could have done what you did. She'd have stayed at home with the kids and hung around the clubhouse. Kayleigh may have gone to college or somethin', but she'd have been happy with a simple life.

You, you're fire and ice and more than a fuckin' handful, nothing like my Kayleigh. Was tryin' to hang onto Kayleigh and realised with help from Master Hoshi that I wasn't lettin' her go and acceptin' what was in front of me. I'd a second chance and threw it away.

When you got shot, I wasn't happy. Reacted and tried to lay the law down, not recognising that you're my equal. You weren't before, you were mine to protect, and I'd never have let Kayleigh pull the shit you do now. Now Artemis, babe, you're my equal, and you're the better person for me.

Kayleigh and I would've been happy, bent over backwards to be happy. Think there would've been a small part of me I'd have kept hidden from her. The ugly, the bloody part that Kayleigh couldn't have coped with. You? I don't need to hide the violence from you. The dark part of me revels in your dark part," Ace stopped speaking.

Ace was right. As Kayleigh, I couldn't have stood the death that surrounded Rage. I would've clung and tried to get Ace away from Rage. That dark part was as much a part of Ace as it was me.

"Got a monster inside me," I told him softly.

"So do I, babe."

"If I don't feed it, shit gets ugly."

"So feed it," Ace told me. I blinked. "Babe, there're a lot of situations out there where you can feed your monster and rescue innocent people. Feed it, let it rage gluttonous. *Fuckin' feed it*," Ace leaned forward and kept eye contact as he said those words. Words that rocked me to my core.

"So you're telling me you can handle the shit I do, the missions I go on. The killing, rescues, standing up for what I believe in."

"Yes. All of it, baby, good and bad."

"I never stopped loving you," I muttered after a few minutes. The air around us crackled, and Ace tensed. "Even when I hated you and wanted your head, I loved you. It's why I never came after you because I couldn't be the one who pulled the trigger."

"You would have this time."

"Yes, I would have because everything I'd buried boiled over. The moment that scumbag forced me onto Rage, and I faced Drake, it began rising inside me. Hate and loathing, despair, and sorrow. That hurt I felt with each knife cut, with each rape, I raged at and wanted you to suffer when they cut the twins from me.

Yes, Ace, this time, I could and would've hurt you. If not for Master Hoshi, you'd be dead by now, innocent of the crime I'd found you guilty of. I'd have destroyed myself by destroying you. Thunder, Misty and Bulldog, the rest of them would've got their final laugh."

"Yeah, babe, they'd have won. This way, we win."

"Do we? Can we build something together?" I asked Ace, not realising the yearning in my voice.

"Yeah, we can. Let me in, woman. Trust me." Ace wasn't begging. He was telling me.

"Trust is so hard Ace, trusted everyone before and look what happened; I find it so hard to trust." Gingerly, I opened myself up a little, so Ace could see me. I didn't know if I could trust Ace, but I wanted to. I'd guarded my emotions so tightly over the years, and Ace was offering me something I didn't know how to take.

Or did I? Master Hoshi and Akemi weren't the only two I'd let in. Buzz, Nigel, Simone, Butch, Angel and Kris, I'd let them in. Including the twins, there were ten people I trusted around me. Could I trust one more? Was it possible for me to let Rage in again and trust them? I shook my head, trying to clear the whirlwind of thoughts.

Ace waited patiently. I looked at Ace, his beautiful face, long hair, broad shoulders tapering to a trim waist and lean hips, muscled legs. Ace was beauty incarnate. I'd never once in the whole time we were together doubted Ace's fidelity. Other women may have looked at Ace and wondered why he was with them. I'd never felt that.

Ace had given me a haven, a place where I could be myself and not fear judgement. Ace hadn't failed me; Bulldog and his band of assholes failed me. Not one of us could have foreseen what happened. It'd happened but did I allow that event, that one horrific event, to scar the rest of my life?

Ace sat calmly but tense. Everything led to this one moment; Ace was willing to accept me, accept what I did and who I was. Ace could love my monster, love me. He was offering that. The question was, could I let Ace or was I doomed to be alone until I died? My monster poked its head up and purred. It gave me an answer I wasn't expecting.

I rose to my feet and looked at Ace, giving him a half-smile. The hope faded from his eyes. I pushed my chair back and walked around the table, where I grabbed his face in my hands. Grinning, I put my mouth to Ace's and kissed him with everything I had.

Ace didn't hesitate and pulled me into his lap and began kissing me back. He sank his hands into my hair and held my head tight as he took over the kiss. Ace controlled it, banking the heat between us, we broke apart, and I looked dazed into his eyes.

"Monkey sex?" I whispered. Ace grinned and stood up, cupping my ass in his hands. I wrapped my legs around Ace as he carried me through the bar towards the offices. I heard hoots and hollers from the peanut gallery. And I raised my hands above my head and threw my head back and let out a cheer. Laughter met me in return.

Chapter Ten.

8th January 2015

Happily, sitting curled up in one of Phoe's huge office chairs, I faced her across the table. Master Hoshi told Akemi he'd four more people who needed employment. And as I was so successful with Angel and Kris, Butch and Simone, Master Hoshi was sending them to me. Wonderful, I wouldn't call my four successful unless them not being serial killers counted.

An idea had come to me. One Phoe once mentioned a plan for and never followed through. I planned to take Artemis legit now, and the vision I had would move us in that direction.

"Talk to me," Phoe said. She wore a pale blush blouse and one of those tight pencil skirts Drake loved watching her in. Phoe's hair was tied back in a messy ponytail, and her seven-month bump protruded like Santa's belly. Phoe rubbed a hand over it.

"I got an idea. You don't have to buy into it. There's enough work for where I wanna lead my people, but this could help you."

"Yeah?" Phoe asked curiously, tilting her head.

"You still looking for a team for child rescues?" I asked. Phoe's eyes grew wide and alert, and she straightened.

"Yes. I can't find anyone willing to take the traffickers on."

"What about Artemis? I'm taking us legal. We'll still bring in bounties and do paid rescues, but I'm getting four new recruits. From their files, well... they enjoy messy, messier than Simone and Butch, that's saying something. The plan is to continue working on the legal bounties and rescues. On the side, we can track shit for Eternal Trust and rescue the kids."

"For real?" Phoe breathed excitedly.

"Yeah, if I take the team away from the black-market bounties, then I'm cutting their work. The team likes money, but they prefer blowing shit up and bringing down scumbags more. I can parcel out bounties and rescues. We'll stay away from security and private investigations. Leave that to Hawthorne, so we don't piss on his patch.

Then during our downtime, I can have my tech guys track leads and find these trafficked kids. My teams will go wherever they need to, to bring a kid back. All I'll ask is you cover costs, which won't be cheap."

"Can do better than that. How much do bounties go for? The ones you chase?"

"Rarely take a bounty for less than twenty thousand, although we aim for ones higher."

"So if I cover costs and then offer a bounty of say ten thousand minimum, and then five thousand for every child rescued?" Phoe mused.

"If the Eternal Trust is found to be paying bounties on traffickers, it would cause a shit storm that will bring the Trusts crashing."

"Ah, but I didn't mention the Trusts, I said me, I can easily afford that. It can't be set up as a payment but set up as a loan or gift. We can sort that. I'll talk to Stuart. He'll tell us how to get around the legal shit, so the Trusts don't get dragged down by this. North will have some input, I'm sure."

"As long as you can keep the Trusts separate from what we do, I'm fine with it. Sure my teams would appreciate the monetary rewards; you want time to think this over, Phoe?" Phoe shook her head vehemently.

"Hell no, I want you to go ahead and set up the rescue plan, too important to delay on. We've a load of missing kid cases that I can dump on you now. I can give you an office at HQ so you can link in. I'll take you on as a consultant for the missing kid cases and get the ball rolling, pay you guys a consultant fee out of my money. Artemis will be employed by me and not the Trusts, but I can set up an office for you at HQ." Now it was my turn to shake my head.

"No, we've got somewhere we work from, somewhere that is safe for us until it's known we're no longer working for black-market bounties. May need your staff's expertise to help us become legal and set up the business if that is okay with you?

If we're coming out of the shadows, we'll need our own place to work from, and we'll need the legal crap that comes with it. We're changing our name, the team voted, and we're now called The Juno Group. I got people who can set up, but we ain't exactly up on legal shit. We've never had to be until now.

We're going to speak to Hawthorne, let him know what direction Juno's going in. We'll let Dylan know what backup we can provide, should he need it and see if Hawthorne is willing to help. If not, then tough shit. Juno's going ahead with this, anyway. The guys so far are on board.

The new four, I haven't yet met, they're due in the next few weeks. Be fantastic to give the teams a focus straight off the mark. I'll take something like ten percent off their earnings to keep Juno running and so on, the rest they can keep."

"Sounds fair to me. Will you personally be going on bounties and stuff?" Phoe asked curiously, and I worked out why she was asking. I offered Phoe a grin and saw the astonishment on her face.

"Yeah, I'll be making a home here with Ace," I said giving Phoe what she wanted to know, and she smiled. I blinked as Phoe's face lit with an inner light and beauty.

"I'm so happy for you," Phoe whispered.

"Can see."

"I love Ace. He took five bullets for me, Ace put his life on the line to save me. He's so intense, dark and handsome, so, well, you know!" Phoe pinked up a little. Well, Phoe had a tiny crush on my Ace, which was okay because I'd a little crush on Drake.

"Ace is all that and more. Ace has a soft spot for you; he wouldn't have taken five bullets for anyone else. He'd have let them hang," I snickered. Phoe laughed and then sobered.

"Will it be hard getting out of the dark side of your business?" Phoe asked, concern lacing her words.

"No. Who wants to go up against Artemis?" I asked, smiling, and glanced up as Drake and Ace appeared in the doorway. Drake moved around to Phoe, who rose to her feet, and he laid one on her; Drake's hand cupped her pregnant belly gently. Phoe fisted her hands in his tee, and when Drake let her go, she looked dazed. Ace came towards me and slung an arm around me.

I tilted my head towards Ace. Ace glanced at me with a quizzical expression, and then Ace grinned and laid one on me too. That was better! By the time he'd finished, my toes were curling, and I was aching inside. I heard a muffled snort and looked over and saw Drake and Phoe grinning at us. Ace nuzzled my neck, and I shivered.

"Business done?" Ace asked, and I nodded. "Lunch?" I nodded again, and grinning, Ace walked me from the room with a head tilt at Drake and a sly grin at Phoe, who began giggling.

"We'll sort out the nitty-gritty later!" Phoe yelled at our backs. Drake laughed.

Ace took me to lunch at a small restaurant five minutes from the clubhouse that made a roaring trade in simple meals. We ordered ribs and fries, and I began telling Ace my plans. Ace listened intently and threw in a few ideas of his own. Still, overall, Ace was encouraging, especially when he realised what it meant for him and me.

"Are you sure, babe? This is what you wanna do?" Ace asked.

"Yes, I want to be a family. We'll buy a house somewhere local. I'll leave the safe house as our offices and leave the cabins there for the guys. The place is wired and easily defensible if needed. For now, if you can support, I don't want anyone knowing where we're working from.

It will take a while to clean up our act, shall we say? Once it's known Artemis is off the market, security won't need to be as tight. We've targets on our backs. Once we've dealt with those, we can be legitimate."

"Need help with those targets?" Ace offered. My instinct was to turn him down. But I realised Ace was trying to meet me halfway and curb those protective instincts. I nodded. Ace's monster showed briefly in his eyes, and I realised Ace needed to let his monster loose a little.

"Think my monster will snap them up whole, but yeah, if you're offering, it might mean getting your hands dirty."

"Got soap and water," Ace smiled, and I relaxed, settling back and took a mouthful of rib.

Ace was serious about getting his hands dirty. He stood at my back as I had several unpleasant meetings with people I'd done previous work for. Being told their favourite hunter was off-limits and no longer available had caused some nasty scenes. Blood had been split a couple of times; I wasn't always the one causing the blood loss.

Ace was content to stand in the shadows and look threatening, something Ace did well. A few scenes occurred before word began getting around, and other meetings went smoother. Buzz and Nigel had been doing their part, refusing dark bounties, and seeking higher-paid legal ones.

Simone and Butch hadn't flinched when I broached my plans. Angel just told me to send him where blood was most likely to be spilt. Which I could tell bothered Ace slightly. Kristoff merely grunted and muttered something about us being family. I could accommodate them as all four bought into the child rescue. It was part of the code we had. Children should be safe no matter what, avenged if needed and most definitely rescued. Precious little lives.

While they had appreciated Phoe's offer of payment, they were willing to do it for free, but of course, money never hurt. None of us was hard up for cash. Buzz and Nigel got a percentage of the bounties they found for us guys and a percentage of rescues.

And knowing my guys, they'd money invested, squirrelled away, hidden and discreetly banked somewhere. Probably under a few aliases like mine was, none of us was stupid. Us now having a mission target, one that meant something, went a long way with the six of them.

Ace met them one at a time as I broached the new way we'd be doing things. He never judged them and accepted what they were to me. Ace gave them a verbal offer to drop in at the bar or clubhouse if they wanted some downtime. I thought Simone and Butch may take Ace up on that offer, but Angel and Kris were solitary. So be it.

It was a week after the meeting with Phoe when my phone rang again. I saw an unknown number and knew
who it was.

"Santos," I answered.

"Did you enjoy my gift?" smooth tones asked.

"Rage MC very much enjoyed your gift," I informed Romeo Santos. Ace sat forward, his gaze intent, and I beckoned Ace closer so he could hear.

"Ah, you gave Jacked away?"

"I gave him to those who had a better claim than me."

There was a pause.

"Interesting, I hear that you are going legit," Santos said.

"My business is going in a different direction, yes."

"A shame. Do we have a ceasefire?"

"What do I get in return?" I asked slowly.

"Two further gifts, my final two." I looked at Ace and saw him nod. Ace's need to get his hands on Thunder was consuming him. Rage had been out daily searching and found zip. They'd traded precious markers, which still led to nothing.

"Deal. If we cross paths again, this deal becomes void," I told him. Ace nodded an agreement.

"Agreed," Santos replied.

"Keep away from Rage territory." There was a pause again.

"That can be negotiated."

"Non-negotiable."

"Deal," Romeo Santos sighed and hung up. A few minutes later, an address was texted to my phone, and I showed Ace. He called Drake and Rage, and we drove fast to it. Didn't want Santos changing his mind.

To my great shock, we found Thunder and one other massive surprise. Romeo Santos clearly had no familial feelings for his father as Miguel Santos lay trussed up. A shiver ran down my spine when I wondered what type of man would serve up his own father. Romeo Santos was a different species from his father. Miguel sought to protect his son, but Romeo sold his father for peace. Shit on a stick, Romeo Santos would cause problems down the line; I could foresee it.

Miguel Santos died hard. Ace and I handed Miguel to Drake, who had a prior claim on him. Miguel Santos had threatened to rape Phoe when her fuckwad ex-husband had kidnapped and tortured her. He'd groped her while Phoe couldn't escape and was tied up. The asshole didn't beg, and he cursed us until Drake put a bullet in his head. For what Miguel

Santos attempted to do to Phoe, his part in shooting Ace and his interference with me, Miguel Santos died fucking hard. Beaten and broken, the guy died.

Thunder suffered. I made sure Thunder suffered for twenty-four hours before my monster was satisfied. Those who had been with Rage when my attack happened were present for him. They each took a go at him. When Rage finished, it was my turn. Thunder suffered far worse than Misty. I made everyone leave me with Thunder apart from Ace and Akemi, who point blank refused to leave. Ace didn't once blink as my monster rampaged, and I set it free.

Every indignity Thunder had done to me was returned tenfold, far worse than Misty had suffered. Ace did not join in but watched without judgement as I paid that bastard back for everything. By the time I'd finished, Thunder had resembled nothing human. I'm not proud of it. It was awful, but Kayleigh was finally avenged, and I gave the knife to Ace when I stood back.

"End it," I told Ace as he stared at the misshapen lump that had once been Thunder. Ace took the knife and crouched in front of Thunder, who managed to open one eye and glared at Ace in hatred.

"How's it feel?" Ace asked. Thunder grunted, unable to say anything as I'd smashed his jaw a couple of hours earlier. "Everything you did to my old lady and look at her, look at my woman. How proud and strong she stands and look at you here, a piece of shit as you always were." Ace slid the knife into Thunder's throat and watched as he choked out on his own blood.

"Akemi will clean up," I told Ace. Ace wiped his hands on a rag to clean the blood off them.

"It's done. It's finished, baby," Ace drawled.

"Yeah, Kayleigh can rest in peace," I told Ace and saw a weight lift off his shoulders. Ace's entire body relaxed, and I knew then what this had meant to him. The chance to put his lost love in the ground where she belonged. Now it was just us, him and me, no Kayleigh between us.

"Yeah, babe, she can," I whispered to Ace as his gaze came to my face. Ignoring the sodden mess of humanity laying at our feet, he bent over and kissed me lightly.

"Us and the twin's babe," Ace whispered.

"Sounds fucking good to me."

"Love you, Artemis."

"I love you too, Ace." Together we walked away from the clearing where we'd done our work. Ace's arm snaked around me and pulled me close, and then let me go as he threw a leg over his bike. Ace looked at me.

"No woman has ever ridden behind me since I lost her. Get on." I grinned at my man and climbed on after him. I wrapped my arms around Ace's waist, and he kick-started the bike, and we roared off towards Rage.

Epilogue.

15th January 2015

I lifted my head from Ace's shoulder as Silvie came running in. Silvie was red-faced and out of breath. We both sat up.

"Phoe's in labour!" Silvie shrieked, and the room turned wired. Phoe was six weeks early. Shit. Boots hit the floor as men raced towards the door. Apache caught Silvie's hand and dragged her behind him, forcing Silvie onto his bike. I climbed up behind Ace, and we roared off. Rage hit the hospital together, causing the receptionist to go wide-eyed in terror and lust as she took in the entire MC.

"Phoenix Michaelson," Ace snapped at the poor

nurse. The nurse tapped at the keyboard.

"Mrs Michaelson's upstairs in maternity, but you can't all go," she exclaimed. Rock threw her a stare over his shoulder.

"Try to stop us." No matter what, the MC would be there to support their Prez. We raced up the stairs and found Phoe's eldest son Micah pacing. Micah and Carmine had both come home for a weekend. Drake was missing, and Carmine appeared from a room.

"In here. We warned the hospital everyone would probably come. They opened up this room for us to wait in."

"Your mom?" Fish asked. Marsha clung to him, wide-eyed and scared. We all loved Phoe. If anything went wrong, Drake would lose it.

"Baby's determined to make an appearance. They tried stopping labour, but it's coming whether we're ready or not. Mom's okay, she's pretty calm, Dad's losing it. They've thrown Dad out once already. Micah calmed him down, and they've let Dad back in."

"They can't stop labour?" Silvie gasped, paling.

"Hey, women give birth every day," I told her with a smile. "Chin up, lady. Phoe will be fine, and so will the baby. Drake may be a hot mess, though," I said with feeling, and a couple of the guys groaned. Hot mess was an understatement. Drake would be climbing the walls.

We waited for two hours before anything

happened. Micah and Carmine seemed content to pace. Apache stayed huddled in a click with a few brothers. Other brothers lounged around. Silvie sat with Jodie and Serenity, who portrayed calmness, Tye was bouncing a ball off a wall, and none of us had the heart to tell him to stop.

Every time a door slammed in the corridor, Tye's head snapped up and dropped. The younger children were scattered around on various laps. Cody and Harley stood close to Ezra, and Lowrider, who had their arms slung casually around their shoulders.

Christian, Jared and Aaron remained near Chance, who had arrived an hour after us with Hellfire. The room was definitely crowded, and although we were drawing looks, no one dared tell either MC to leave.

There was a commotion, and Drake appeared carrying a bundle in his arms. At Drake's side hovered a midwife fretting. Drake strode into the room, and everyone stopped talking and moving.

"Meet Dante Chance Michaelson, five pounds exactly, twenty-one inches long, ten fingers and ten toes and his mother's blond hair," Drake said proudly. Micah was at his side within seconds, looking at his baby brother. Chance sucked in air loudly, his eyes melting.

"Mum?" Micah asked, touching a finger to his baby brother.

"Mom's fine, they are tidying her up, and then you can visit," Drake soothed. One by one, the kids appeared at Drake's side, peering at their new brother, then Chance was in before anyone else. Chance peered over his cousin's shoulder and then clenched a hand on Drake's shoulder.

"I call godfather," Chance stated to Drake.

"You think we've named our kid after you, and you'd be anythin' but godfather?" Drake asked, amused. Chance kept his eyes on the baby, and it was so sweet. The big man was awestruck.

"Did good brother. Gonna find my girl," Chance said finally and strode in the direction Drake had appeared from. No one stopped him. Everyone knew better than to get between Chance and Phoe. They'd both slit your throat if someone tried to keep them apart.

Ten minutes later, everyone had got a look at baby Dante. Drake was being harried back to maternity so they could do what they needed to do. A hand slipped around my waist and lay flat over my stomach.

"Missed the first time," Ace muttered his gaze, seeing something in the past.

"Always a second time," I told him, and Ace blinked and looked at me.

"Thought you couldn't carry again?"

"I had Master Hoshi. He made sure they saved everything possible. Yeah, I can get pregnant and carry a baby." I told Ace. I saw love and desire flare in his eyes, desire for another child.

"Let's have a few months together before baby-making starts," I warned Ace. Ace bent and gave me a sweet kiss.

"Yeah," Ace drawled, but his eyes told me a different story. I gazed up at my old man, who smirked, and I laughed.

Characters.

There are many characters in the Rage books, so I thought I'd give everyone a helping hand with whom is who. This is a list of those in this book. As more of the Rage brothers find their girl's, I'll add them to this page!

Rage MC

Drake Michaelson. DOB 1975. His father started Rage MC and died before Drake was old enough to become President. He became VP and then, in a hostile takeover, became President. Phoenix thinks he looks like Tim McGraw with longer hair. Drake has a lanky leanness to him but has well-defined muscles. He sports dark brown eyes with laughter lines, and he's six foot four. In January 2015, his son Dante Chance Michaelson was born. Drake considers Detective Antonio Ramirez and PI Dylan Hawthorne close friends.

Apache. DOB 1967. He is one of Drake's enforcers. Ace is his only son. Apache was widowed when Ace was young. He has bright green eyes and is six foot two. He is a Native American. Apache is described as absolutely stunning, with gorgeous, high cheekbones, raven black hair that hangs past his shoulders. Silvie

Stanton has been in love with him for nearly quarter of a century.

Ace. DOB 1983. Ace is Drake's VP. He's described as looking like a young Lou Diamond Phillips. Like his father, he is Native American. Ace has bright green eyes, six foot two. He is described much the same as his father, absolutely stunning with gorgeous, high cheekbones and raven black hair that hangs past his shoulders. Ace was in love with Kayleigh Mitchell and thought she'd left him. Ace discovers that Kayleigh hadn't left him but instead had been tortured and left for dead. He has two children Nova and Falcon.

Fish. DOB 1978. Fish is Drake's sergeant at arms. He's been married to Marsha for many years. They can't have children. Fish was heartbroken when he thought Kayleigh ran away. He'd taken Kayleigh on as his own when she was eleven. Fish is devastated when he discovers what happened to Kayleigh. Fish has a bushy beard and untamed hair which he keeps in check with a bandana. He is tall and broadly built and has an innate kindness.

Texas. DOB 1970. Texas is an older man; he is the MC's secretary. He designs bikes and does specialised paintwork. Texas has a daughter. He had information he wasn't aware of concerning Kayleigh's disappearance. Texas has a robust moral code, but he is aware of what the MC is capable of. He once alludes to cleaning up after their messes.

Axel. DOB 1951. Axel was one of the founders of the club. He is the Chaplin of the MC. He has blue eyes, and he is heavily bearded and very loud. He's built like a mountain. Axel has wild hair which hangs to his shoulders. Axel disappears in The Hunters Rage. There is mention of his messed-up kids, and Axel has gone to resolve an issue with them.

Gunner. DOB 1976. Gunner is one of Drake's Enforcers at the MC. Gunner is described as having grey eyes.

Slick. DOB 1978. Slick loves books and is happy reading quietly. He has soft brown eyes and is heavily muscled. Slick was in love with Kayleigh, but he never let on as he knew she belonged to Ace. He has a tattoo of her on his left pec of a circle of thorns with pink, blue and purple roses and an image of Kayleigh kneeling in the circle with two hearts on chains threaded through her hands. One heart has Ace's name, the other has his, and her name threads through the thorns. Slick is kidnapped by Artemis in revenge.

Manny. Manny was suspected by Artemis of being involved in Kayleigh Mitchell's death.

Lowrider.

Ezra.

Mac. Mac was suspected of being involved in Kayleigh Mitchell's death.

Rock.

Lex. Lex was suspected of being involved in Kayleigh Mitchell's death.

Blaze. Prospect.

Slate. Prospect. Slate was 'put to sleep' by Master Hoshi when he denied Master Hoshi access to the clubhouse.

Jett. Prospect. Jett was drugged by Artemis when she infiltrated the clubhouse.

Hunter. Prospect. Hunter was drugged by Artemis when she infiltrated the clubhouse.

Rage Old Ladies.

Phoenix Michaelson. DOB 1979. Drake's old lady/wife. She's English and left England to escape an abusive relationship. She has five children she gave birth to and adopted eleven. Phoe is exceedingly well off and runs three National Charities. The Phoenix Trust, the Rebirth Trust and the Eternal Trust. She has been married three times, the first husband died and her second was a bigamist. Drake is her third husband. Phoe is blond and green-eyed and is five foot tall. She met Hellfire MC first and is loyal to them, and Chance Michaelson is her closest friend.

Marsha. DOB 1979. Fish's old lady and the only old lady until Phoe meets Drake. She's known to be kind and caring. She's distraught when she discovers the truth about Kayleigh's disappearance, and her emotions were so intense she destroyed a room in the clubhouse.

Silvie Stanton. DOB 1982. Silvie's treated like an

old lady even though she doesn't have an old man. She's kind and generous, and the MC has a lot of respect for her. Silvie has blond, curly hair. She knew Kayleigh Mitchell when Kayleigh was brought to the MC. Silvie is in love with Apache, but Apache ignores it.

Kayleigh Mitchell. DOB 1987. Died 2004. Kayleigh was a small, slender blond with blue eyes. Raped and abused by her stepfather, aged eleven, she ended up in the care of Marsha and Fish. Just before her seventeenth birthday, she discovered she was pregnant with Ace's children. She was tortured and left for dead by Thunder and Misty and several other members of Rage.

Artemis, aka Kayleigh Mitchell. DOB 1987. Reinvented 2004. She has red curly hair, green eyes (contacts); she's small, dainty and muscled. Artemis has a heart-shaped pixie face full lips. Artemis looks at Master Hoshi as her father and Akemi as a brother. She's a famous bounty hunter and runs a team that operates under the name Artemis. Artemis was part of an organisation called Revenge before she left and created the Artemis team. She has combat skills and has killed many times. She coasts the dark side of life as well as the legal side.

Hellfire MC.

Chance Michaelson. DOB 1970. Chance is the

Hellfire President. His father started Hellfire. Chance looks like Tim McGraw with long hair. He is Drake's older cousin. They were brought up together and are as close as brothers. They both fought to get their clubs clean from the filth that infected them.

There are a lot of comments that Chance and Drake could be twins. Chance is very protective of Phoenix and loves her without barriers. He has the same lanky leanness as his cousin. Drake has brown eyes, and Chance has bright green eyes with laughter lines. He is six foot four with his hair hanging past his collar.

HQ Staff.

Emily. Emily is Phoe's personal assistant. She is young and wild and likes colour.
Stuart. Stuart is the Director of Legal; he is a little uptight, and Stefan takes great delight in teasing him.
North. North is the Director of public relations.

Non-HQ People.

Liz. Liz is head of the home security team. She doesn't do security for the Trust but for the family. Liz came from England on a job offer from Phoenix. She is dedicated and hard-working.

Rage Children.

Nova and Falcon Conway. DOB 2004. They look like their father, Ace. Nova has countless gold medals for mixed martial arts. Falcon prefers swimming and baseball while also winning awards for mixed martial arts.

Micah. DOB 1995. Lives in Miami. He is English. Micah is working an apprenticeship in Miami designing street cars under a famous designer.

Carmine. DOB 1996. half African American, half white. He is from Maine. Adopted 2010. Plays for the Cubs. Lives in Chicago.

Tyelar. DOB 1996. He wants to play for the Blackhawks. Tye is half Mexican and half Caucasian. Tye is from Maine. Adopted 2010.

Jodie. DOB 1997. She likes tennis and is close to Serenity.

Serenity. DOB 1998. She is from Maine. She plays tennis well but also likes ice hockey and was adopted in 2010.

Harley. DOB 1999. Harley's from Maine and was adopted in 2010.

Cody. DOB 2000. Carmine found Cody living on the streets in Colorado. He was adopted in 2011.

Christian. DOB 2002.

Jared. DOB 2004.

Aaron. DOB 2005. Aaron was born after his father died. He never met him.

Eddie and Tony. DOB 2010. Eddie's full name is Edwina Joanne Michaelson. The twins are African

American and were adopted in 2012.

Timmy and Scout. DOB 2014. Adopted 2014. Their mother was a drug addict. They have severe illnesses which Phoe hopes medical care will cure.

Garrett and Jake. DOB 2014. Adopted 2014 Their mother was a drug addict. They have severe illnesses which Phoe hopes medical care will cure.

Dante Chance Michaelson. DOB January 2015. Six weeks early.

Members of Rage MC who left or died.

Thunder. He's now dead by Artemis and Ace's hand. He was in on Kayleigh's torture and was known to have no moral, and had a kink for pain. Thunder was captured and turned over by Romeo Santos.

Misty. She was a skank in Kayleigh's eyes. Misty died when Artemis caught her and tortured her like Kayleigh was tortured. She had been Ace's on and off lay over the years and kept it from Ace that she had been in on Kayleigh's torture and rape.

Gid. Was a trusted brother until the truth came out that he had been involved in Kayleigh's disappearance. Artemis killed him after gaining what she thought was the truth from him.

Jacked. Remained a trusted brother until the truth came out, and Artemis was handed him by Santos. She handed him to Rage to deal with him. He's believed to be dead.

Sticks. He left the club when Drake got control of it. He was part of the torture and rape of Kayleigh Mitchell. Artemis didn't remember until he was brought to her by Master Hoshi. Believed dead.

Bulldog. He was the next president after Drake's father died. He took the club down a dark path which led to many illegal activities. Drake wrestled control back from him. Ace killed Bulldog. Bulldog was behind Kayleigh's torture in an effort to break Ace and weaken Drake's standing in the MC.

Ghost. Ex-member supposed dead.

Prof. Killed by Artemis for his part in her death.

Prince. Killed by Ace for helping shoot Manny. Ace slit his throat. His body was dumped at Bulldog's new clubhouse.

Preacher. Killed by Artemis as Preacher was the one who came up with the idea. He died hard.

Mad Dog. Was the shooter of Manny. Ace tortured and then killed him. His body was dumped at Bulldogs.

Skill, Mayhem, Crow and Farmer are dead. All believed killed in the battle to regain Rage and make it clean.

Hammer, Smokey, Archer, Breaker and Iron left Rage over the infighting and blacked their ink.

The Artemis Group.

Buzz. Buzz is competent on a computer, but he is more the office manager and designs his own weapons. He was a weapons specialist for the army as well as a weapon designer. He is loyal to Artemis and the twins. Artemis found him when she came across him in a fight that he was losing.

Nigel. Nigel is a hacker. He has a wiry and slender build. He's often mistaken for being a geek but is as deadly as the others. Nigel's known to have hacked into government databases.

Simone and Butch. They are two hunters at Artemis, and they will only work with each other. Butch has special force training, and he moves like a ghost. Simone is much like Artemis in character but not looks.

Angel. Angel is a hunter with serious head issues. There is no line he won't cross except for hurting a woman or child. He got captured by Miguel Santos, which led to a rescue and Artemis dismantling Santos's empire until his son called a truce.

Kristoff. Kristoff is another hunter. He was a street kid who crossed paths with Artemis before she hired him when he was about to get nailed by police. Kristoff looks upon the team as family.

Akemi. Akemi is Japanese. He is tall and slender with well-defined muscles. Master Hoshi calls him his son, and Artemis thinks of him as a brother. There are no lengths they will not go to for each other. He is polite and respectful and can use a Kantana.

Master Hoshi. Late fifties early sixties, he is lean and trim. He's five foot four; his face is lightly lined, shaved head and has brown eyes. Artemis thinks of him as a father. He is in charge of the organisation called Revenge. Master Hoshi is responsible for Artemis being who she is now. He cares for her and calls her daughter.

Mrs Humphries. Artemis's housekeeper.

Jonas Valden. DOB August 1999. Approached Drake to join Rage at fifteen. His father is a well-known tattoo artist, Rio Valden.

Zac Valden. DOB 2002. The younger brother of Jonas. His father is a well-known tattoo artist, Rio Valden.

RCPD.

Antonio Ramirez. He is over six-foot-tall and has black wavy hair, olive tanned skin. Ramirez is Mexican and has brown soft, gentle eyes; he's described as lean hipped and long-legged and broad-shouldered. He is a good cop, and Drake thinks a lot of him.

Eric Benjamin called **Ben.** Partner of Ramirez.

Hawthorne Investigations.

Dylan Hawthorne. Owner of Hawthorne investigations. He is extremely clever and will bend and break the rules as he wants. Dylan thinks of Drake as a close friend and takes Rage's back during the Artemis war. He discovers information on Artemis.

Leila Gibson. She is Hawthorne's computer genius. She managed to get a trace on Artemis, which led Rage to Artemis, through the Stacy Conway identity.

Santos Empire.

Miguel Santos. In his late fifties and is mean and power-mad. He is known to be one of the worse crime lords in Rapid City. However, the police are unable to catch him. Artemis goes after him when he tries to get her to kill an innocent man, and she begins a war with him. He is killed by Artemis when his son Romeo Santos hands him over.

Romeo Santos. Is an unknown player. He has taken over his father's empire, and in a move to gain peace hands Artemis Jacked, Thunder and his own father.

Authors Byword.

Thank you for reading the Hunters Rage. This is a darker novel of Rage, and while more violent and traumatic than Rage of the Phoenix, the story of Ace and Artemis had to be a dark one, I felt. The struggle to get Rage clean couldn't have been victimless. Can't only kill the bad guys, I'm afraid! Rage pulling away from drug and gun-running and everything else wouldn't have been bloodless.

Ace was a natural victim to have. He'd found love early and recognised the girl for him. He had everything within his grasp, and no one's life is perfect. Ace at twenty couldn't have it all! Kayleigh, while a survivor, was just that; she wasn't strong enough to have survived what Rage suffered through to get clean.

It is medically possible for the babies to have survived at twenty-eight weeks. However, the start of Falcon and Nova's life would have been difficult.

The next book, the Rage of Reading, is Sinclair and Jett's story. A shy, socially awkward woman with a brother of Rage? What could possibly go wrong!

Thank you for reading the Hunters Rage. Do check out the other titles in this series and take a gander at the Love Beyond Death Series, book one of which Oakwood Manor is out now! If you enjoyed this book, please leave a review at,

Goodreads and Amazon

Check out Jett in the Rage of Reading in the next book of Rage MC.

Thank you!

Elizabeth.

Made in the USA
Las Vegas, NV
09 June 2022

50000204R00173